IDLE THOUGHTS

Vaughan W. Smith

Fair Folio

Sydney, Australia

Fair Folio
www.fairfolio.com.au

Idle Thoughts / Vaughan W. Smith. -- 1st ed.
ISBN 978-0-9874694-1-0

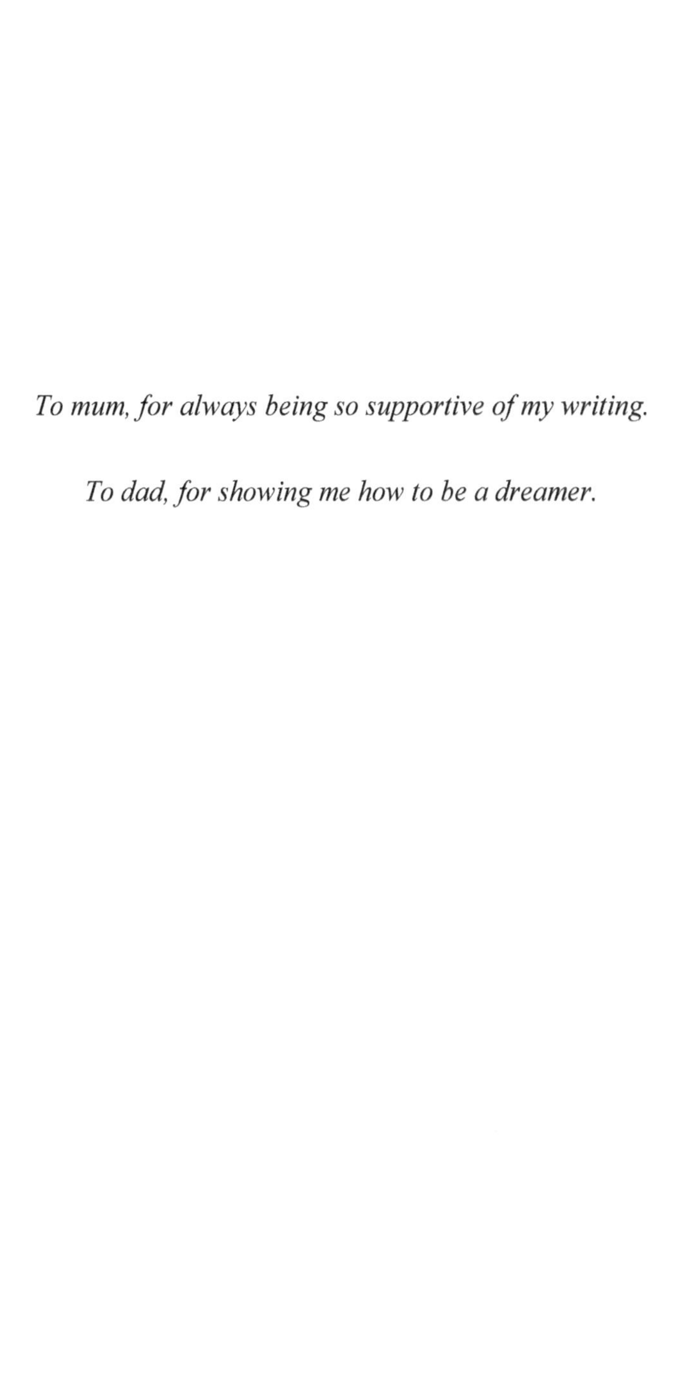

To mum, for always being so supportive of my writing.

To dad, for showing me how to be a dreamer.

CHAPTER ONE

HUMBLE BEGINNINGS

I awoke with a start and sat upright hurriedly. I had that moment of panic when you don't know where you are. After that momentary disorientation I stood and rifled through my jacket pockets. I found a small white card with the words 'Vale Club 6pm' on it. I checked the silver wrist watch on my left arm and read the time as a quarter to six. My destination was only five minutes away so I did a quick inventory of what I had on me. I found a wallet, a blue and white chequered handkerchief and a pair of white gloves.

Opening the wallet I saw a nice wad of cash and photo identification for Earnest Rodriguez. I paused for a moment to take in the room around me. It looked dirty and run down, consisting of only the bare essentials. I dismissed the room and strode out of the door and downstairs to the lobby of the budget hotel. The lobby was empty as I walked on to the street. Groups of people were rushing around and the traffic was moving slowly. Darkness was slowly creeping along the street, with some lights already lit. I wandered out onto the road, waiting for a few cars to pass before dashing across and walking up the street. Within a block or two I stopped and looked up. A dilapidated red neon sign confirmed that I had arrived at the Vale Club.

I pushed through the front doors and into a dank and dark room. It smelled of cigarettes, leather and something else I couldn't quite identify. I saw a man at the bar regarding me with some thought so I walked over. He was a large balding fellow with round glasses.

"The piano player I presume?" he asked. I nodded in response. A carefully placed smile appeared on his face and he beckoned for me to follow.

We weaved our way through the haphazard arrangement of tables and chairs, past the dance floor and to an undersized raised section in the far corner of the room. I took note of the empty glasses I saw, the number of patrons and the height of the largest chair. Three people in particular, sitting together, captured my attention: an older man wearing a monocle, a blonde beauty in a red dress and well-dressed youth wearing dark glasses. As I reached the far corner of the room I spotted the piano, a meager brown upright. The man from behind the bar unlocked it with a tiny brass key, opened the lid and then gestured at me. I understood his meaning, pulled out the stool and sat down.

I sat completely still, looking at the assorted black and white keys hoping something would come to me. My mind was stubbornly blank. I absent-mindedly dug through my jacket pockets and ran my hands over the gloves. Wearing them seemed like a good idea, so I took them out and slowly put them on one finger at time. When I couldn't stall any longer I hovered my hands over the keyboard, and placed a single finger down experimentally. A note sounded and set off an amazing chain reaction. My hands had a life of their own, playing with dazzling alacrity and power. I let the music wash over me.

Two things concerned me as I played. I felt as though the eyes of the old man with the monocle were boring a hole through my back. The other was a particular black key that had some sort of troubling significance. I recognised it as E flat, but nothing more, and the reference itself held no meaning for me. I tried to put the special key out of my mind and kept playing. The song rose in intensity and I could feel the eyes of the whole room focused on me. It was a rush, but I didn't quite feel in control. Then it happened quite suddenly. I had pressed the fateful key and picked up a unique vibration from the piano. At that very moment I knew that a poisoned dart had been fired from a secret compartment and was aimed at the old man. As if on cue he coughed abruptly, masking the sound as the deadly weapon pierced his chest.

The young man seated next to the dart victim turned to look, as if he sensed something was wrong. The woman in red flinched and knocked over an ashtray. I played on; the song had to be completed. With a thundering chord I finished and an abrupt silence fell over the whole room. Time seemed to slow and I turned to see the old man collapse in his chair, with his companions quickly tending to him. I saw some embers from the ash tray begin to grow into flames and knew I had to leave as quickly as possible. I turned and headed directly for the fire escape in the opposite corner of the room. Gun shots rung around me and I ducked my head instinctively. My heart rate increased and soon all I could hear as I ran was its loud beating and the crashing boom of my every step. I furiously pressed down on the door lever, and as I burst out into the cool night air a single sound followed me from the club and pierced my cone of silence: a woman's scream.

I darted to the nearest street corner to assess my situation. Darkness had fallen while I had been inside. The street had taken on a more sinister look, and I noticed several police and emergency workers flooding the area. All my instincts told me that I had to get away. A car quietly sidled up to me from the dark lane I had run along, its lack of headlights catching me by surprise.

"Get in quick!" a voice hissed at me from inside. I scanned the street and decided to take my chances with the stranger. He said nothing and turned around the car quickly, weaving through tiny streets without his lights. Several minutes later we emerged on a main road and rejoined regular traffic. A sense of relief swept over me and a tenseness I had not realised I was holding on to melted away.

"Where are we headed?" I asked.

"The warehouse," he replied curtly. I didn't ask any follow-up questions. The rest of the drive continued in silence until he stopped the car.

"Wait here, I'll be right back," the driver said. He crossed the road and entered the warehouse through a narrow entrance mostly obscured by boxes. I started to think back on the events I had just experienced, but stopped myself. I had to focus on the task at hand, and be ready to react. I had no idea what would happen next. Within minutes the driver returned, tossing a bulging envelope onto my lap as he sat down.

"I don't know what kind of job you pulled, but our mutual employer was extremely pleased," he said.

"Who might that be?" I asked.

"You don't know who you're working for? I don't know whether to laugh or be impressed."

"I'm Earnest."

"Tony," he said in response as he started the car. After we had reached the main road he spoke up again.

"I have the address but can you possibly give me directions?"

"Sorry I'm not familiar with this area," I said, shrugging my shoulders. He snorted and slightly shook his head tossing his dirty tufts of hair around. He then pulled out from the curb and drove away at quite a speed.

I sat quietly, observing the terrain, trying to make note of the surroundings or any significant landmarks. However the darkness worked against me and Tony drove like a maniac. A great tiredness swept over me, and I alternated between being unable to keep my eyes open and being jolted awake by a sharp turn or sudden stop.

"Is Earnest your real name?" he asked.

"I don't remember," I said. He muttered something under his breath and turned his attention back to the road.

"What's your part in all this?" I asked him.

"I'm the driver, been serving the rich and infamous for years now. But I'm not blind, I've seen a thing or two. I gotta say, there's something different about you." I didn't quite know how to respond to that so I let it sit. From that point we drove on in silence. I stared out into the road, not looking at anything in particular.

"Here we are, number twelve," Tony announced suddenly, jolting me out of my minor trance.

"Thanks," I said. He looked at me strangely and licked his lips.

"Let me know if you need any help, by the looks of that envelope you sure can afford it."

"Sure," I said, and went to leave.

"Don't forget this!" he called out as he grabbed my arm. I awkwardly bent down and retrieved the envelope and closed the car door. Tony drove off without a moment's hesitation. I looked over at where I had arrived. It looked like a normal enough house, with a tidy front yard, a white picket fence and a paved path. I opened the gate carefully, however it swung noisily into the fence afterwards. I continued on, trying to be quiet without looking suspicious. The front door was white, with a silver knocker at mid-height and a giant metal stud sticking out below that. I knocked three times, clearly but not violently. I could hear no response from within the house. I knocked another three times and waited again with the same result. It occurred to me that there were several explanations: I lived alone, I lived with others who were out, or this was somebody else's house. Each seemed equally likely. I sat down on the front step and leafed through the contents of my envelope. Apart from all the money, it had a small folded piece of blue paper. I opened the note and it said the following:

Look under the mat.
Regards,
M

I was torn. I wanted the message to mean what I thought it did, so I could get in without a fuss. However, I also hoped that if it was my house, it wasn't so easy to get in. I stood up and grasped around under the welcome mat and found something metallic. It was a key, which was both a relief and a disappointment. I put the key in and turned it clockwise. The latch unlocked with a clear 'click' and I pushed open the door. I was immediately assaulted with a musty smell, suggesting that it had been locked up for a lengthy period.

I shuffled around in the hallway and found a light switch. From there I wandered the house, turning on all the lights and opening whatever windows I came across. It was nicely furnished, with two bedrooms and a study. Something didn't seem right though. Once I had completed a lap a realisation dawned on me, there were no personal items at all. Nothing identified the owner; it was completely generic. A wave of weariness hit me again, so I wandered over to the bathroom and splashed some water on my face. Something in the mirror caught my gaze, only it was just my face. I peered at it, and a man with dark locks, piercing green eyes and pale skin stared back at me.

"I'm not an Earnest. That's not an Earnest," I said to myself. Saying it felt right.

I walked over to the study and sat down at the desk resting my face in one palm and letting the events of the day wash over me. I had killed a man, linked up with a getaway driver and been paid for the deed. There were multiple problems there, but the main one was that I had no memory of anything before waking up in the hotel. I acted on instinct, from one moment to the next with no knowledge of the events I was participating in. It raised quite a few questions.

I had a decision to make. In my mind there were two options. The first was to cut and run, take the money and get as far away as possible. Build myself a life somewhere else and hope that in time my memory returned. It was the coward's approach, but not without its merits. The second was to continue along with whatever I was involved in and get to the bottom of it. Play along, where appropriate, until I had an opportunity to do otherwise. The idea of getting answers was good, although the huge amount of unknowns was not.

The tipping point was the old man who I had killed. It weighed on me like a stain I had to remove. Which meant running away was not an option, I had to confront things head on and make them right. The more I thought about staying and investigating, the more I was convinced. I needed answers and I wouldn't be satisfied until I had them. To assist with my task, and taking my strange situation into consideration, I also decided to write down everything that happened to me, and my thoughts. No matter what happened, the record of events from my perspective would assist me in my investigation and reveal my true intentions, should something happen.

Sleep whispered to me, so I dragged myself over to the bedroom and fell into the bed. My questions were not enough to keep me awake. One thought stuck with me though: 'I hope that my resolve and intent are not stolen away by the night'.

CHAPTER TWO

A PLAN FORMS

Unfortunately I awoke in a different location from where I went to sleep. After the previous day's events, I really wanted a sense of continuity. Thankfully, though I do not know how I ended up there, nothing was taken from me. I still had my money, items and the notes I had written down during my experience. I found myself in a cheap hotel, but not the same one as before. I assessed the information available and came up with the following: I was in a new location, there was a change of clothes available and presumably another job to do. The clues or instructions I needed would be in those new clothes.

I changed into a plain black leather jacket, faded jeans, a white t-shirt and other casual attire. It looked like no formal outings were on the cards. I rifled through the clothes and found a wallet and a train ticket. The wallet had identification for a man named 'Roger

Smith', and again the photo looked like me. The train ticket was to a 'Central Station'. Unlike yesterday there didn't seem to be a specified time. I tried to think back and I definitely had no knowledge of a prearranged time either. I was quite puzzled, since there was no indication of what was planned and when. At least previously I was informed of a time and place. I decided not to rush myself, and begin with the information I had. I casually strolled down to the hotel foyer and spotted a phone. I dialled the number Tony left for me and waited patiently. After what seemed like a long time I heard a distinct metallic click and then a voice.

"Tony here," he answered.

"Tony, I have a request that you may be able to assist with," I said.

"Who is this?"

"It's Earnest, we met yesterday."

"Oh right, how about you give me a real sounding name now?" he replied.

"Fair enough," I said, stalling for time. He was right though, I needed a name for myself that was distinct from any aliases that might be assigned to me. The only problem was actually coming up with a name. What would I call myself?

"I'm Sean," I told him.

"Well, Sean, what are you after?"

"What I require is a secure storage space with easy access."

"That makes sense," he replied, "I have a rather convenient suggestion for you."

"What's that?"

"Grab yourself a locker at Central Station. It's a public place and very accessible."

"That should work, I'll actually be passing through that area today," I told him.

"I know, I have a message for you."

"Go on," I said, rather intrigued by this development.

"It says to catch the five forty-three train on platform six."

"Done. Will you be joining me later?"

"No, I have other jobs."

"Next time then," I replied and hung up. I then took a moment to think over my plan. I would secure a storage space and make sure I was on that train. However, I had to assume that Tony might be more involved than he let on. The fact that he had a message for me helped support this theory. I decided it would be wiser to get myself two storage lockers, one at Central Station as he had suggested, and another at a nearby station. That way I could keep a few items of minor importance in the Central locker to avoid suspicion, and my personal things in the other one. Things like this very document, which I value above all else right now. It is the only record of my true intentions.

Next my thoughts drifted to my other task: I would do whatever was necessary to prevent what they had planned for me. I must admit, I was starting to feel a little more sure of myself. I thought that if I put my mind to the task, I could save a life this time; by failing to take it. I stepped outside, picked a direction at a whim and started walking. I checked my watch and noted that I had hours to spare before my rendezvous.

Along the way I stopped to asked a man on the street the way to Central Station and it turned out I was already heading the right way. I was standing at a street corner idly waiting for the lights to change, and I glanced across the road. There was a large post office bustling with people. What really grabbed my attention however were the rows of post boxes out the front. It was a great idea, what better storage area than one you could post things to? That would also eliminate the problem of delivering items to my storage and let the postal system do the job for me. I just had to ensure only small parcels accumulated in the box so it didn't get too full.

Half an hour later I walked out of the post office with a key to the largest post box they had available, and a rental period lasting an entire year. I located mine and put the first part of this document inside. I was quite happy with that result, but I still had to organise additional storage at Central Station to complete my preparations. Let me pause for a minute to explain my train of thought. It might appear as though I was being quite paranoid here, by arranging a decoy storage place to match what Tony had suggested. However, last two days I have awoken in places not knowing how I arrived there. Not to mention seemingly thrust into the middle of events I still don't entirely understand or indeed know the full implications of. So in addition to being extra cautious, I think these actions were also a way for me to exercise control. When lacking complete control of your circumstances, the small things that you can influence become important. They take on a special significance.

After a time I arrived at Central Station. The station was larger than most, and looked quite old. The tiles on the floor were scratched and grimy, and the walls were dull with a poorly disguised layer of dirt. It didn't take much effort to find the tellers who were renting out lockers. Unfortunately they didn't have a year-long rental period so I settled with a month. I was a bit disappointed but considered that if things worked out maybe I wouldn't need it in a month's time. I walked over to the lockers, looking for mine. The key was number 153 which ended up being at head height and on the end of a whole block of lockers. I opened it to see how big it was inside, and decided that I should store something within. Fishing through my pockets I chose the folded piece of blue paper I received that first day in my envelope of money. It seemed fitting, as it was also an important clue for me. Who did the 'M' on the note represent?

With that business taken care of all I had left to do was make my way to platform six and catch the specified train. Checking my watch I saw that I still had an hour to pass before the departure time. It seemed like a good opportunity to scout out the area, to see if there were any surprises in store. I walked around the station looking for anything out of the ordinary. In hindsight it was a bit of a pointless exercise. Not only did I not know what to look for exactly, but I'm not sure I would have recognised a problem. However it was reasonable that I continued on and went through the motions, due to my frame of mind.

As the appointed time approached I walked back to the platform, sat down on a seat and waited. I felt something strange, like there was a stirring in the air. Yet nothing appeared out of the ordinary. A thought lingered in the back of my mind, that perhaps there had been a mistake and nothing would be occurring. A part of me really wanted to believe that. However I knew that was just a childish wish on my part, and had no basis in reality. If only it had been true.

There was an even distribution of people along the length of the platform, and quite a bit of jostling. Some maneuvering was by those trying to get a better position and the rest by people still arriving. I guessed they were all on their way home from work. This thought made me even more nervous as I tried to predict what was in store for this train ride. I decided that the best course of action would be to wait near the middle of the platform and get on whichever carriage was closest. I thought that any planned events would be at one of the ends of the train, and not in the middle. My primary concern was preventing trouble, and I thought that by placing myself in what

I considered a safe area I might help avoid a messy situation.

Before long the train slowly pulled in and waves of people poured out of the doors. At the same time huge crowds were pushing onto the train and it was quite chaotic. It was like a sea of people both surging out and washing into the train. I'm still surprised that nobody was crushed. I managed to shove my way in and was squashed into the corner near the carriage doors. Just as they were closing a woman ran in. I recognised her instantly. She was the same woman from the Vale Club, the one wearing the red dress. This time she was in more casual attire, but it was definitely her. I wanted to say something, to apologise for what I had done. She wasn't far away, and I reckoned that if I squeezed past a few people I would be next to her.

As I was thinking of what to say, I noticed that she was pushing her way through the people. She was moving away from the doors and deeper into the carriage. I decided to follow her and went in the same direction. Soon she was at the end of our carriage and continuing through to the next one. I kept following her whilst attempting to be as discreet as possible. She quite often turned back as if she had forgotten something, and each time I stayed out of sight. I didn't want her to notice me and jump to the wrong conclusion. This continued until we were in the last carriage. It was less crowded than the rest. She made her way through the standing passengers to a man sitting down with a cane and briefcase and spoke a few words to him. He nodded and she sat next to him. He looked like the blind man she was with at the Vale Club.

I paused a moment to build up some courage and review what I would say, then approached the two of them slowly and carefully. I was so nervous that I imagined there was a blockage in my throat that made swallowing difficult. When I was standing close and about to speak she turned and finally spotted me. Calling out angrily she retrieved a gun from within her clothes and aimed directly at my head. I had hoped, perhaps foolishly, that I would have a chance to speak before things escalated.

I looked into her eyes for what seemed like a long time and I knew she was about to fire, so I ducked down and headed further back into the carriage and started to run to the next one. Turning to look behind I could see that she was following intently. Things were now officially not going as planned. I continued moving through the carriages trying to keep myself from a clear line of sight so she couldn't shoot me. While partially hidden I checked my watch and noted that the time was 5:57. I was thinking to myself that I was out of time and that I had to get out at the next station. That thought stopped me completely for a moment. What had brought it up? What was going to happen?

By that stage I had made my way back to the middle carriage and there was no sign of the woman. The train was pulling up to a station and I pushed my way through to the doors. As the doors began to open I stepped forward but was blocked by someone. I looked up and saw that it was her. She was intent on stopping me from leaving the train, but her weapon was not drawn. I knew that if I didn't move soon, the doors would close. It was a stand-off and I hesitated, unsure on how to proceed. Suddenly it was like a switch was flipped inside me and I leapt forward taking both of us out of the train doors in a messy heap. The doors closed and the train started to pull away. I stood up and collected myself and she did the same. Only she drew her pistol again, keeping it hidden.

"What have you done this time?" she accused me. Before I could answer her there was a great explosion from the rear of the train. Following it were the sounds of additional blasts and as I looked over I saw great spheres of fire cascading along the length of the train as it started to tilt on its side and veer off the tracks. The heat from the explosion and ensuing fires was so intense it extended all the way to us. The air itself was so hot it was like we were enclosed in an oven.

My attention was diverted again by the sharply contrasted chill of metal against the back of my head. I knew what it was, and that I didn't have much longer to live.

"At least I saved you," I said quietly then closed my eyes and braced for the shot. It never happened so I opened my eyes slowly, turning to face her. I saw that her face was streaming with tears. The blind friend of hers must surely have perished in the blast.

"I'll kill you next time!" she declared, then wiped her face and left.

As you can imagine I felt fairly defeated. Despite my best efforts, another catastrophe had occurred, this time even more disastrous than the last. Instead of making amends with the mysterious woman, I had killed another of her comrades, or at least appeared to do so in her eyes. I had managed to save one life, but was involved in the deaths of countless others. My earlier confidence and self-assurance were completely shattered and I knew that the recollection of that event would stay with me. There was nothing else to do so I started walking away from the tragic scene behind me. My slow pace was in stark contrast to those rushing past me in the opposite direction.

I passed through the station as if in a trance and reached the ticket gates. They didn't even care if I had a ticket or not. I didn't even know what station I was at. As I stepped on to the street it finally dawned on me that I really had no idea where I was. As I contemplated which way to go I was approached by two heavy-set men in expensive looking suits.

"Come with us, sir," they offered in a manner that I thought unwise to refuse. I was hustled into the back seat of a black luxury car, which drove off immediately.

"Our employer would like a private word with you," one of them explained. I merely nodded and stared out the window. All I hoped for was that something worthwhile came out of the meeting, to redeem the day in some small way. I didn't recognise the area we drove through, but that in itself wasn't surprising. After close to an hour the car pulled up abruptly and I was ushered out of the vehicle and into a very plain-looking building. We descended three flights of stairs and entered what looked like a makeshift office.

A bald round man sat at a desk and watched me closely. He gestured to the chair opposite without saying a word. I sat down quietly and waited for him to speak.

"That was quite a show you put on today," he remarked. I didn't know how to respond so I remained quiet.

"It's unfortunate that you didn't achieve the primary objective, but the destruction of the manifest should be enough. Were they both taken care of as well?" he asked. Since it was a direct question I had to think up an answer and quickly.

"The woman survived but I left her. Additional action wasn't part of the plan," I said calmly. I surprised myself by how collected I sounded. Inside I was a mess of nerves and uneasiness. My guts were churning away relentlessly and I felt sick. At any moment I could have keeled over and emptied my stomach of its contents.

"I must say, you are quite the professional. Always following the plan to the letter."

I nodded assent, as I didn't trust myself to answer him as confidently as before.

"So far your plan has succeeded surprisingly well. Phase A has been completed on schedule. You have my blessing to continue with Phase B."

"Very well," I replied, trying to play along.

He stood up and paced around the room slowly.

"I must admit, I'm not sure what to make of you," he said softly.

"You come from nowhere with an elaborate plan, and even manage to pull it off. I don't know anything about you, and I know everything about everybody with your talents." He made a hand gesture at the two men standing by the door and they left. Shortly they returned with Tony in tow.

"You remember Tony?" the man asked.

"Of course," I replied.

"Even Tony doesn't know what to make of you. He did give me something useful though."

The man walked over to the desk and removed a small item from the top drawer. He held it out in his hand and I saw that it was a folded blue piece of paper. The one I had placed in the storage locker at Central Station.

"Do you recognise this?" he asked me.

"Yes," I answered. My mind was racing with the pangs of betrayal and at the same time my paranoid intuition was completely vindicated. What if he had found my writing instead?

"What I can't understand is that why you would go to the effort of securing a locker and then placing this inside. Why are you keeping this note that I left you? What else are you planning?" he demanded. And there it was, the small piece of positivity that I wanted. This man was the

'M' in the note. A bit of my hope was restored, and a new resolve forged.

"It is merely a record of our correspondence. Surely it's fine to keep it in a location your representative recommended and not on my person," I replied in the hope that he accepted the answer.

"Just remember that I am watching you," he told me.

"Take him back, Tony," the man commanded. As I left he spoke once more.

"I'm not sure if you know, so I'll remind you just in case: nobody crosses Markus and lives to brag about it. Keep that in mind."

The car trip back was awkwardly quiet, Tony said nothing and I didn't offer any discussion myself. I wasn't sure where we were going, but it was most likely the same location where Tony dropped me off previously. I was thinking over the events that had just happened, and the information I had gained. I had a name for my employer, Markus. I also knew he was a detestable man, although that was easily deduced from the acts he had commissioned so far. However it also looked like I had planned out something bigger with the man. It was hard to believe that I could be the architect of such a plan. At the same time though, it did explain my intimate knowledge of what would occur. But it didn't seem right that I would be the sort of person to eliminate people so coldly. I remember thinking that maybe I didn't know myself as well as I should have.

The car stopped and as I went to leave Tony handed me another bulging envelope. We didn't speak and I got out and closed the car door carefully. I walked over to the house, and it was indeed the same one I stayed in the other night. I fished the key out from my pocket and unlocked the front door. Everything inside seemed to be exactly as I had left it. An interesting thought came to me: what if Markus and his cronies were not the ones that moved me from here the previous night? What if another party was involved, or if I myself had relocated thinking the location unsafe.

That there was the root of my problems, too many questions and not enough answers. I needed to start finding out what was going on. I had a lead though, that man named Markus. The clear way forward was to investigate him, and find out who these people were that Markus was targeting, through me. Were they better or worse than him? I opened the envelope and inside was money and what looked like another note. When I read it I discovered that it wasn't actually a note, but an invitation. It seemed that a Frank Masters would be attending a charity ball the following night. I sincerely doubted that Frank Masters existed, so I decided to go in his place.

As this day and my account of it has come to an end, I feel I owe an apology. As this tale begins to take shape, I cannot drop clever hints or foreshadow what is to come, which I'm sure a good writer would do. Who knows what tomorrow will bring? I can complain about many things in my current life, but I must admit it is far from mundane.

ELDERLY MAN DIES IN CLUB FIRE

By Jacqueline Somers

At approximately 5:45pm yesterday the Vale Club, located in RedBelle, caught fire and claimed the life of sixty year old man Arthur Morgan. His daughter was also caught in the blaze but escaped with minor injuries.

Fire fighters battled for over an hour to contain the inferno which nearly engulfed nearby buildings. The cause of the fire is still unknown, but authorities are not ruling out arson.

Three other people were hospitalised with minor burns and smoke inhalation. The club owner, one Jerry Montgomery, referred to the fire as a "Tragic accident that nobody saw coming." This was the first fire in the club's twenty years of operation.

"When rebuilding we will ensure the best fire safety practises are employed," Mr Montgomery promised. This is the fifth club to go up in flames this year, up from three last year. Experts believe that many of these clubs do not have sufficient fire safety measures in place, due to their age. Pubs and Clubs are an especially high fire risk due to the abundance of alcohol, carpet and wooden furniture.

HUNDREDS DIE IN TRAIN DISASTER

By Jacqueline Somers

A Metro Train on the East Line was derailed by a series of explosions yesterday just past Shermouth Station. Over five hundred people are confirmed dead and more are still being found amongst the wreckage. Injuries have been counted in the hundreds. Police believe it to be a terrorist attack but no groups have come forward claiming responsibility.

The incident occurred just past 6pm and is believed to have begun in the rear of the train. The initial blast triggered smaller charges throughout the remaining carriages which witnesses described as a giant fireball.

"It was like nothing I have ever seen before", said Frank Davis, a passenger who had alighted at Shermouth Station. "I turned around when I heard the explosion and couldn't believe my eyes. The train was covered in fire and tilting on its side. The screeching sound when it derailed was deafening."

The train travelled for another one hundred metres before coming to a complete stop. Ambulances and fire fighters were on the scene in minutes but many had already died. Rescue efforts are still ongoing.

Metro Rail chief Mitchel Anderson had the following to say. "We are doing everything in our power to determine how this tragedy occurred and punish those responsible. We are working closely with the police to examine all potential leads. I am also making it my priority to get the train line back into service as soon as possible."

This incident has been referred to as the greatest train disaster in recent history. The East Line is now completely blocked while excavation and rescue work continues. Bus services have been organised to replace trains in the meantime. A press conference is being held tomorrow to communicate the extent of the tragedy and the details of the inquiry being launched.

CHAPTER THREE

A PARTNER FOR THE BALL

I awoke again in a strange and particularly cheap hotel. I felt that maybe a pattern was forming. My first waking thought was how nice it would be if I could actually use the money that I was accumulating to stay in better accommodation. In fairness though there was probably a method to the selection of nasty establishments. I checked the wardrobe of the room and there was an expensive suit hanging up there, with proper identification for my new friend Frank Masters inside. The charity ball wasn't until later that night, so I had the rest of the day to make preparations. Since there wasn't much to do, I decided to get myself a proper meal and go from there.

I walked downstairs to the reception area of the hotel and paid for another night on the room. I left immediately and looked up and down the street I was on, searching for a nice café or small restaurant in order to get something to eat. There was nothing nearby, so I had a small wander to check out the area. I stumbled across a place called 'The Morning Star' and their advertisement for all day breakfasts won me over. I sat down at a table and found the daily newspaper sitting there. After ordering the breakfast special I flipped through the paper to pass time. I think my food arrived quite promptly but I didn't notice as my attention was completely focused on one of the articles. It was concerning the train disaster from the previous day.

There was no mention of any suspects, although there were over five hundred reported deaths and hundreds of injuries. I was absolutely floored. Of course it made perfect sense for a train explosion to have that kind of grisly toll, but having the cold hard numbers right there in front of me made it worse. However, in addition to the wave of depression this news brought with it, I also gained an idea. I called the waitress over and requested the previous day's newspaper. Luckily they had one and I scanned it quickly, looking for any reference to the Vale Club incident. There was a brief article about the fire and the death of a sixty-year old man. He was listed as an Arthur Morgan, survived by a daughter. She had to be that woman I saw on the train and at the club. I could finally put name to the faces from that fateful night. The name of the man I killed would certainly unlock some clues as to why Markus wanted him dead. I swore to myself that I would find a way to atone for all the deaths I had caused. I paid for the meal and asked the waitress if I could buy the newspapers off her. She gave me an odd look but agreed and I folded them both carefully before walking out with them under my arm. I thought it only fitting that I include the articles with any documents I leave behind, as a reference of sorts. I also wanted them as a reminder of the consequences of my actions. The stakes were high.

I went for another walk, thinking about my next step. What I needed was information on Arthur Morgan. Information about him would lead to information about his family and associates. That should logically follow on to if they might be targets and how to contact them. My thoughts then drifted ahead to the charity ball. It was clear that this event held an objective that Markus wanted completed, and it was surely related to the people who had already been targeted. Maybe I could find a source of information there.

The problem, however, was that I had what seemed to be another plan that relied purely on making an appearance and hoping something eventuated. The number of dead I was already burdened with suggested that it wasn't exactly a good strategy. I knew this time I really needed something better than 'show up'. I spent the better part of the afternoon trying to come up with that 'something'. Despite my intentions the best I could come up with involved mingling and finding out about the people attending. That was merely something that would happen regardless, and didn't constitute much of a plan. Again I would have to rely on my instincts. The thought of that didn't help my confidence either.

Back at the hotel I found a pair of scissors and cut out the relevant newspaper articles and put them in an envelope together with my writing from the previous day. If I were to ever compile my writings into something bigger, I would want the articles to be included with the events as I saw them. With the addition of a stamp and address it was ready to be sent. The one remaining task was to get changed into the dress suit and make my way to the ball. Before getting ready I took a moment to reflect on my mission. It was intended to relax and focus me a little, but in reality the opposite happened.

Soon after I was in a cab on my way and my mental state could be best described as completely nerve wracked. I had no idea what the night would bring, and I could only hope that I would be able to avert any major disasters. As the taxi pulled up I looked out and noticed that we were outside a very expensive hotel. There was a large crowd of people around and those entering were very lavishly dressed. I instantly felt out of place and I hadn't even gone inside yet.

I paid the driver, got out and walked as confidently as possible up to the doors. Once I was through the doors I showed my invitation and was directed to a great hall. It contained a dance floor, a modest stage, a bar and plenty of tables and chairs. The room was not particularly crowded yet, either I was too early or the majority planned to come in later. I scanned the room looking for anyone that I could recognise, but nobody stood out. My gaze ended up on the bar, thinking it would be a good place to start, so I strode over.

The bartender asked me what I wanted to drink and I told him to surprise me. The drink that arrived tasted terrible but I got small buzz out of it. I asked him what it was and he referred to it as a martini of some kind. Despite asking what it was, I wasn't really that interested in the answer. As I sat there carefully sipping it, a lovely young woman with long flowing brown hair sat down next to me. She already had a drink with her, so it seemed as though she was looking for something else.

"So what brings you here tonight? What's your connection to the foundation?" she asked.

"I received an invitation and decided to come along," I said, happy that the truth was also the best answer.

"Is that so?" she laughed, "your honesty is refreshing."

"Perhaps you could help relieve me of my ignorance, and tell me a bit more about the foundation," I suggested.

"The Marchilde Foundation was created to help find homes for children who are either homeless or from broken families. This ball is to raise money to improve the facilities for those children who haven't found homes yet."

"That's a noble cause," I remarked, "how can I contribute?"

"There is a charity auction later in the evening, or you can make donations throughout the night. However I recommend the auction. It's great fun, and the money is for a good cause."

"I'll make sure I stick around," I told her. She smiled, got up and left to talk to someone else. I guessed that she was trying to secure donations and get people involved in the auction. The auction seemed to be the focal point of the night so I felt that I should be there. I asked the barman for another drink, and turned to take another look at the room. It was filling up more now, with a slow but constant stream of people entering.

I went for a wander around the hall, trying to pass time. I was pretending to examine a display about the foundation when I heard someone approach.

"Turn around slowly, with no sudden movements," the female voice commanded calmly. I recognised it instantly. I complied with her request and saw that she was in another red dress, this one much more spectacular than the last.

"We should stop meeting like this," I quipped. She did not seem amused.

"Are you following me?" she asked.

"No," I said, "I had no idea you would be here."

"What are you doing here?"

"Why don't we sit down and have a quiet talk," I suggested. She walked over and took a seat at a nearby table. I sat down opposite her and thought of where to begin. I decided to be honest, but hide the fact that I knew next to nothing. I think that piece of information would cause more trouble than it was worth.

"What's your name? I honestly don't know it," I asked.

"You killed my father, but don't even know that? You bastard, why shouldn't I just kill you right now?"

"I know his name, but not yours," I remarked rather calmly given the circumstances. I started wishing that I had maintained this level of composure on the train.

"It's Alexis, are you happy now?"

"Well, Alexis, I have a few important personal matters that I must take care of. Once they are done, I will submit myself to you to do with as you wish."

"What do you have left to do? You have run out of people to kill that are close to me."

"I can't say," I told her honestly.

"Why should I trust your word?"

"I saved you," I replied.

"Saved yourself more likely, I was just in your way."

"Then how do you explain me seeking you out on the train?" I countered and she did not know how to respond. I decided to follow it up with another question.

"Why are you here tonight, what's your connection with the foundation?"

"Nobody here has any connection with that silly cause, this ball is just a front. You, of all people, should know this. I'm here to take revenge."

"Do you want my help?" I asked. As soon as the words left my mouth I couldn't believe that I had just offered to help her, since she obviously intended to kill someone. Maybe I thought my seemingly bumbling ways would stop her from doing it, or perhaps I just felt I owed her something.

"I have no interest in any help that you could offer. Stay out of my way!" she told me forcefully before leaving the table and storming off. I now had a clear objective for the evening: keep an eye on her and see what trouble she got herself into. In the lead up to the main event, I did just that and paid close attention to her activities. She didn't seem to converse with anyone and kept to herself. I got the impression that she was waiting too, for either the auction itself or something afterwards.

After two teasingly slow hours the auction was about to begin. I paid close attention to each item being offered but none piqued my interest. Garish collector plates, odd-looking sculptures, bizarre paintings and weird gadgets came and went. Suddenly the lights dimmed and a thundering sound could be heard, steadily from behind the stage. With a crash it ended, the lights returned to normal and the stage was cleared except for the auctioneer and a small golden box. I knew instantly that this item was important and must be won. It was introduced as a mysterious box that would be presented to the winner by the foundation president personally.

The bidding started at one dollar, and went up rapidly. The general thrill seekers soon fell by the wayside and it was left to a handful of rich gentlemen to continue the bidding. Until of course a lovely feminine arm was raised to make a bid. I looked over and recognised the woman as Alexis. What did she want with this box? Then it came to me in a flash, it was not the box she was after but the man presenting the box. He must be the one that she wanted for revenge. I mentally calculated how much money I had accumulated recently and decided I was still in the running. I made a bid which forced one of the other gentlemen to bow out. Alexis turned abruptly and when she saw it was me glared furiously. I decided that I must be on the right track.

Up and up the bids went, and my limit was soon approaching. The others had decided that this amount was too much for something sight unseen and Alexis and I were the only ones left bidding. For every bid she made, I went slightly over. She became frustrated and kept upping it by more and more each time. I had a decision to make. Should I keep going past the point where I could legitimately pay and bluff to beat her? Or should I bow out when I hit my limit? She did seem quite determined and I concluded she would probably continue past her limit, if she hadn't already, just to win. So when my highest possible offer was beaten, I stopped bidding and nobody else contested her. She flashed a forced smile and with that the auction was over.

I followed her discreetly once she had won and came to a small exit at the edge of the hall leading out to a separate section I had not noticed before. It was guarded by two burly men who let her through. By my guess the foundation president and the mysterious box were both back there. If that was true, I seriously doubted that they would just let me in. I looked around for a distraction that might let me slip past. There were two very drunk gentlemen not far away who looked like they might make good targets. I noticed one of them had a blue silk handkerchief protruding from his suit pocket. I wandered by, quickly snatching the handkerchief and dropping it right in front of the foot of his friend. As luck would have it, the man took a step forward in an animated fashion and slipped on the handkerchief, tumbling down to the ground and taking his friend with him. All I had to do was sit back and watch the show.

I didn't have to wait long, the man I pilfered the handkerchief from started laugh at his friend's clumsiness. The friend noticed the handkerchief beneath his foot as he got back up, of course, and accused the first man of dropping it on purpose. This soon escalated into an explosive argument, nicely fueled by alcohol. The two guards, obviously bored, walked over to break it up. I used this opportunity to sneak into the private area and find Alexis.

As I progressed further I noticed that the corridor I was in ended and branched off into two paths. If viewed from above it would appear like the letter T. Each end led into a different room. I picked the left path and walked into the room at the end but soon discovered that it was empty. That meant that Alexis had to be in the other one. As I went to leave the room I heard voices in the hallway.

"I thought I saw a guy walk down here," the first voice said.

"I guess we should check just in case," the second voice replied, sounding a lot closer than I had expected. I had to hide, and quickly. I looked around the room and noticed a rather large air vent in the wall near the ceiling, which looked just big enough for me to crawl inside. I managed to pry the cover off and squeeze in. Replacing the cover was far trickier but somehow I got it back on moments before the door to the room was kicked open. The two guards walked in, looked around suspiciously and then left. I wondered whether this vent or duct I happened to be in was connected to the other room. I quietly shuffled along on all fours until I discovered a bend. I followed it and found myself staring into another room. I saw Alexis and a man with jet black hair in his forties. It looked like they were having an argument but the words were a bit muffled. I inched closer and listened more carefully.

"You've had this coming for a long time," Alexis said.

"Surely you don't think this was all my doing," the man replied.

"I'll get every single one of you if I must!"

"How can you do that, if you can't even kill me?" the man laughed at her. I looked down and spotted the golden box was between them. He kicked it away, and it ended up fairly close to the vent opening. Drawing a gun from his suit he stepped closer and aimed it squarely at her forehead.

"It ends here my dear, any last words?" he asked. Alexis spat in his face and closed her eyes. There was no time for thought, so I burst through the vent and scooped up the box in a smooth motion. That proved distraction enough as the man turned to face me with surprise plastered all over his features. Alexis must have noticed, since she used this moment to kick the gun out of his hand and bowl him over with her shoulder. I opened the box and thrust my hand inside. I felt a cold handle which suggested it was a gun, so I pulled it out and pointed it at the man as he stood up.

"Stop right there!" I told him. He ceased his movements and Alexis ran over to pick up his gun.

"Who are you?" he asked me.

"Just a man," I told him and put the gun into the inner pocket of my suit jacket.

"I'll leave this to you," I told Alexis then left the room. I walked down the passage, exiting the secure area and past the guards. They stopped me and asked me what I was doing back there. I replied that I was looking for a toilet and to my dismay found none. I felt they wanted to question me further, but the sound of a gunshot clearly echoed through from the back and they ran in. I calmly walked away back into the crowd. The two guards weren't armed so I wasn't worried about Alexis being in any trouble. My only concern was reaching the exit as quickly as possible without drawing any unwanted attention.

I stepped out into the night air and appreciated the slight breeze. I wasn't sure what to do next, so I just walked down the street. It just felt natural. Before long, another luxury black car pulled up beside me. Stocky suited men got out, escorted me into the vehicle and handed me a phone.

"Yes?" I said into it.

"I've been informed there's quite an uproar at the charity ball. The target was found dead and the suspect is a single female working alone." I recognised the voice as the man called Markus.

"That's correct," I said.

"You continue to impress me. Leaving the girl alive has been hugely advantageous."

"You doubted me?" I asked him. I tried to make myself sound as confident as possible, to convince him I was the real deal. Even though I just got lucky, but there was no reason for them to know that.

"Yes I had my doubts, but I can see they were unfounded."

"Is that all?"

"No, did you acquire the gun?"

"Yes, I have it right here," I said, playing along. I did have a gun with me, perhaps it was the one he wanted. It had come from the golden box after all.

"Give it to one of my associates and you will be paid," he said before hanging up. I did as requested and received the now customary bulging envelope in return. I got out of the car and continued my walk as they drove off.

Looking back it was clear to me that the plan had been to kill the foundation president and take the gun he was offering in the gold box. There must have been something special about that gun. What concerned me was that if it was so valuable why was he putting it up for auction? That question would be something to think over later. I felt that the night was a partial success. I saved Alexis and secured the item expected of me. I did not prevent the death of that man, but I didn't kill him myself. I just hoped Alexis had a good reason for doing it. There was just something about her that I couldn't quite quantify, she had an importance that I couldn't quite pinpoint.

As I write down these current events many questions are on my mind: what is the connection between all these people and why does Markus want them dead? Is Alexis right about the foundation being a front? If so, then maybe the foundation president was a competitor for Markus. Although I don't know what Markus is really into, it can't be good.

The multitude of questions and the lack of answers makes things rather frustrating. However I'm slowly collecting pieces of the puzzle, which is progress for now. I just need to use these corners and edge pieces to complete the outline. It is easier to piece together the middle when you have an idea of what it is you are forming. Writing this account is an invaluable way of organising my thoughts and identifying the important pieces. What I wouldn't give to see the puzzle box though, and have an idea of what the end result is supposed to look like.

PHILANTHROPIST MURDERED AT CHARITY BALL

By Jacqueline Somers

Wealthy socialite and philanthropist Andreas Willis was shot dead last night at a charity ball. Two security guards working were also killed. The event was a fundraiser for the Marchilde Foundation, an organisation that provides help for underprivileged children. A young woman spotted leaving the scene is the prime suspect.

The shooting occurred shortly after the completion of the Charity Auction, in a room adjoining the main hall. Witnesses reported that the security guards ran to that room hurriedly around 9pm and saw a woman emerge alone minutes later.

The woman was described as tall with long blonde hair, blue eyes and wearing a red dress. Police are planning to release a composite image to enlist the public's help in tracking down the culprit.

Police Commissioner Jim Conradi had the following statement: "We have a number of good leads that we are diligently working on this case. We will see the killer brought to justice."

Andreas Willis established the Marchilde Foundation over 10 years ago, after retiring as CEO of the Mid City Bank. His foundation has helped over 200,000 children since its inception. He is survived by his wife who is expected to take over presidential duties. A public memorial service is being planned and the details will be announced in the coming days.

CHAPTER FOUR

A STROLL IN THE PARK

I opened my eyes once more to unfamiliar surroundings, and it was no surprise. Well a little surprise as it turned out, since for once I was staying in a nice looking place. It was a definite improvement over the previous shabby hotels. I wondered whether this upgrade in accomodation was a result of my desire for a better environment, or for some other purpose. I found the latter to be the most likely.

Rifling through my belongings I found another note. This one was a little more cryptic than those before it. It directed me to 'look underneath the seat dwarfed by oak in Clarence Park'. I walked over to the windows of my room, opened them and looked out. I saw that there was an expansive park across the road. Even the most cautious gambler would have put money on that being the park in question. I felt an icy breeze come through the nearest window and I was glad to find a heavy brown coat amongst my possessions.

I wandered downstairs and noticed that this hotel had a restaurant attached so I ordered some breakfast. I requested the current day's newspaper and leafed through it. I found an article on the incident at the charity ball. The thought crossed my mind that this could be the start of an odd ritual: breakfasting and reading about events I was involved in the previous day. There weren't many details in the piece, but the name of the man killed was mentioned. He was Andreas Willis and had been the president of the foundation since its inception. It didn't immediately suggest any connections with Alexis and her father, or even Markus. I bought the paper off them, thinking that I should really start frequenting news agents, and took it back upstairs to my room. I did a quick inspection of the room and spotted an invoice on the desk, it seemed as though I had already paid for two nights in advance.

I couldn't think of anything else that needed immediate attention so I chose to follow the note's instructions and see what I could find in the park. After crossing the road I found myself at a large sandstone gate with a sign above it which confirmed it as Clarence Park. As I expected it was no coincidence that I was staying opposite the park mentioned in the note. The park consisted of a winding network of gravel paths with an assortment of plants and trees along each side. Most of the vegetation had a compact plaque at its base, explaining its name and the region where it originated.

I wandered through the park taking it all in and learning the layout. Once I felt I had a working knowledge of the main routes, I turned my attention back to the note. It seemed fairly simple, what I was looking for was a seat in front of an oak tree, or perhaps even the biggest oak tree. Finding it was a different matter, but at the least logically it should stand out as an uncommonly large tree. I remembered noticing a few big trees towards the middle of the park, from my earlier exploration, so I headed back in that direction.

It must have been a popular park as there was a steady flow of people walking through it, and sitting on the various seats. There were even some lying down on blankets on the grass in the more open sections. I arrived at the centre of the park and looked around. I noticed in particular two large trees around the next corner and walked over to them. Both were roughly the same size, but one of them had a much smaller seat in front of it. The word dwarf from the note came to mind and I went closer. Bending down I read the plaque and noticed that it was indeed an oak tree. Luckily the seat was unoccupied so I sat down and took in the scenery. It was a nice spot to sit, you got a good view of the people going by and each of the main paths leading to the different areas. Hoping to remain inconspicuous I decided to stay seated for a time and pretend that I was enjoying the atmosphere. As it happened I did appreciate the spot and felt myself relax somewhat.

I bent down as if I had dropped something and fished around under the seat with one hand. I found a tiny folded piece of paper stuck to the bottom of the seat. There was no mistaking it, the note was what I had been directed to find. I retrieved the note and discretely slipped it into my coat pocket while continuing to take in the view. I remained seated, scouring the nearby area but saw nobody paying me any special attention. After a few minutes I took out the note and opened it. There was only one line on it, which read as follows:

The inquisitive man takes a break to swim with the dolphin.

I sighed inwardly, it was another clue. I could only hope this trail of clues wouldn't continue for too long. I pondered the note deciding that it must be referring to another location nearby. From my earlier loop around the park I recalled passing two water features. They would be a good starting point.

I made my way over to the nearest water feature. Looking at my watch I noticed that it was nearing midday. That explained why the crowds were getting bigger, as people must have been coming in to find a nice spot to eat lunch. When I was closer to my destination I saw that it was actually a fountain. The water ran through a lion's head and collected in a shallow pool below. The whole thing was probably the size of a large basin. I examined it from all angles and could not find any traces of dolphins, concluding that it was definitely not the place. I must have gotten some weird looks for my fascinated inspection of the fountain, but I admit I didn't notice. I think that was for the best, I felt uncomfortable enough already.

I set off in the opposite direction towards the other water feature I had seen. Chances were it was what I was after. If it wasn't, then I would have to form another plan. As I continued along I considered who would leave a trail like this and for what purpose? Whoever it was, it seemed probable that they were nearby watching me. Why else would you orchestrate such a stunt if you could not observe the results. Although that line of thinking could have easily been my paranoid tendencies taking shape.

I arrived at a circular shaped basin, wrought from copper. It was filled with water and had small dolphins along the sides in such a way that they looked like they were jumping out. It fit the description perfectly. I peered into the water, but couldn't see much. I removed my coat, rolled up one sleeve and dipped my arm in. A chill ran up to my shoulder as it entered the water. I fished around slowly and methodically despite the cold, as I didn't want to miss anything. The areas around the dolphins were my main concern, so I started my search there. While checking around the last dolphin I found something small and metallic. I grabbed it and pulled my arm out of the water. I shook my arm vigorously once it was out of the water to try to warm it up, and dry off a little.

Once I was satisfied I looked over my find and saw that it was a generic round badge. I turned it over and read the front, dropping it immediately due to the shock of what it was. I bent down to pick it up again immediately and walked over to a nearby seat to compose myself. The badge had the words Vale Club printed on the front, in the same style as the neon sign. I wondered who had left it and for what reason. It was definitely placed there as part of the treasure hunt. I opted to take it at face value and travel to the Vale Club once more to see out the trail I was following.

I left the park and hailed a taxi, directing the driver to take me to the club, that very same club where this tale began. I wondered if it was possible that the venue was back open, surely the fire damage would have been pretty extensive. There had to be either something there or someone waiting. As the taxi took me closer I started to get anxious, what if there was a trap in store for me? It didn't matter though, I had to continue regardless. There would be no answers otherwise. We arrived and I paid the driver, getting out across the road from the club. It was mostly destroyed as I expected, and definitely closed. I crossed the road and walked up to it, reading the note on the front door which explained the renovations and repairs taking place. There was no hidden message that I could see. I continued past it, wondering what was next.

"Here to gloat over your deed?" Alexis asked me from behind. I quickly turned to face her, and tossed over the badge as a form of explanation. She caught it but didn't bother looking at it.

"So, you're the one working for Markus then," she said, "I knew he had someone doing his dirty work, so I organised this little game to see for myself. It's rather convenient, and now that I think about it, it makes perfect sense that you are his lap dog."

"Not at all, I have my own agenda," I replied coolly, trying to sound confident. In reality I was flustered and my heart rate was rising quickly. I had no idea how to handle the situation.

"Ah yes, you and your personal matters, and your reasons. Pathetic rationalisations to explain away the fact that you have no spine," Alexis replied full of venom. She turned her back to me and walked away a little. I think she didn't know what to do, she had probably expected someone else. If that was the case though, why make the meeting at the Vale Club, the scene of her father's death? She already knew that I was the one who killed him.

"Good riddance, they can take you," she said breaking the silence.

"What are you talking about?" I asked her. However I soon got the picture when two cars pulled up and a group of men with guns poured out.

"This is the man," she told the men and pointed at me.

"Markus's operative?" one of them asked. He was taller than the rest and not as stocky.

"Yes, as agreed," she replied. There was nowhere to run so I let them shove me into the back seat of one of the vehicles. As we drove off I looked back and her eyes met mine. I could not read the look on her face.

My captors weren't especially talkative. The man I identified as their leader was in the other vehicle, so these were probably just grunts. Using the relative quiet to my advantage, I tried to figure out the recent events. I wasn't sure what they wanted with me exactly, or why Alexis had lured me there for them. I wasn't any further with my deductions when we arrived either. They blindfolded me before taking me out of the vehicle. It was odd being led around without my vision but I decided to not cause any problems and go quietly. There would be a time for action, but not yet.

They placed me in an empty room initially, so I used that time to rest and prepare for whatever was next. After a while the door opened and a well-dressed man entered. He was in an expensive dark navy pinstripe suit with well-groomed black hair under a matching hat, but what really stood out was his intense blue eyes.

"I'll cut straight to the point," he said, "was I your next target?"

"I don't even know who you are," I replied.

"Don't play games with me, we know that Markus has been eliminating us one by one."

"What makes you think that I have any part in this?" I asked him.

"The girl told us everything. How you killed her old man, pulled the train job and then took out Andreas while leaving her holding the bag."

"Are you referring to the charity event?"

"Of course I am."

"You seem to have gone to some trouble, so why am I here?"

"We want to know why Markus is targeting us. He must have some reason for taking action now, of all times. I also believe that as long as we have you here, he won't make any more moves against us."

"What makes you think I am close enough to Markus to know what he is planning, or for him to even care if I am captive? I have no idea what connection there is between you all," I replied honestly, but also in an attempt to bait the man. With some luck he would get frustrated and reveal more information.

The man paced around the room, occasionally looking at me, then ignoring me again. He finally stopped and addressed me.

"I want to be civil about this matter, but you also need to cooperate. I will take whatever steps are necessary to extract the information I want, and believe me they will not be pleasant," he said. I took a moment to think about his generous offer, and decided it wouldn't hurt to feed him something. I reasoned that I shouldn't need to make it all up either, there were bits and pieces already revealed to me. It might even be a good opportunity to fill in some of the gaps.

"He seems to be after certain objects, but I don't know their relevance," I told him.

"Keep going."

"The incident on the train was to get the contents of a briefcase," I explained then added, "eliminating the old man before that was probably related."

"Yes, yes this is beginning to make sense. Keep going," he instructed.

"The purpose of the charity ball job was to retrieve a gun."

"And you succeeded?" he asked.

"Yes."

"He must have discovered something we missed," the man muttered to himself. He pulled out a scrap of paper and pen from within his jacket, scribbled something down and returned them.

"Will I be able to go?" I asked him, "I have cooperated."

"Lord no, I can't have you running around causing trouble. You will remain here until I have dealt with Markus and that woman." I did not mind the idea of remaining captive if it prevented further lives being taken, however I couldn't wait there knowing they would go after Alexis. I had no idea what they would do with her, or me either once Markus was out of the picture.

"Wait!" I called out as he was leaving. He stopped and faced me. I stepped closer before speaking again.

"I still don't even know your name."

"Thomas," he replied and turned to leave. I knew that was my only chance of escape. Instinctively I reached over and pressed a point on his neck which caused him to collapse quietly into a heap on the floor. A quiet voice in the back of my head asked how I was able do that, but it was quickly silenced due to the gravity of the situation. My freedom was all that mattered. I retrieved all the items stored in the pockets of my coat and stuffed them in my pants pockets. Then I swapped my coat for his jacket and took his hat. To complete the picture I dragged him over to the small bed, put my coat over him and lay him down facing away from the door. I hoped that it would buy me some time should anyone check in briefly, and I might also pass as him from a distance. With any luck I could leave the place undetected.

I left the small room and closed the door behind me. There were no guards posted, so my disguise was not tested yet. I made my way through a network of corridors and went up every time a set of stairs presented itself. Of course I would have to come into contact with people eventually, I just hoped it was not in the confines of the underground section where I would be more easily detected. Thankfully either the array of bland hallways was not particularly vast, or I got lucky, since I soon emerged into the lovely and fresh night air. I was at a location that looked like a large complex of warehouses with lights scattered here and there. I looked around carefully while I walked to see if anyone was watching me, or reacting strangely. At the same time I didn't want to appear like I didn't belong. I spotted some parked vehicles in the distance and made my way over to them. As I got closer I saw that I was right and walked a direct line to the nearest vehicle. However my good fortune had finally failed me and there was another man out there. He saw me and started walking over. Most likely he was approaching because he recognised the outfit, so I tried to play it cool.

I turned my head briefly in his direction and when I saw he was still approaching I made a dismissive gesture with left my hand as I continued walking to the vehicle. He stopped immediately and turned to head the other way. With any luck he didn't want to cross his boss and was leaving, rather than rushing off for the alarm and countless reinforcements. At any rate I didn't want to hang around to see which it was. I tried the driver's door of the vehicle and it opened, which was a good sign. I entered and closed the door behind me, looking for the ignition. My luck didn't carry that far however, as there were no keys. I wondered whether I could start it some other way.

With some effort I pried apart the compartment covering the ignition and found a tangle of wires. I tried not to think about it too much and just started adjusting where they were plugged in, and connecting wires haphazardly. I think there was some method to it, but I did not consciously know it. The sound of the car roaring into life was like victory bells and I drove the car towards the exit of the complex. I arrived at the gate and discovered that it was open, the man I saw earlier was in a little room next to it and waved me through. Perhaps my luck had never left me.

Now that I was clear of my captives, one problem remained. I had a stolen car, and no idea where to drive it. I had memorised the address of my house, if you could call it that, but did not know the way there. I probably could have found my way if I was close, but I had no point of reference. There was also the option of the hotel that I had booked. However I didn't know if Alexis had spotted me leaving there, so I didn't want to risk it. I ended up driving for a little while, and when I found a suitably remote spot I decided to ditch the car.

I hailed down a taxi not far from where I left the car and directed the man to drive me to my home address. This time I noted important landmarks in areas I had been before. I wanted to ensure that I could navigate the area myself if I needed to. The taxi driver tried to make conversation, but I didn't even bother with any small talk. At last we arrived at the place I called home. Once I was inside, I remembered that Thomas had written a note for himself and placed it in his jacket, which I was still wearing. I pulled it out and read the contents:

Secure Milson's artifact, most likely at Mantiver HQ

That was interesting, although I will admit it was rather convenient that he would scribble down such useful details. Surely a man of his position could remember without a note. Either way, I decided it was my best lead and to consider the greater puzzle with it included as a piece. My analysis was as follows:

It seemed safe to say that there exists a group of men who between them have a collection of artifacts of some nature. The gun I retrieved from the charity ball had to be one of these artifacts. Markus is known to the group, perhaps even one of them, and he is targeting the rest to steal what they have.

What of Markus and his plans though? Perhaps he thought me dead. That seemed like it might just be for the best. That could be an opportunity for me to escape from this mess before it escalated further. I entertained the thought for a moment, revelled in it, but ultimately discarded it. I could not go through with that. At the very least I wanted to do enough good to settle the account for the acts I had already been a part of. Leaving at that stage would have made me worse off than at the beginning.

I pondered my options and only one stood out: seek out this other artifact and get it before Markus. Maybe if I secured one I could discover why they were being collected, and even use it as a bargaining chip down the line. It was nice for a change to be deciding myself where to go next, even if it turned out to be an illusion of choice. When you think about it the only difference is that I found the new direction myself, rather than having it thrust upon me.

That line of thinking distracted me from what was really worrying me. The way I instinctively disabled that man and started the vehicle. They were highly honed skills with very specific applications. Your average person would not know them. It was more likely that anyone with those talents was from an unsavoury line of work. The only logical explanation was that I was not new to the tasks which I have been doing since the beginning of this written account. I can only hope that what I did previously was for good reasons and for good people.

One question rises above the others: what defines a man? His actions or his intentions? His past or his present? The answer still eludes me but it helps me to write down these thoughts and order them. Let's see what tomorrow brings.

CHAPTER FIVE

SECURING AN ADVANTAGE

I awoke in my house where I had fallen asleep, which was certainly a new experience. How sad it sounds when I write it, that waking up in the same place that I went to sleep was unexpected. I sat up and planned my day. I would find myself a good business suit, go out to this Mantiver company and gain access. Once inside I would try and find Milson and the artifact referred to by Thomas. Hopefully then I would have an opportunity to learn more, or at least secure the artifact as something to bargain with.

It was a simple plan in essence, however pulling it off would be anything but. I started off by searching the house for anything useful. I found what looked like an appropriate business suit for the occasion which took care of one problem. Next I needed to find the address of the company. I lucked out again by finding a phone book with their address and contact number listed. I was amazed by the fact that my plan could actually go ahead. All that was left was travelling there, and a taxi sounded like the best option. I had come to rely on them as my main mode of transport. The only real drawback was the cost, which wasn't really an issue for me so I saw no reason to stop using them.

On the way there I thought of ways I could get access to their restricted areas. The most obvious option was to get into a less secure area, and find my way from there. My first hurdle would be getting that initial step inside. I was still lost in thought when the taxi parked across the street, signifying our arrival. The Mantiver company had an expansive complex of tall buildings consisting almost entirely of glass panels and looked very impressive. I thought to myself that perhaps getting in was going to be even harder than I had imagined.

I entered the building and noticed people everywhere. That was positive as the crowds would help me blend in. I stood still for a moment, observing the people and trying to spot employees of the company. I noticed a few signs which provided directions to the various areas. Taking all that information in, I chose to ask at reception about a meeting in what seemed to be the busiest area and see where it got me.

"Good morning," I said to the receptionist.

"Good morning and welcome to the Mantiver Corporation. How can I help you today sir?" she replied.

"Well I have a .. meeting.. in the Blue Lab," I explained awkwardly. Her face lit up and she smiled secretively.

"Oh are you the security consultant? Your partner is already here, I gave her a basic pass to get in." She pointed to the corner and I saw a figure in dark glasses with long blonde hair. A part of me hoped it was Alexis, but at the same time a part of me hoped it wasn't. I thanked the receptionist and walked over to find out.

"You're late," she told me. I instantly recognised the voice. My fears were confirmed.

"That's funny, I don't remember making any plans," I said.

"You didn't, I just expected you earlier. After you eliminated Thomas this had to be your next target."

"I did no such thing!" I contested strongly, "I merely excused myself from his hospitality."

"You're a real class act," she laughed, "switching places with him so when they came in to execute you they killed their boss instead. It was a great touch." I was quiet for a moment while I took in the information. I guess my instincts to leave were right. Yet it also meant I was responsible for another death.

"Why save me when you are working for Markus?" she asked, her tone suddenly serious.

"I'm not working with him by choice," I replied. As soon as I said that I realised the truth of it. Regardless of what had already transpired, working with Markus was not something I wanted to do. Upon reflection it seemed obvious, but I hadn't thought of it that way.

"Work with me and maybe I won't kill you," she offered. Thinking it over I guess it was the most conciliatory she could be given the situation. I inwardly rejoiced at the chance to start setting things right.

"Sounds fair. By the way, what did you say to the receptionist?" I asked.

"That my partner would be arriving later, and would test her with a terribly lame excuse to gain access. I gave her your description just in case. I would have gone in without you soon, but you just made it in time."

"So what are you after?"

"The same thing as you, I want their artifact."

"What is it? What's the significance?"

"I'm not sure either, but it's why my father was murdered," she said before abruptly turning away. Her confident front had crumbled momentarily. It was an understandably uncomfortable subject for her. I couldn't imagine what it was like for her actually talking to me after what I had done. I moved on with another topic.

"What's your plan, and how does it involve me?" I quickly asked.

"Get in, split up and find the artifact. Meet back after one hour and plan our next move. The security consultant angle should keep us out of trouble from the underlings since they won't question it. Your unique skills might come in handy if they have any strange security measures."

"Sounds about as well thought out as my plan," I joked and I managed to get half a smile out of her. With that we went through the main doors and into the first secure area.

"It's this building right?" I asked warily, remembering the other buildings in the complex.

"I think so, but we will find out for sure soon enough," she replied. We came across what looked like some offices but what was of more interest was the nearby elevator.

"This is where we split up. You go upstairs and I'll head downstairs," she instructed.

"Sure," I said. She pressed the down button and walked into the nearest lift that opened. It was then I remembered that I didn't have my own security pass. I couldn't help wondering if this was another setup at my expense. I could picture it perfectly, me fooling around and making a nice distraction while she got away with something. I couldn't discount the possibility that she would betray me again. Yet I still felt I owed her, so I did what I could regardless of what might happen.

My first step would be getting a security pass from the area I was in and seeing how far I could take it. I would have to play on the fact that there were so many employees milling around. If required I should be able to bluff that I'm from another area as long as I have a pass. It looked like they relied on a basic electronic security system to lock the doors and secure the lift, but with the proper access card that would be no problem. All the office areas I came across appeared to be locked but there was a constant flow of people going in and out. That made it easier.

I noticed a stairwell near one of the transparent glass main doors, so I used that to my advantage. I stood at the entrance to the stairs, speaking one side of an imaginary conversation while keeping the office door in my peripheral vision. When I noticed movement I wrapped up my fake chat and went to use the door as the other person was leaving. The idea was that I could get in without drawing attention or using an access card. It worked perfectly and the man on his way out even held the door open for me as I went through. Now I was in, I needed to find a wayward access card to call my own. That would get me to a higher floor, and one step closer.

I strolled through the office trying to belong there. I passed several cubicles of people talking loudly and kept an eye out for a card. I came across a kitchen area with lots of people standing around chatting. This meant that there should be some unattended desks, so I grabbed a half-full coffee mug from the bench and continued on. It was a smart move as people paid even less attention to me with the new prop. As I was close to completing a lap of that particular office I noticed a partially closed drawer with a neck strap hanging out. It looked exactly like the type you usually have connected to an access card. I sat at the desk, put down my coffee and fished around in the drawer. What I had spotted was indeed an access card, although it was otherwise unmarked. I would need to test it to see what access it had. I hung the lanyard around my neck, got up and walked out of the office without being challenged by anyone.

The first part had gone off without a hitch, although eventually some poor employee would discover that his or her card was missing. Hopefully the coffee left there would imply that someone sat down at the wrong desk by mistake. I hoped that the absence of obvious foul play would buy me more time, which was reassuring as I had no idea how long I required. I stepped into the nearest elevator and passed the access card over the sensor. There were thirty floors in the building but only the first ten lit up. Of course I wasn't sure what floor to target, but it seemed logical to aim for the top and work my way down if required. Floor ten it was.

I stepped out of the lift into a very different environment. It appeared a lot more reserved, and the people walking around seemed more purposeful. That made me uneasy, as they would surely be a bit more discerning about who was about and ask more questions. I had to rethink my approach as my trick with the previous access card wasn't likely to work again. First I looked for an empty desk, to sit down out of the way and plan my next move. I spotted one in the corner and walked towards it. Step by step I crossed the office and nobody seemed to pay much attention to me, so I felt in the clear at least for a short time. I thought about how much easier it would have been at night. I made a mental note to consider why I didn't think of that earlier.

"Who might you be, slacker?" an older woman with greying hair asked me. I froze, unable to respond. The security consultant explanation was playing out in my mind but I just couldn't utter the words. At the same time I didn't think it would work on her, which might have been the reason for my temporary paralysis. I slowly turned to completely face her, hoping something clever came to mind.

"You must be the new guy, skulking over to the corner to avoid doing any work," she scolded me. I smiled at her sheepishly and internally cried out in relief, that was a better alternative than the many others that were running through my mind.

"Come with me, I have a job for you!" she commanded and walked off quickly. I sprung into action and followed her. It was all I could do.

She led me to a cramped office in the opposite corner, with glass walls so you could see out into the rest of the floor. There was a constant stream of people rushing in and out of the glass office, and it seemed to be the main hive of activity. There was paper everywhere, on tables, chairs, filing cabinets and in the hands of the people scurrying around. She told me to wait by the door and stepped around the chaos expertly, searching for something amongst the papers. She plucked a bundle of paper about as thick as my thumb, seemingly out of nowhere, and handed it over to me.

"I need this report taken upstairs to Milson's office," the woman instructed me. "Here's a special access card to get to the floor. This is just a simple errand, take too long and I'll come looking for you. The receptionist there will give you a receipt to acknowledge she got the report."

I nodded and walked off with purpose. What a lucky break, I had gained access to the floor with Milson's office. It was only logical that other important things would be stored there. The pressing problem was that I had a time limit, if what that woman said was true. She looked too busy to go after me personally, but it could be problematic if she sent someone to see where I had gone. Still, it was an opportunity and I was determined to make it count.

I walked over to the lifts, more confident now that I had a legitimate reason to be there. The elevator seemed like it took forever to arrive, eating away at my limited and constantly expiring time. I used the card and every floor lit up as available. It was at that moment I remembered that the woman had not actually told me which floor I was supposed to go to. I decided to pick the top floor and see what I found there.

The elevator ascended and people got in, and then got out, so that it was empty again by the time I neared the top. I looked at my watch and realised it was lunch time, which explained why I was hungry. I had been hungry for a while, but only noticed when I had a chance to relax. At last the elevator doors opened and before me was my destination. The top floor consisted of a lavishly decorated reception area and a large room with equally imposing double doors. The reception desk was unattended, I thought that perhaps they were out to eat.

I walked up to the desk and peered over it, there was definitely nobody around. I went over to the office doors and knocked sharply twice in quick succession. A minute later I knocked again in the same way, but there was no response. I tried opening the doors but they were tightly locked. I then noticed there was a card reader to the side of the doors and realised that I needed access to get in. I had a go with the access card that had worked in the elevator, but as expected it was denied. I looked at my watch, I wasn't sure how long 'too long' was, but it felt like my time was running out and I hadn't even completed the errand, let alone gotten anywhere interesting.

My only option was to find a way into that room. I looked around the reception area and found a letter opener. I picked it up and then went over to inspect the card reader securing the door. It was the same as the rest in the building. Again I acted by purely instinct alone, and used the letter opener to pry the reader off the wall. I pulled it completely off, but it would not come away entirely as it was still attached to something by a series of wires. Behind the reader was a hole just big enough to fit an arm through. Without a second thought I did just that, sticking my right arm in and following the wires back to a panel of some kind. My fingers explored it briefly, then I retracted my arm to grab the letter opener and pressed it up against the panel in a few different ways, targeting different metallic objects. I heard a definitive click, quickly removed my arm and pushed hard on the nearest of the double doors.

It opened with ease, and I let out a huge sigh of relief. I used my foot to keep the door open and I placed the reader back in its spot. It wasn't properly secured, but hopefully it would pass a casual inspection and delay any suspicions until I was long gone. I dashed in and let the door close behind me. I was in an extravagantly decorated and fully furnished room, complete with lounges, a giant desk and elaborately cushioned chair. This had to be Milson's office, or at least someone very important if not him.

Leafing through the papers on the desk I quickly verified that I was in the right place. The next question was whether the item I sought was here, and if I could find it in time. Of course there was also the minor problem of not knowing what the artifact looked like. I started off by doing a quick sweep of the room on the lookout for any safes or other secure storage areas. Whatever this artifact was I doubted it would be in plain sight. At first glance there wasn't anything that looked like a safe, so I was either in the wrong location or it was more carefully hidden.

Time was short, and I could just picture someone bursting through the door any minute and then demanding an explanation. I sat down in his chair and grasped around for any secret switches or other strange things accessible from that position. My hands ran over something on the underside of the desk surface. I tried pressing it and felt a gentle vibration from the desk with a clanking sound for accompaniment. I checked the drawers again and this time found an extra compartment in one of the bottom ones.

I opened it up and reached inside. I felt a cold metallic object and pulled it out to take a look. It was a small intricately made clock that fit entirely in the palm of my hand. The feel of the metal reminded me of the gun I had earlier retrieved from the charity ball. I shoved it in my jacket pocket and tried to put the room back to how it was when I arrived. I left the office, remembering to take the report with me, and I placed it on the reception desk. As I returned to the elevator I noticed it was just arriving.

"Oh Milson!" a female voice laughed as the elevator doors opened. A man and a woman stepped out, both looking dishevelled and then quite embarrassed when they saw me. I mumbled something about a report left there, and I darted into the elevator. I think they took my awkwardness as being due to seeing them in that state, and not for some other reason.

Once safely inside the elevator I rode all the way to the ground floor to see if Alexis was around. I was pretty sure I had what we came for, and even if I didn't there would be no second chance. I stepped out and looked around, but didn't see her. I hurried over to the office where I originally pilfered the access card, and dropped it near the door. That way I believed that it should find its way back to its owner. Feeling hungry I followed the signs and found the cafeteria. I bought two sandwiches and an apple juice and returned to a seat with a view of the elevators.

Midway through my second sandwich I saw Alexis stepping out of a lift. She looked stressed and in a rush. Once she caught sight of me, she became visibly annoyed.

"Well look at you!" she remarked, "here I am breaking a sweat and you are just sitting around stuffing yourself."

"I was hungry," I replied before taking another bite from my sandwich. She looked at her watch.

"We have to go, right now, otherwise we will be late for our next appointment." I nodded and finished off my food, bringing the drink with me. She led me over to the elevator and presented an access card of her own, taking us down. It reminded me of the special access card I still had, so I dropped it in the lift. We soon emerged in a car park and I followed her through a maze of vehicles until she stopped suddenly.

"This is it, get in!" she hissed at me. I got in the passenger side and didn't say a word. Within a few minutes we were clear of the building, the entire complex and then out onto the street. She pulled over to the side of the road, and then turned back to look at Mantiver HQ. She fished something out of her bag and pressed it. I looked over at what she was watching, and then saw an explosion consume the basement of the main building. The structure rocked, but stayed up. However the car park fell in on itself.

"Payback is a wonderful thing. As an added bonus it will slow them down," she remarked.

"You do realise that you just brought even more attention to us?" I said, annoyed and surprised by her actions.

"I hope they think it's me," she said. It didn't make any sense, but I felt that she didn't want to elaborate further. She started the car back up and drove off. I couldn't take my eyes off the destruction behind us.

"Did you get it?" she asked me.

"I think so, but I can't be sure since I didn't know exactly what I was looking for."

"What was it?"

"A small metal clock." She seemed to ponder that for a moment.

"I think that's it, I wish we still had the manifest."

"The manifest?" I asked.

"A list of all the artifacts and a description of each. It was in the briefcase we were transporting on the train. The one you blew up." Again it came back to me, and since I couldn't argue otherwise I had to assume that I was at least partly responsible for the rail incident.

"If Markus was willing to blow up that list if he couldn't get it, then he must have some other source of information on them," I remarked. As far as I could see it was the only logical explanation.

"Good thinking, that's our next target," she said.

"Our next target? I thought you wanted me dead?"

"I may as well make use of you before that happens. Besides if you do a good job maybe I'll spare you," she replied in a matter-of-fact manner. That wasn't exactly an inspirational line. However I felt that it was the least I could do, to help her in this. It wasn't all bad either. Helping Alexis was probably my best bet of finding out what was going on. I could also get back at Markus for what he had brought me into. There's always the chance that I volunteered for this, that I'm as much in the wrong as him, but he still has a lot to answer for.

As I write these words, my main concern is that I trust in myself, and keep the doubts to a minimum. They have their uses, but left unchecked they will consume me. Alexis herself is a puzzle. It appears as though she's now my partner, of sorts, which I still don't know how react to. I think the extent of her planning is to cause as much pain as possible to the people she hates. However she definitely needs some help. Such anger will get her in more trouble, of that I am sure. If possible, I would like to help prevent that.

In retrospect I employed more skills of a dubious nature today. What's really surprising is that Alexis expected me to. Does she know something more about me? She doesn't seem the type to place blind faith in others. Regardless of that, I don't know where she has taken me. Now that today's events have been written up, I am about to go to sleep in this strange dwelling. It is a shoebox of an apartment on the outskirts of the city. It might even be her home. I must hurry and finish this account as quickly as possible, so that Alexis doesn't find me writing it. That would be too hard to explain.

I hope that I can continue this tale, but I honestly don't know what will happen. Maybe Alexis will sell me out again. I wouldn't hate her for it either, since I took something that can never be replaced. There's a lot of uncertainty in the world, well at least in my world. No matter what happens though, I will move forward. It is only through action that I can find answers. No amount of thoughtful pondering will provide the solution. My fate, what becomes of me, is all decided by my actions. It is not predetermined.

TERRORIST STRIKE DESTROYS MANTIVER CORPORATION HQ

By Jacqueline Somers

The main building of the Mantiver Corporation was destroyed by an explosion at approximately 1:30pm yesterday. After the initial blast the building crumbled in stages and eventually collapsed. Twenty employees are missing, suspected dead, including the Mantiver Corporation CEO Walter Milson. No terrorist groups have claimed responsibility for the attack.

Police are still sifting through the rubble but suspect the bombs were set off in the underground parking garage. Emergency crews were quickly on the scene and rescued the people trapped inside with a quick and daring rescue operation. This heroic effort kept the casualties to a minimum.

The incident occurred while many employees were on their lunch break. The complex consists of six buildings but only the main building was attacked. The Mantiver Corporation are known for their genetic research and pharmaceutical products.

Acting CEO Jeremy Rafters had the following statement. "Our hearts go out to all the families of the employees harmed by this senseless attack. We are striving to discover the cause behind this tragedy and those responsible. I promise to keep the public up to date on all developments."

This is the second terrorist strike in a matter of days, the previous one destroying a Metro City Train on Tuesday. Police did not comment on any possible links between the two attacks.

CHAPTER SIX

DIFFERING PERSPECTIVES

Well, this is a first for me. I've never been the type of character to reflect too heavily on things, and I have never kept a journal or anything like it. But after reading what he had written, I felt I had to add something. It's only right that I tell my part of this tale, and fill in some gaps that would never be filled in otherwise. I'll start from the top.

It all began with the death of my mother. She died in a restaurant, caught squarely in the middle of a gang shootout. She was no saint, but she was a good person and didn't deserve to go like that. Her death changed my father and I, we became angry with the world. Being a teenager I just bottled it up, but he took action. I have always respected him for that, though I never told him.

He dived headfirst into their world. Before this he was just a plain old shoe salesman, but he found one of the crime families and did whatever jobs were going.

During this time I never saw him, I think he pretended I didn't exist to both help himself with what he was doing, and to protect me from any reprisals. Despite his absence, he was still very protective of his little girl. Our neighbour kept an eye on me, and I appreciated having someone around, though you would never hear me admit it back then. My dad worked his way up their ranks very fast and earned their respect. I have no idea how he managed that, but looking back I think I'd rather not know.

Years passed and he became well-known in their world. At that time tensions flared up again and my father convinced the crime family he was with to go after one of the groups that killed his wife. A bloody war ensued, probably no better than the one that took my mother, but he didn't care about that anymore. He got his revenge, well at least half of it. But it wasn't enough for him, in his eyes they were all equally responsible. He didn't have to wait long.

Shortly after the bloodshed ended, the other family responsible for her death made a move against my father and his men. They saw an organisation weakened by fighting, which equated to an opportunity to scrub out a competitor. They ambushed several key members to kick things off, sending my father into a rage. I'm not sure whether he wanted an excuse to go all out, or he had formed real bonds with those people, but he took action. He hunted down each member of that rival family himself, one by one, eliminating them. That was the end of it, his revenge was complete and the feuds done with.

Then he came back to me, explained his actions in full and apologised for it all. It was good to have my father back, but he had changed. He was never the same as the man who I remembered from my childhood. He tried to go back to selling shoes, but he no longer had the patience for it. He was also constantly concerned that people might be targeting him. Whether these were legitimate concerns, or paranoia setting in, I'm not sure. But those attacks never eventuated.

It seemed he was unable to completely leave that world, so he set up his own small group. He took on odd jobs for the various families. His reputation from the earlier bloodshed preceded him, and nobody really wanted to cross him. As time went on he had found a place for himself where he didn't take any sides, and avoided the messier conflicts. It was at this time, when he had finally settled down, that he looked for a new purpose.

I don't know how he first stumbled across them, but his new purpose was found in the promise of these artifacts. He established some sort of link between them, and used that to research and find more. He never collected them as far as I know, but over time he created a detailed dossier on them. It consisted of the last known location of each, a description and some personal notes particular to that item. This was the stage at which I became involved.

I can't remember why I joined him, but I had no alternatives. It was like the choice was already made for me, and there were no other options. But at the same time I didn't feel like I was forced into this line of work. It's hard to explain, so I hope you understand what I mean. When it comes down to it, I know nothing else. It sounds a bit sad when you put it that way.

We had another working with us, he was Elias. He was blind since birth but had loving parents that took care of him. He was a clever guy, and growing up became fairly self-sufficient. Unfortunately as a young teenager his parents were killed. They were executed by a hit man called Stefan, but there was no contract on their heads. My father was after the man and finally tracked him to a seedy strip club. Stefan used his friends there to give him enough time to slip out, with my father close behind. A wild chase followed.

Stefan had made many enemies due to his work and was looking to leave town anyway. He didn't want any additional reason for people to follow him so he avoided a direct confrontation with my father. However my father's reputation amongst those people was not for nothing, and he followed tirelessly. Finally in desperation Stefan broke into a house and took the people within as hostages at gunpoint. My father saw him go in, so he called out for Stefan to surrender peacefully. Of course he did not and threatened to kill the hostages if my father so much as set foot inside. My father ignored him and burst into the house. Who knows what Stefan was thinking that day, but he went ahead with his threats. Two gunshots echoed around the house and then silence.

The only people left in the house were the recently deceased owners. Stefan had bolted after shooting them, using their deaths as a distraction to give himself time. By the time the house had been properly searched and secured he was long gone. At this point, when things already seemed at their worst, it got worse still. Elias arrived home. The only consolation was that he was not able to see his parents like that.

My father sat down Elias, explained what had happened and promised to the boy that he would take care of him. The boy cared not about his own welfare, he just wanted revenge on the man who killed them. Maybe he also wanted revenge against my father, for forcing the situation. Together they made an agreement that my father would teach Elias the tricks of the trade, as well as he could, and provide the youngster with the revenge that he wanted.

Years later they tracked down Stefan and paid him a visit. With my father's help, Elias finally had an opportunity for vengeance. He was left alone in a room with the man, while my father waited outside. After an hour he emerged and my father asked how it went. Elias said nothing and walked out. My father went in to see for himself, and Stefan was unhurt but silent. Honouring Elias's decision, he untied the man and left. When I joined my father in this business he told me the story before I met Elias. I couldn't understand why anyone would have made that choice, so I asked Elias myself when I had the chance. I still remember the exact words he used.

"I made him understand that I held his life in my hands, and I could end it if I wanted. I needed him to feel that helplessness that my parents would have felt right before they died. But I'm no killer, so I left."

I guess that's the kind of person he was. I don't think I could be so merciful to the killer of my parents.

So that was our group. My dad was the mastermind and muscle, I worked various roles to assist as required and Elias took care of the information. Elias had a great disarming quality to him, due to his blindness. People opened up to him more, and gave him the benefit of the doubt. He could get into places others couldn't and get away with things nobody else would even dare doing. He excelled at overhearing conversations and extracting important details from civilians who had noticed things but had no idea of their significance. The manifest itself was a testament to his hard work, without him it would not have been compiled.

We couldn't chase after these artifacts non-stop, we still needed to eat. So my old man solicited jobs to keep money coming in. These jobs never involved innocents, just people who everyone would be happier off not having around. I think during these years my dad mellowed out a bit, but he still had this crazy obsession with the artifacts. I hope to one day find out why he was so obsessed. I mean why else would he work with Markus?

I'll never forget my first encounter with Markus. I knew straight away that he was bad news. I never understood why my father tolerated him, it seemed so obvious from the start that he had evil intentions. He came across as so self-absorbed and seedy it made my skin crawl just being in the same room as him. He shared an interest in the artifacts, and either had some or knowledge of them. My father worked with him to an extent, sharing some information to gain what Markus had access to. I think Markus was probably holding back a lot, and his latest actions suggest strongly that he has some long-term plan. It was likely he was even working towards it back in those days.

Which of course brings me to the mysterious stranger who has shaken things up so much, and taken the lives of the two people closest to me. Right from the start, as much as I hated him, he intrigued me. He seemed so different from the rest. That is why I followed him, watched him work and did as much research on him as possible. He was a ghost, and I found nothing about him. The real break came when I noticed him posting a letter. I intercepted the document and not only was it the strangest letter I'd ever seen, I noticed that it was addressed to a post box. My natural curiosity got the better of me, and I broke into it to see who he was corresponding with. I naturally assumed this was his contact point with his handler or employer, whether it be Markus or some other player I wasn't aware of.

The truth was far more shocking. He was writing to himself, and it was an account of everything that had happened to him since that day my father died. If the text was to be believed, he was an innocent caught up in this mess. Well, not completely innocent, since he seemed on an unconscious level at least to know what he was doing. He must have acquired his skills somehow, as they are quite refined. But still he appeared to be an unwilling participant. This revelation has really forced me to question my feelings about him. He is responsible for my father's death, perhaps not as much as Markus, but he was still the instrument. But he wants to protects lives, and has even saved me a few times. He wishes to atone for his deeds. Can I honestly hate such a man?

I can't confront him about any of this, because then he will know I have betrayed him and read his writing. By itself that isn't a big deal for me, but I have this feeling that I shouldn't mention it. It is instinctive, that I should act like I don't know any of this information. I learned a long time ago to trust my instincts, so I will remain quiet on this subject. I have decided to leave this document with the rest of his documents in the post box. This way either he will find it eventually if he goes through his post box, or whoever else reads his story will find it. I feel a little guilty about this invasion of his privacy, so my words will serve as payment. In a way I also like the idea, that someone out there will know my story as well, as told by me. I can only hope that this tale has a happy ending.

CHAPTER SEVEN

MARKET VALUE

It's been a couple of days since I last wrote, and lots of things are happening. I haven't had much of an opportunity to put pen to paper, as I didn't want to let Alexis see me writing it. The act of writing isn't that suspicious, but it would lead to questions and curiosity. If I know anything about her, it's that she is tenacious and would find out one way or the other. I'd really rather her not know the extent of my ignorance. It would be fairly embarrassing, and I wouldn't know how to explain it.

I awoke the next morning of my own accord, and not roused by burly men as I had feared might happen. Alexis had taken me to a safe house of hers. It might have been her own house, she didn't specify. Although I doubted that was true, because it reminded me of the house where I stayed first. There was nothing really there in the way of personal effects. It may have been a house, but not a home. A small house too, as there was only one bedroom and I ended up sleeping in the lounge room on a cheap sofa bed. While it certainly looked fine, after waking my back felt like I had been shoved into a garbage can and rolled down a long and bumpy hill. I made a mental note to sleep on the floor if I spent another night there.

I ended up waiting around for a while, since Alexis was busy organising something. Of course she didn't bother filling me in on what was happening. It's funny though, it didn't really bother me. I had come to expect no information and having to work things out as they happened. When she did eventually come over to chat, she found me at the window watching the rain. I find it fascinating really, one big shower cleaning the world by force, like a mother washing a reluctant child.

"I've arranged a meeting," she told me.

"With who?" I said.

"A man who can identify the artifact we have. He runs a local market stall appraising antiques as a front."

"So what's the plan then?"

"The meeting is tomorrow. He won't be there today but I want to go in anyway and scope out the location. I don't want any surprises."

"That's very forward thinking of you, I thought you were a bit more impulsive," I remarked.

"Even I do a little extra preparation if I have some time to kill," she replied with a smile. I thought back to the Mantiver HQ explosion and wondered how much was calmly planned out, and how much was off the cuff.

She did have the escape organised, but she didn't know where the artifact was. I think, realistically, she planned a big boom and left the rest to chance. I just happened to show up on the day and find it, while she carried on with her plan.

She drove us over to the markets and during the trip I started to get the feeling that rather than us being partners, I was more her sidekick. I wasn't particularly worried about it for some reason, but rather amused. None of the people I'd really interacted with so far had been that talkative, but I think she was probably the quietest of them all. I still felt a strange tension hanging around, so I didn't force any conversation and just let the silence prevail. The rain was tapering off, but outside it was still very wet. I thought that it should make the markets a lot less crowded. I wasn't sure if fewer people would hinder or help our plans for the day.

We arrived and I noted that the markets were located in an open square surrounded by shops of various sizes and the occasional apartment building. The stalls themselves were small canopies stretched over four poles in a square formation, with rectangular benches between the poles. The goods on sale varied from simple electronics all the way through to hand-made clothing, fruit and vegetables. Alexis grabbed my hand and pulled me along through a small crowd of people outside a stall. One of the few things she had said during the car trip was that we would have to appear as a couple to blend in better. A 'cover' was how she had referred to it. I knew it was completely fake, but it was nice walking with her that way, hand in hand. I think it worked too, as far as I could tell nobody paid any attention to us. I noted that we had stopped and focused on what was ahead. It was a closed stall that was unstaffed.

"This is where he said his stall was, he might be telling the truth about this at least," Alexis whispered into my ear. She walked over to the stall next door and pretended to eye the merchandise until the man there was finished serving customers. She asked one or two questions about the goods which looked to be cheap necklaces made of odd items, then started on the real questions.

"What's that place next door?" she said.

"Oh that's Albert's Antiques," the man replied, "he isn't here on Wednesdays but should be in tomorrow if you want to take a look."

Alexis thanked him and we walked on by without paying any attention to the antiques stall. That concluded the first pass of the location, and we had verified that the stall existed. The information supplied by the man to Alexis about his situation appeared to be true. It didn't prove much, but helped provide a little more confidence in dealing with him. At the very least it wasn't an operation he had concocted purely for the meeting.

"Check the exits and meet me back here," Alexis instructed.

I wandered around the perimeter and took note of the potential exits. There was a corridor leading to toilets, and a major entrance at each end of the markets. It looked like some of the stores around the edge were more permanent fixtures with upstairs sections so it might even be possible to get access to the roof and escape. I found a service ladder around the back of one of the buildings that confirmed my theory as a viable option, should the need arise. If someone had both ends blocked, you could get around them that way, but it would be risky if they saw you trying. There was nowhere to hide up there.

Happy with my assessment I returned to the meeting spot, but Alexis wasn't there. To pass the time I looked at the stalls nearby. One was peddling leather bags, the other old worn books. The books piqued my interest so I browsed through them, not on the hunt for anything in particular. I knew that if I spotted something interesting it would just grab me. It caught my eye that one of the books was very thick but had no cover. I picked it up to take a closer look. At the same moment Alexis walked over and told me it was time to leave so I just gave the stall owner some money and took the book with me.

Once we were back at the car, she spoke again.

"I saw one of Markus's henchmen casing the place, he might have seen me."

"Why would they be here?"

"For the same reason as us, or to catch me. He must have heard about the Mantiver HQ attack. It wouldn't be a stretch to believe that I had made a play for the artifact and would come here next for verification. The man here is well-known in these circles."

"I'm still missing, presumed dead, right?" I joked.

"I hope so, that will give us an advantage. But if I could find out you are alive, we should expect Markus to be able to as well."

"You still plan on going ahead, knowing that there might be an ambush?"

"Of course. Maybe I can take out some of his hench-men while I'm at it. Plus I'll have you watching my back," she responded with confidence. She certainly seemed to have faith in my abilities, but what would she think if she knew the truth about me?

I had some time back at her safe house to take a proper look at the book I had bought on a whim. It was titled 'The Count of Monte Cristo'. I started to read it, and was soon after completely enthralled. I didn't even notice Alexis walk over to see what I was doing.

"What book did you pick up?" she asked.

"The Count of Monte Cristo," I replied. She smiled.

"That's the best revenge story ever told. I've read it three times," she told me. The book was huge, reading it once would take a very long time, let alone multiple times.

"You must really have enjoyed it, it's quite lengthy," I remarked.

"I guess I'm just a sucker for good old-fashioned ret-ribution," she replied, again with a grin. This made me feel rather uncomfortable, given the circumstances. I began to wonder what kind of retribution or vengeance she was plotting for me. I nodded at her and went back to reading. The pacing of the book was quite good, just as I was finishing each chapter and considering putting it down, something else happened and I had to read on just a bit more. It was refreshing to read something so interesting and fantastical, rather than reviewing my own words.

I liked the main character Edmond Dantes. I admired how he took control of his own destiny, and how carefully he orchestrated his return and subsequent revenge. I had to read through to the end to see how he completed it. As I read it that night I wished I was as capable as him, but then I reminded myself that he's just a character in a book. Books can be constructed in any way, for any end. All things are possible, limited only by the imagination of the author. Sadly my account is not a work of fiction, so I can't just alter it to be more exciting or make myself look better. I owe it to myself and anyone else who reads this tale. Nothing else of consequence happened that night, I just read far too much and then slept.

The next morning was overcast, but at least the rain had stopped. My plan to sleep on the floor had been a partial success. I decided when I awoke that taking the slim mattress off the sofa bed and sleeping on that on the floor would have been better still. It was something to try next time. I walked through the small house looking for Alexis, and found her in the kitchen staring out the window. She turned around when I approached.

"Ready to go?" she asked.

"Sure," I replied without too much enthusiasm.

"Got the artifact on you?"

"Yes, do you want it?"

"No, keep it. Less chance of them getting their hands on it," she told me. We left the small house and drove back to the markets. It was still quite early, and I asked her if there was a specific reason to leave at this time. She mentioned that the fewer people the better, so we could potentially get more time with the antique guy and have an easier time noticing any of Markus's men. I pointed out that we would be easier to spot as well. I think that was unavoidable though, as they would be watching that stall regardless, if they were indeed even there.

"Here's how it will play out," she began, "when we arrive we will split up and approach the stall from opposite ends of the market. You go directly to the antique guy, speak the pass phrase and give him this money." She then tossed over a wad of cash which I caught awkwardly.

"What's the pass phrase?" I said.

"Inquire after a blue dragon. He will inform you he has none, but there is a yellow dragon he can part with. Tell him a yellow dragon is better than none and hand over the cash," she explained.

"What happens next?"

"He will take you to the yellow dragon. Use that opportunity to show him the artifact."

"What will you be doing?"

"I will slowly make my way there from the opposite entrance, examining stalls on the way. Hopefully if there's any goons they will notice me and be distracted. If it goes to plan, they won't be watching the stall closely, if at all."

"What's the signal if things go sour?"

"Hmm," she mused, "I remember seeing a PA system in that area. Get over there and say 'Oranges are now out of season'. If I hear that I'll come running." I wondered to myself how much help that would really be if I was in enough trouble to require assistance.

With that the briefing was concluded. We were parked near the markets and left wordlessly in opposite directions. I took my time walking in as I wanted to ensure Alexis entered the markets first at the far end. If there were people watching, I preferred as little attention as possible. I could feel sweat dripping down my back, just at the thought of what might happen. I think my walking pace was slowed even further than it already had been by my worry. At the same time I was trying to look calm and casual, and not the nervous wreck I felt inside. I remember thinking that perhaps I should have gotten better at handling such a situation by this point, but maybe my ignorance had served me well before, better than I had realised.

I scanned the rooftops as I approached, and saw nobody. This didn't bring the relief I wanted, because it meant that there could still be people out there, just well hidden or further ahead. I reached the southern entrance of the market, and walked through. The first step was done, now I just had to keep going. I was glad to have surveyed the place beforehand, it gave me more confidence in the area and my route. There weren't many people around, and those that I saw seemed to belong. Again I had to trust that I would recognise someone out-of-place. Each step took me closer to uncertainty.

I could see the antique stall, only it seemed to be bigger than I remembered it. I could see that there was an extension on the side, and a larger canopy above. The extra section was totally enclosed and not open like the rest of the stall. It made sense, I'm sure the owner would want a little privacy for his goods and not feel safe leaving them there when the stall was closed. Especially if Alexis and Markus knew of him. I walked closer until I was right behind it. I took in the area under the pretence of looking up at the sky and everything looked fine. I went around to the front and noted that a young man was working there. He didn't seem the type to be running that kind of place, however I thought it best to stick to the script. I inquired after the blue dragon and waited for his response. I got one immediately.

There was surprise in his features, like he had been caught off guard. He hid it quickly and asked me to come in and take a look at their collection, in particular a yellow dragon. I stepped through a gap in the tables and followed him through to the private area, which as I guessed was full of stock. An older man was standing there with his back turned, examining something.

"This man here was seeking a blue dragon, but I told him that all we could offer was a yellow one," the younger man said.

"Thank you," the older man said without moving, "now go back out to the store." There seemed to be some urgency to his command. He turned to watch his colleague leave then shifted his attention to me.

"Can you afford a yellow dragon?" he asked. I handed over the money and he seemed satisfied.

"Come with me," he said after pocketing the money. He bent down and moved something around on the floor. I heard a dull metallic scraping sound, and then noticed an open hatch in the ground. He began to climb down a ladder below it so I followed him.

At the bottom of the ladder was a simply furnished room full of antiquities and tools of various kinds. The old man walked over and sat down in an aged red leather chair.

"Now we have the proper privacy, let me take a look," he asked. I walked over, took out the metallic clock and handed it to him. His eyes lit up, and he took it gently, turning it over several times and examining it from various angles.

"This is definitely one of them," he remarked.

"What are they for?"

"The objects themselves, I think just for decoration or everyday use. They were designed to fit in amongst regular items. What makes them special are the engravings on each piece. Each piece has an identifying mark and a message."

"What happens when you get them all?" I inquired.

"Nobody knows for sure, there's a few theories and stories around. I haven't paid any attention to that, I think they're just fairy tales. My fascination is with the craftsmanship of each item."

"Where did they come from?"

"There's no one source, they have popped up from all over the place. I can't really fill you in much about their origin because I've only seen maybe two or three pieces," he said apologetically. I had the feeling that he was telling the truth, but at the same time holding something back. He seemed a little nervous as well, I could tell something was up. Since he didn't seem to be offering much more information, I decided not to waste any more time. I strode over and took the clock from him, thanking him for his help.

"Don't go yet, I'm afraid I need more time to properly analyse this piece," he said with concern in his voice.

"I'm sorry, you don't seem to have the answers I'm after," I told him and continued on my way. As I was climbing the ladder out of the small room I could see the exit at the top slowly disappearing. It looked like someone was closing the hatch, or blocking it with something. I instantly doubled my speed for fear of being trapped.

As I neared the top I hooked my legs into the ladder for stability and used both hands to push against the blockage as hard as I could. It shifted and I heard a cry of pain. Not wasting any time I climbed out and caught a glimpse of the young man from behind the counter in a heap in the corner. The metal hatch had landed on his leg and he was in agony. He noticed me then and glared. As I left he called out.

"It's too late they're already on their way."

It didn't take much guessing to come up with who 'they' were. I had the information we came for, so the best plan of action was to evacuate with haste and let Alexis know of the situation. I then remembered the PA system she mentioned and looked around for it. I located a more central stall with a pair of large speakers and a microphone. That was it. I ran over, discovered that the system was actually off and frantically searched under the counter for some switches to turn it on. At the same time I poked my head up occasionally to see if there were any suspicious people converging on my position. I heard a low hum, which sounded promising, and tapped the microphone once. The tap was greatly amplified so all I had to do was remember the correct message.

"Oranges are out of season, grab some before it is too late!" I announced over the microphone and then darted off.

We hadn't explained the finer details of what would happen after I called for help, but I figured we would meet at the car. It seemed like a good idea to take my time if at all possible, and give Alexis a chance to secure the area around the car before I arrived. Of course at the same time I needed to get to safety, hanging around would lead to complications. I decided to try to get to the rooftops and survey the markets from there. There still weren't that many people around, so I decided it would be more prudent to avoid them all. I was concerned that I might not blend in as well with the low number of people in the markets. In hindsight I don't think heading up to higher ground was the best option.

I headed to a store I had mentally marked the previous day, and went up to the second floor. Out the back there was a fire escape that went all the way to the bottom as well as up to the roof. I raced up the external stairwell and climbed the ladder at the end, peering over the edge at the rooftop. It looked clear. I got up and crept across the roof while searching for other people. Sensing it was safe I moved over closer to the edge so I could look over the markets better. I crouched down and scanned the crowds. I saw movement near the far exit of the market, guessing it was Alexis making her move. There was nothing else that caught my eye, so I decided to head over to the car and check out the situation there.

"Don't move or I'll shoot," a voice behind me calmly commanded. I stopped and waited for further instructions. As afraid as I was, anger was the main emotion I felt. I was mad at myself for taking this chance before properly assessing the situation. Angry for making another novice mistake. I clenched my right fist deliberately before releasing it. I was not going down without a fight.

"Turn around slowly with your hands up," the voice commanded again. It sounded like a middle-aged man. I complied with his request, trying to think of a plan in the meantime. The man was definitely one of Markus's goons, I remembered him as one of the enforcers at that warehouse. He had a gun pointed at me and now my back was to the edge. It wasn't a particularly favourable position.

"Hand over the artifact, nice and carefully," he instructed. I reached into my jacket with my right hand, hoping a plan would suddenly form. There was nobody here to save me. However what happened was not a plan, but I don't know what it was.

I slowly retrieved the clock but just as it emerged from my jacket I threw it straight up in the air. The man's eyes tracked it intently. I lunged out with my left arm grabbing his gun hand and swung him towards the edge. He reacted quickly and began to struggle but I continued to position him so that our places were completely reversed. He moved in to hit me with his head, but I used my left foot to kick out his right leg from under him and in the same movement strike him directly in the chest with my right palm. He began to crumple and then toppled backwards off the roof plummeting soundlessly until he landed with a hard cracking sound.

It was then I remembered the artifact but before I could begin to worry about it I noticed something out of the corner of my eye and stuck out my left hand. I caught the object and knew instantly that it was the artifact. Of course this all sounds quite ridiculous, but that was what happened, as strange and bewildering as it was. I must have stood still on that roof holding the artifact for a good minute or two, just trying to make sense of it. Then all of a sudden I snapped out of my temporary trance, and ran along the rooftops to the end of the market.

I found a ladder that branched off into another fire escape. I peered down but didn't see anyone waiting for me. Descending as quickly as possible, my thoughts were now on Alexis. I hoped she had made it to the car safely. I would soon find out. The markets were abuzz with people now, due to the man who fell. That commotion helped me slip out, as many more people were pouring in to see the spectacle. I pushed past them and dashed off to the side when I was out of the exit. I could see the car in the distance but nobody around it. Caution seemed best so I took my time approaching and keenly scanned the area. As I was closing in I heard a scuffle nearby. I quietly ran up to the corner as fast as I was able to see what was happening. It was Alexis surrounded by several thugs, struggling furiously. I was about to try to help when she saw me and went limp. She flashed me a disapproving look and let them escort her into their vehicle. I noted down the licence plate number and rushed over to her car. If I could get it going I would be able to follow them.

Just as I was trying the door I noticed the car was sitting a bit low. I looked down at the closest tyre and realised that it had been slashed. A quick lap around the car confirmed that all the wheels were ruined and unusable. Even had she made it back, escape would have been impossible. Maybe she had led them away to ensure I was safe. I thought about stealing another car to follow her but it was too late, they were gone. I walked to the main road and hailed a taxi, directing the driver to take me to a hotel in the centre of town.

I booked a night and stared outside for a while, not knowing what to do. I wrote down the events from the last few days and that has helped a little. It is clear to me that Markus has her, and he must know she had an accomplice. There was a good chance he would suspect me. He would have no qualms killing her, but I did not feel like that was his intention. For a man so obsessed with the artifacts it would make more sense for him to be keeping her as a bargaining chip to get another artifact. Once I had thought through this, it became apparent that he would want to make a trade with me. I decided to drop by my original safe house the next morning, and see if he had left something.

The way forward for me has never been so clear. I have two goals: one is to rescue Alexis and the other is to take down Markus. A bonus would be solving the riddle of these artifacts. The puzzle of my past is something that can be teased out later and I have more pressing matters now. The circumstances may not be brilliant but it is nice putting the rest of my problems and concerns into the background for a time. The world will be the ultimate judge of my tale, deciding whether I'm a hero, a villain, or just something in between. I fear that by the end, I won't know myself. But I will have done what I thought was right.

MAN FALLS FROM ROOFTOP AT CRANLY MARKETS

By Jacqueline Somers

A thirty-five year old man toppled to his death from the rooftop of Beckley's Lingerie at Cranly Markets yesterday afternoon. His identity has not been publicly released by the police at this time. Witnesses spotted another man on the roof at the time of the incident although they were unable to identify him.

The police found a handgun at the scene which they believe belonged to the deceased. Officially the incident is being branded a gang related homicide.

CHAPTER EIGHT

MOVING PICTURES AND ARTIFACTS

I awoke and headed directly to my old safe house. It was my starting point to see if Markus had made contact. On the journey over I thought about what I would do if he hadn't tried to contact me, and drew a blank. However I somehow knew that he would, I just hoped it was intuition and not some other lost memory from my plans with him. Of course that was probably an irrational hope.

I arrived at the house and it seemed undisturbed. I entered carefully, looking for any signs of forced entry or disturbances. After closing the door I turned and noticed an envelope on the small table in the hallway. It was full, in a way I had begun to associate with lots of money. As it turned out that was correct, but there was also a note. The contents of the note were as follows:

I have the girl. Everything is proceeding as you predicted. Initiate the next phase, the show must go on.

Unfortunately, it looked as though the events so far might have been part of the plan. However this gave me no real direction, and Markus didn't even ask for the artifact. However I soon came to the conclusion that there was no way anybody could have planned it all out so meticulously. I could not be the architect because it couldn't be done. Especially a plan that relied on practically zero contact and communication.

That conclusion left me with two possibilities: either there was some way such a plan was possible that I had overlooked, or Markus was using the idea of a plan to keep me under his thumb. What kind of person would admit to knowing nothing, instead of going along with things as I had? It would be easy to manipulate someone this way, especially if they had gaps in their memory.

Money in the wallet suggested another job, so I chose to head back into the city to see if I could pick up any leads. In addition I hoped that perhaps on the way I would recognise that place where I had met Markus briefly. It was for this reason I was carefully scouring the surroundings as the taxi sped me along. Then came a vision, be it providence or a lucky coincidence. I saw a poster plastered on the back of a seat on the side of the road. It was an advertisement for a movie titled 'The Show Must Go On'. I asked the taxi driver about it, and he said that only one cinema in the city was showing it. I told him to take me there. That movie title was too close to be pure chance, it had to be what Markus was referring to.

Relief swept over me, as I now had a new direction to pursue. The fact that the relief would only be short-lived made it so much more powerful. I was happy to just revel in the moment while it lasted. I think that's when we are happiest, when we have a goal or direction. Some target, real or imagined, to aim for. But it's not about the goal itself, it's about having a purpose. If we attain the goal, the satisfaction is only temporary. We set another one and go again. So it seems, for me, at the very least.

I found myself standing outside the George Brothers cinema complex. I wandered around looking at the movie posters in their foyer, looking for one in particular. I found it, but then realised that finding the poster itself did not prove much. It merely confirmed the information that the taxi driver provided. I instead found a board with a list of their showing times, and it just so happened that there was a session of the movie I wanted in the early afternoon. I bought a ticket for it and then looked at my watch. I still had an hour or so to pass, so I walked outside to find myself a newsagent. The paper had a celebrity scandal plastered all over the front page. On the second page was an article about what occurred at the markets. As was now customary I purchased a copy to include alongside this document. I then made my way back to the cinemas.

Inside the complex I found where the 'The Show Must Go On' was being screened, but the doors were closed. I was a bit early but decided to go in anyway and get my bearings. As I walked in there were two ushers cleaning the cinema. They both stopped what they were doing, and turned to face me. I could tell they were annoyed by the intrusion, and that it was something that happened often. Regardless, they politely asked me to wait outside until the session time.

I took a seat just outside the doors, and watched the people come and go. While waiting I saw a few other people go in as I had, and chuckled to myself. All came back out soon after, looking suitably chastised. As I sat there I thought about what might happen in the cinema, if my guess was right and I was meant to be there. The only logical idea that came to mind was a meeting of some kind, or an exchange. A cinema would provide a public place that was also discreet and dark.

At last the doors opened and the two ushers emerged laden with rather full garbage bags. They announced that the cinema was now open, but the tone they used was almost what you would use to address a difficult child. The people waiting outside wasted no time and walked in as soon as possible. I followed them in to secure myself a good seat, and decided on right up the back, towards the middle. I managed to get myself one in the back row. It was important that there be nobody behind me to help reduce the chances of any surprises. As the people filed in and sat down I watched them all. After the initial rush no one else seemed to be coming in. I guess the movie wasn't that popular. The people who had entered spread themselves fairly evenly through the cinema, with the occasional pocket of activity visible.

I couldn't remember seeing a movie before, but the experience wasn't foreign to me. I must have seen one before, and remembered on some level. While the various advertisements and trailers played I tried to keep an eye on the other people, but it was getting darker and was harder to do so. Soon the curtains at the edges drew back, further revealing more of the screen. The lights dimmed completely as well and the main feature began. I thought to myself that maybe nothing was going to happen, and wondered whether I should stay or leave.

That decision was soon made without any effort on my part. I felt a presence nearby and saw some movement. Someone sat down next to me.

"So you were up here," a voice said quietly. It sounded like it belonged to a man, although I did not recognise it.

"Do I know you?" I said without turning to face the person.

"No, but we share an employer in common," the voice replied.

"M?"

"Yes."

"What do you have?"

"I have information on another artifact that must be secured. All the information is here in this envelope," he explained and then thrust an object in my direction. I took it and shoved it into one of my pockets. The information would come in handy, regardless of how I chose to proceed.

"Is that all?"

"Yes, I'll let you enjoy the movie," he said and then left as quietly as he had arrived. I opted to do just that, and not think about the information or what it meant. I would have plenty of time to mull it over afterwards. The movie itself chronicled the efforts of a bumbling group of misfits trying to put together a musical. Many of the other patrons laughed heartily throughout but I did not find it as amusing.

However I still walked out of the cinema refreshed, and hailed a taxi to take me to the nearest hotel. I secured myself a room and when I was inside I opened the envelope and examined its contents. Inside were a photo of a man and pages of notes. The man in question was a James Madison and according to the information he had a few items of interest. The first was an artifact that he carried with him everywhere. Unfortunately for me, the information didn't specify what it was, but I doubted it would be much of an obstacle. I had even less information about the artifact in my possession when I went after it, but I still managed to acquire it.

It was also noted that he carried another important item on him at all times. A special key. The key opened his personal vault, and if this information was accurate James Madison was in possession of the largest number of artifacts ever collected in one place. It was clear why Markus had this man followed and investigated. He wanted those artifacts. However from my quick examination of the information available, I found there to be a few problems. The first and most obvious problem was that there was no information on how many artifacts were in this vault, or how large they all were. It could be difficult to extract them all myself.

The other problem was to do with Madison himself. He would notice if I stole any of the items in his possession, and as soon as he noticed it would thwart any attempts to access his vault. The trick would be to somehow relieve him of those items either without suspicion, or in a way in which he could not cause a commotion afterwards. A solution to the first problem was easily solved, but the problem of dealing with Madison would be trickier. Although I decided that with a bit of luck the same solution could work for both.

I had determined that an extra person helping out would be ideal for raiding the vault, so that I could cart away whatever was within with more ease. One individual stood out as perfectly suited for the job, the driver I met the first night, Tony. He could be trusted for this task, since it was to benefit his employer. I also believed that not only could he drive me around, but if I could bring Madison to him then he could keep Madison from causing problems. A plan was beginning to form rapidly.

Also amongst the information passed to me by the man in the cinema was a detailed schedule of Madison's movements and appointments. According to his routine, he would be at a private showing of a movie that very night at the cinema I was just at. That would be the ideal time to strike. If I could extract him from the cinema without being seen, it would be trivial to relieve him of a few items and have Tony keep an eye on him. Then we could move on to the vault and once the mission was completed let the man go.

I called Tony and secured his help. He didn't know the full details, but I was pretty sure that's how he was used to operating anyway. I also thought it a good opportunity to write an account of what occurred today. Before I continue I want to explain a little about why I decided to perform such a heist.

If this information I have is correct, then Madison has a large collection of artifacts, which equates to substantial leverage with Markus. Acquiring such a collection may also provide details as to the nature of the artifacts themselves. The one I have already is not enough by itself. This information would be invaluable, as it would reveal to me something about Markus and the others who are after the artifacts. I'm still a bit blind in that regard, with no idea of why these items are so sought after.

Soon the appointed time was nigh so I went downstairs to meet Tony. He seemed friendly enough when he greeted me but I still wasn't so sure about him. I would have to be careful, just in case. The first part of the operation was at the cinema, so we drove there first. I had Tony drop me off around the corner and then instructed him to wait for me in a nearby side street at a particular time. He nodded assent and then drove off.

Madison would book out an entire cinema for a private viewing once a week. There would be a minimal security presence with him inside, if that, so it would be easy to extract him. However I would not be able to waltz right in the cinema doors, as there would be security on them. I also couldn't use the fire escape as the doors can't be opened from the outside. That left one option, the projection areas.

I can't explain how I know this, but I seem to know about cinemas. Each cinema in a complex has a projection area that shows the film. These projection areas are usually connected to other projection areas to assist projectionists moving around the cinemas. They remind me of secret tunnels providing access to the whole complex. Each projection area also has an entrance into the cinema itself. So the plan was to go see another film in a different cinema and find my way into the projection area. From there I could enter the cinema where Madison was without being seen. I just needed to find a movie with the right timing.

I had a few hours before Madison was due to arrive, but that worked well for my particular schedule. I asked an usher about movie finishing times, telling him that I wanted to be out by 8:30pm. He recommended a movie called 'Two Roads, Two Tales' that finished at 8:25pm. That sounded perfect so I thanked him, walked over to the box office and bought a ticket. My window of opportunity would be after the film finished but before the next film started. I remembered from my earlier visit that the staff would come in to clean the cinema, but from my experience most people don't hang around for the credits to finish. The time before the staff arrive, and after everyone else has left would suit my purposes. The one thing I couldn't completely account for was the movements of the projectionists. I had to hope that I avoided them once in the secure areas.

I watched the movie that I had bought a ticket for and it was pretty good. It was a story of two brothers who left their home together but took different roads. The film was about their stories, and how they differed. I had spotted the door leading to the projection area when I entered the cinema, so I edged towards it as the credits began to roll. As the last person left I pulled out a lock pick I had gotten from Tony and went to work on the door, trying to get it open as soon as possible. Thankfully my brain seemed to go on autopilot once I started, so I felt confident in my ability to bypass the lock. However it was taking longer than I expected and I was really beginning to worry. I could just imagine the staff coming in and asking me what I was doing.

The lock clicked open and I stood transfixed for a moment, amazed that I now had access. I quickly collected myself and went through the door, closing it behind me carefully. I heard a door slam in the distance, which must have been the projectionist leaving the area. That was a lucky break, had I been quicker in getting in things might have been problematic. There were two possible exits from the projection area I had entered so I picked the one opposite where I had heard the activity. There weren't any signs around showing where each cinema was located, so I would have to check each one I came across. Luckily Madison was seeing the same movie I had seen when meeting Markus's operative, so I would know it when I saw it.

The first projection area I came across was playing an animated children's movie. While passing through I took care to look for signs of other people. It seemed safe so I proceeded. When I left I found myself in a corridor that split off into two directions at the end. I had to decide whether I should take the left or right path. I tried to do some calculations in my head but I wasn't sure how many cinemas were in this complex. I was pretty sure that the cinema I was aiming for was down one of those two paths. I picked the one on the left and was just about to go through the door when I caught sight of movement ahead of me. I quickly turned and went back to the fork, picking the other way. Once I was inside I noticed that thankfully it was empty. However there was someone nearby in that other projection room so I would have to be quick and quiet. I focused my attention on the film being displayed, as it seemed familiar. It didn't take long to verify it was the movie Madison was watching. I looked down into the cinema trying to determine how many people were there and where they were seated.

It was hard to distinguish shapes due to the darkness, but I thought there were at least four people inside: two up the front and two up the back. None were seated together so each had about an equal chance of being the target. There was a small blind spot underneath the projection room, where another person could be seated without my knowledge. By a process of elimination I concluded that the ones at the front would have to be guards, as nobody would hire out a cinema and sit that close. I would have to enter the cinema to tell who was the target from the remaining people. It was then I recalled the creaking sound that had occurred when I entered the first projection area. If the noise entering the cinema from this room was the same, I would be spotted immediately.

At that point I remembered that a loud sequence was coming up in the movie. Opening the door at such a time would minimise the chance of being discovered. As I was reviewing my plan in my head I heard a noise behind me, there was someone coming down the corridor to this room. I had absolutely nowhere to hide, although from the layout of the room I figured that crouching down near the door to the cinema might escape immediate detection. I hoped to exploit that and buy some extra time to enter the cinema at the appropriate time. As I crouched down I noticed there was a round mirror on the ground nearby. It was the kind that usually hang in the corners of public areas to give visibility of other areas. It looked like the supporting bracket was broken so perhaps it was there for maintenance. It gave me a view of whoever was entering the room, but at the same time it would also reveal me if they paid any attention to it.

I saw a man enter, dressed in a collared shirt and pants. He seemed to turn to look at the movie, then continued walking. I would have to make a move soon, although I wasn't entirely convinced the sounds of the movie would mask my exit in this room as well. When the man drew a silenced pistol I knew something was up. He wasn't a projectionist or even security, he was an assassin. There was little doubt as to his target, so I had to do something. I fished through my pockets for anything that could be used as a weapon and found nothing. I gritted my teeth and resolved to use the element of surprise as a poor man's substitute. As he stepped closer I leaped out at him, praying I wouldn't get shot.

Some divine being upstairs must have heard my desperate plea because he was completely surprised by my attack. He dropped his gun as he fell, but quickly reacted and shoved me off, scrambling to recover it. I kicked my leg out and caught him, toppling him over again. As I went for the gun he tried the same thing with his leg but I anticipated it and did a small hop. I landed in a roll and grabbed the gun trying to turn around as quickly as possible to get the advantage. I was just quick enough and he put his hands up slowly. Something looked familiar about the man now that I had a second to appraise him properly, but I couldn't place it. I looked away briefly to see where the movie was up to and he pounced. Somehow I reacted in time, purely by instinct, and fired catching him in the shoulder. He stumbled backwards and then toppled onto the giant metal platter of film that was feeding into the projector. His fall made the film scatter and start looping itself around him. He scrambled madly to get free, but only entangled himself further. It looked like he was going to be strangled to death.

It seemed like a horrible way to die, so I went over to try to rescue him. He must have taken this as a direct threat on his life, as he flailed terribly whenever I approached, practically sealing his fate. It was then I realised that if he was left as is, the movie would soon be interrupted and any chance of stealth would be lost. So I left him there, to try to accomplish my mission. I justified it in my mind by thinking of what the other man would have done in that situation, and highlighting my attempts to save him. But really I could have done more, and in that moment I chose not to. I would have to live with that.

Time was not on my side, so I slipped into the cinema at the first opportune moment. The entrance to the cinema from the projection area came out towards the rear, in an open section between rows. As I emerged I crouched down low and let my eyes adjust to the darkness. I identified the two guards near the front easily, then looked up the back to try and spot the rest. Of the two remaining people, one was in an aisle seat near the main exit, and the other was back against the corner. I didn't see anyone else in-between. I figured that the best way to proceed was to creep up the wall and aim for the man in the back corner. If he wasn't the target, he could be quietly taken out of commission.

I crept closer to the man and got a better look at him. He was in a suit and didn't look like a guard. He was probably Madison, but I couldn't make a positive identification in the dark. However getting him out past the three guards would still be a challenge. It was then that providence struck, and again lady luck smiled on me. The movie started to flicker and slow down, the picture disintegrating and then becoming only blackness. The man in the back corner yelled out to his guards to remedy the situation immediately. The guard up the back left through the main doors back into the cinema complex. His two compatriots down the front opened the fire escape and went out, presumably for a smoke.

This was my chance to strike. While the remaining man's attention was diverted towards the main cinema doors I crept up and placed the gun, which I took from the assassin, right up to the back of his head.

"You need to come with me," I told him quietly but urgently. He nodded and said nothing and I motioned towards the open fire escape doors. He made his way down to the bottom of the cinema calmly and quietly. I still don't understand how he was so unperturbed by the situation. I had planned to use him as a hostage on the way out if required, but as he exited the doors his guards had their backs to us and we walked right on by. Once we were out I recognised him from the photo I had been supplied. Madison didn't attempt to call out at all, he probably realised it would just exacerbate things. Tony was waiting nearby with a car and Madison and I got into the back.

"Have any trouble?" Tony said.

"Not at all," I lied. Something about the way Tony asked, piqued my curiosity. It was then I made the connection, that the assassin with the gun was the same man who delivered the information and mission earlier. Was he sent there to kill Madison, or kill me? Was he there for the guards? Was Tony in on some greater plan? I quickly put those thoughts out of my mind, as such questions would only hamper my other task. Still it made me feel like some extra precautions were in order.

"Empty your pockets," I told Madison. He appeared to comply, but only removed two objects.

"I believe these are what you are after," he said as he handed them over. One was a silvery pen that felt strangely cool in my hand, definitely an artifact. The other was the most bizarre key I had ever seen. It appeared almost like a regular key, but the round section one would normally attach to a key ring seemed to be a strange rubbery plastic.

"The key only works if I am the one holding it," he informed me.

"You are being very cooperative, so I'm sure you can assist us with that," I remarked.

"It does not matters what you take, I will just regain them in time," he told me like he was stating established fact. If these artifacts were as sought after as Markus had made out, any man who had assembled such a collection would stop at nothing to see them returned.

"Then you already know who is behind this," I commented. He nodded his head.

"Yes, I do."

"How big is your collection?"

"I only have five pieces in my vault."

"Are any of them remarkably bigger than the rest?"

"No, they will be easy to transport."

"Good, we will be arriving there soon," I said. I turned over the key and pen in my hands and then put them in my pocket. I still thought that Madison was being way too cooperative, which made me nervous. I knew I would have to watch him carefully, as we would be returning him to his own home to secure the other artifacts. There was still a good chance he would try to engineer something.

We pulled up around the corner from his mansion. The main gates were open and the grounds at least seemed deserted. My information told me that the entrance to his vault lay not in the house though, but in a small building off to the side. Leaving Tony behind, the two of us made our way there directly and my sense of dread grew with each step. Still, I had to press on and see it through. We arrived at what appeared to be an ordinary garden shed, but I knew better. Inside were steps down leading to a massive round metal door. On it was a small panel with a keyhole. It was time to see what was inside.

I retrieved the key from my pocket and carefully placed it in the lock without touching the strange section at the back.

"Your turn," I told Madison. He walked over and turned the key. The sound of pressure releasing and mechanical movements flooded the small space. The door slowly swung out and almost filled the room. Inside were shelves around the walls, a few tables and chairs scattered about and a large examination table in the middle. On it were placed five metallic objects, which would have to be the artifacts. I motioned for Madison to enter first, and he did without hesitation. I was just about to walk in when I got the feeling that something didn't seem quite right. It was the musty odour outside the door, the dust and cobwebs. It really didn't appear to be an entry that saw a lot of use. A man like Madison, he would have to be down here every day. I pulled the door closed as I entered the vault.

"What are you doing?" Madison asked, disturbed.

"Hoping you have another way out of here," I replied. I picked up one of the metallic objects, which was a spoon, and instantly knew it was one of the artifacts. I hunted around the room and found a large metal briefcase. Opening it revealed a soft black material inside with various depressions. This was probably how he transported them. I began to load the objects into the case and then shut it.

"Time to leave!" I announced and looked at Madison intently.

"We can't, you closed the only door out of here and it only opens from the outside," he explained.

"Nonsense, that door hasn't been used for a long time, yet this room looks like it has been visited daily. Opening the main door probably summoned the cavalry," I told him in a matter of fact manner. His reaction confirmed my suspicions, so I began looking around for an alternate exit.

Of course then it hit me, Madison had not moved the entire time we had been inside the vault. If there was another way out, he would have instinctively moved over to it, especially if he expected his men to burst through the main door. I know had I been in his position I would have tried to slip out while my captor was occupied. I turned and looked at where he was standing. Behind him was a desk and what looked like an ordinary shelf.

"Move!" I told him. He reluctantly shuffled to the side.

"No, the other way," I instructed and pointed. He complied and this time moved away from the desk. I wondered to myself if it could be the same thing, and put one hand under the surface of the desk and felt around. I found something and pressed it in. The shelf and the wall behind it rotated ninety degrees, exposing a small tunnel behind.

"You even use the same trick," I commented and motioned for him to go into the passage ahead of me. I grabbed the large silver case and followed him closely. As we progressed I heard banging sounds behind us. I imagined it was the guards attempting to force entry into the vault. The tunnel had lighting, although minimal, so it was easy enough to navigate through. Before long we arrived at another door.

Madison waited patiently before it. I brushed past him and inspected the door. It looked normal so I tried opening it. It was a bit stiff, but opened and took us outside. I nudged Madison forward and he walked through. I expected that somebody would be waiting outside, as surely Madison wasn't the only one who knew of this exit. My left hand was trembling slightly but I ignored it and walked out. Lo and behold there was someone outside, but it was Tony.

"There you are! This place is crawling with guys we gotta get out of here," he said.

"Lead the way," I replied. I know I can't pretend to be a super spy, but even to me Tony's presence at this precise spot seemed incredibly convenient. He led us around the perimeter of the mansion and out to his car.

"You can put the case in the boot," he offered as we approached.

"There's no time, let's go," I said and got in the back along with Madison. I had no plans of letting the case out of my sight.

"Where are we headed?" I said as we drove off.

"Markus's storage facility," he replied. I began to consider my next moves carefully. After a few minutes we pulled into an empty car park. We all got out, Madison and I standing around wondering where to go next. I walked over to Tony to ask him what the plan was when I saw him draw a gun from his pocket. He aimed it at Madison and fired twice, once into his chest and the other into his head. Holding the metal artifact case with both hands I swung it at Tony's head as hard as possible. He was knocked down and did not seem to be getting back up. I checked his pulse and breathing and he was still alive, most likely unconscious.

I found a phone in the car and called the police, telling them that there was a murder here. I hung up and threw the phone to the ground after giving them the nearest intersection. I started walking, with any luck the police would get here before Markus's people did, or even before Tony woke up. I couldn't believe it, all this death over a collection of artifacts. I ran through a quick tally in my head, I now had the five in the briefcase, the clock back at my hotel and the pen taken from Madison. That came up to seven artifacts. There was also the gun that I had given Markus, which meant eight artifacts accounted for. I hailed a taxi with ease and soon enough I was back at the hotel, feeling very tired but at the same time completely wired. It was hard to relax.

Writing down the events has helped, but I'm still not quite back to normal. I had some very close scrapes today, and there's going to be many more before this matter is resolved. I seem to have this knack of appearing comfortable and competent in all these things that I do, but that is purely an illusion. My recent success was one big fluke, and when I look back at what I did it all seems incredulous. Yet I know it happened, I somehow survived it all and ended up with the artifacts. They are my next lead, as I have nothing else to work with. Even if Markus contacts me again, I am even less sure of his intentions.

The question is, whether Madison was the only target, or if I was as well. The assassin in the cinema was the same one who gave me the information. Why include me at all if he was going to do the job himself. The only reason I can come up with is they wanted me out of the way too. Would Tony have shot me next? I wonder if Alexis is still alive. I need to find a way to get to Markus, and find out what his plans are. I need to see how he operates, and where Alexis is. I think if I can save her from this, then my debt to her will be largely paid. It will never be fully paid, but I will rest easier and I think perhaps even be able to forgive myself.

My aim for tomorrow is to examine these artifacts I have, and try to discern something about their function. This information will help me ascertain Markus's goals, and maybe even tell me something about his organisation. Knowledge of what the artifacts provide will help me guess what resources Markus would have acquired in preparation to use them. If these resources are specialised in any way, I can track him through them.

RECLUSIVE MILLIONAIRE SLAIN IN CAR PARK

By Jacqueline Somers

Aloof and reclusive fifty-five year old millionaire James Madison was found dead in a parking complex last night. He suffered two close range gun shots, one to the chest and the other to the head. Emergency services were notified of the shooting and found another man at the scene who has been brought into police custody.

Police said the wounds were consistent with gang style executions. The man found on the scene has been identified as the main suspect and is being held for questioning at Riverfield Police Station. James Madison is the second high-profile murder in as many weeks. When asked whether there was any connection between these murders the police had no comment.

CHAPTER NINE

GREAT MINDS

I had a vivid dream, so much so that I can still remember it now. The overarching story or the links between scenes however I can't remember. Though that could just be the nature of dreams, perhaps there is no logic linking all the images. The reason I mention this dream, is that it seemed inspired by the events of the previous night. I saw Tony killing Madison over and over in different ways, from different angles. Each time I was powerless to do anything, either restrained by fear, handcuffs, a cage or other similar things. Each time Tony said it was 'part of the tale', just as he dealt the final blow. Then it would reset and I would be in a different place but with a phone ringing. Always the phone ringing. I knew what answering the phone would entail, but I would pick it up anyway. Tony was on the phone, and he would tell me to come meet him. Then the cycle would continue again. Another death to witness.

Thinking it through there were to me two possible explanations for this dream. The first was that I was just traumatised by the event. The other was that on some level, I believed that I should seek out Tony for information, regardless of the consequences. I know the first seems so much more plausible when you think about it, but I was puzzled. I had done and been involved in some terrible things so far, why would this one affect me so? I still had the artifacts to research, but I just couldn't focus on them. So I decided to go find Tony and see what he had to say. Sometimes you just need to go with the flow, and see where it takes you. I just needed to be careful.

I bought myself a paper to see if there was any mention of Tony or the murder. There was a small article about it that mentioned the suspect was being held at Riverfield Police Station. That was simple to find, but it would not be easy to get in to see him. A police station is not the kind of place where you can just walk in and do whatever you want. I had an idea though, to pose as a reporter trying to get a followup on the story. It was a bit of a long shot, but it was a start.

I arrived at the police station, and stood outside gathering my courage. For some reason this was more daunting than any of the other tasks I had done. It sounds silly considering the events I had already taken part in, but there was no denying the feeling. I think that this time it was because I was willfully defying the law and attempting to deceive them in plain daylight. Steeling myself I entered the building, rehearsing my lines in my head and at the same time imagining all the ways they could go wrong.

I opened the glass doors and stepped into what looked like the reception area. There was a police officer sitting behind a large counter and a few people seated in chairs nearby. I introduced myself as being a reporter following up the story on the murder of James Madison.

"What paper you with?" the officer asked me without looking up.

"Ganford Gazette," I replied.

"We already have one here from there," he said, pausing what he was doing to assess me. I racked my brains to come up with a name, then I remembered the articles I had collected.

"That would be Jacqueline," I told him.

"Maybe, I always forget her name," the officer said, "Frank take this guy to interview room two." Another police officer walked over and I followed him through a few corridors until we reached a small square room with the door partially open. He left me there and walked back, mentioning something about other duties to get to. I took a deep breath then strode through the door like I belonged there. Inside was a large desk with three chairs around it, two up against one side and one on the other. There was a slim woman in short brown hair sitting down on one on the seats, studying some paperwork. She looked up as I walked in.

"Who are you? You don't look like the guy I'm waiting for," she commented. Her gaze was unnerving and I froze for an instant. Then I remembered the story I had prepared and started it up.

"I'm Will, from the Gazette. I'm here to assist," I said.

"I didn't tell anyone I would be here, who sent you?" she asked pointedly.

"I didn't know you were here, until the police officer at the front desk mentioned it." She didn't seem entirely satisfied by my answer but didn't question me further on the subject.

"Fine, I'm Jackie. Sit down here and be quiet, I'm waiting for a suspect." That suited me just fine, I thought that if I played it right, we could part ways after the interview without any trouble. I thought it was worth asking her some questions beforehand though, to confirm.

"Who is he? He must be important to warrant all this attention."

"His name is Tony Phillips. He's accused of murder. He's pleading innocent and wants to get his story out to see if there were any witnesses. I thought it would be an interesting yarn so I came over to hear him out." That certainly sounded like the Tony I wanted to see, and if it was him it saved me a lot of hassle. However conducting the interview with her would surely be a lot more than I had bargained for. As I went over the details from the previous night in my head, I heard some footsteps approach. An officer pushed a man into the room roughly, and he stumbled over and sat down in the spare chair across from us with a grunt. It was Tony, no doubt at all.

"I'm Jackie and this is Will, we're from the Ganford Gazette," Jackie introduced us. Tony sat up and had a good look at us. As soon as he saw me, he went slightly pale and couldn't contain his surprise. I think Jackie noticed but said nothing.

"I'm Tony and I've been set up," he said, although it lacked conviction.

"Why don't you explain what happened then?" Jackie asked. Tony licked his lips nervously then began to speak.

"Well it's a fairly simple story. I was catching a taxi home last night after a few too many drinks. I passed out in the taxi, I'm not sure how long I was out. When I awoke I was outside near a car I didn't recognise. My head hurt and as I sat up I noticed a dead man nearby and a gun on the ground. Before I could react at all I was surrounded by police and then brought in."

"Interesting story," I commented. Tony avoided looking at me.

"Whoever framed you, why did they pick you?" Jackie asked directly.

"I have no idea," he replied.

"Someone obviously went to a great deal of trouble to do this, can you remember any other details?" Jackie probed. I wasn't sure if she bought his story or not.

"No, there was nothing else to it really," he said.

"What do you want me to do with this information?"

"If you could include my version of events in whatever story you write, and ask for any witnesses to come forward that is all I ask," Tony concluded. It didn't really add up, I couldn't see how that would help him at all. My only thought was that it might be a coded message of some sort. But surely Markus would be aware of his capture already.

"I'm going to visit the sergeant, to check if there's any other details I can release. See what else you can get out of him before I get back," Jackie requested as she left the room. Once the door had closed I began to speak.

"We don't have much time. What's this article nonsense all about?"

"I have nothing more to say to you," he replied.

"Where's he holding Alexis?" I demanded. He looked at me and said nothing.

"There's no way out of this for you Tony, we both know you did it. All the evidence is stacked up against you as well. Not even Markus can make this go away, although I doubt he would risk it anyway."

Again Tony remained silent. My efforts were having no effect.

"Now is your last chance to do the right thing. If you're afraid of giving away too much just tell me where to look, I'll find what I need myself," I pleaded. Tony took a deep breath and exhaled slowly. I could not tell what he was going through exactly, but it seemed like he was conflicted.

"They're all connected. Find the connection, and find Markus's real name. Once you find that, the trail is clear," Tony said softly, almost under his breath. It looked like he might have spoken again but Jackie burst through the door.

"Time to go!" she announced. She came in to grab her things hastily and then walked out. I got up and left as well. I turned to look back while closing the door, and Tony looked despondent. I still wasn't sure of his role, and if there was really a good man under all that. He had seemed so genuine the first time we met, but distinctly different the other times.

Jackie was waiting for me just outside the interview room, which seemed odd after she left so quickly.

"C'mon, let's go get a coffee and discuss this story," she suggested. I agreed with her to help facilitate my exit and followed her out of the station. A wave of relief swept over me as I left the police station behind. I had managed to get in and out without any incidents. It was a short walk to the coffee shop and as we arrived, I pondered whether I actually drank coffee. When she asked me what I wanted, I just said to get me whatever she was getting. While she was queuing up to purchase them I spotted a quiet table and sat down looking out into the street. I was thinking about what Tony had said. It made sense that Markus was not his real name, but an identity.

"Look at you, real casual there," Jackie commented as she walked over. I looked at her questioningly.

"We'll go over it in my office. I need to run it by the editor anyway," she said and motioned for me to follow. I considered just leaving, but figured it might be better to play along a little longer. I didn't want to repeat the mistake of unnecessarily exposing myself that I made at the market rooftops. As I caught up she handed me a coffee cup and mentioned that the next ones were on me.

The newspaper office was across the road, and she took us up to the third floor. I tried to appear calm and relaxed but it was hard. My cover story had me being one of them, and any person could potentially call me out. Jackie's office was at the end of a hallway and consisted of a large desk with chairs either side, an imposing filing cabinet and papers everywhere. There was also a pot plant looking rather sickly off to the side, I doubted it got much sunlight. The lone window in the room seemed overshadowed by another building so minimal natural light came in. Jackie dropped her notes on the desk and asked me to look through them while she spoke to the editor. This seemed like a good chance to slip out so I gave them a brief glance and then walked over to her office door and looked out. The hallway seemed empty so I decided to make a break for it.

I remembered the way we walked so I went back the most direct route. Soon I was back in the large entry area for the third floor. I scanned around quickly then went to leave.

"You seem lost," a voice said behind me. I turned and saw it was a young woman, but one I did not recognise.

"Oh I was looking for the bathroom," I replied.

"Sure it's this way," she said cheerily and gestured for me to follow. We walked around the corner to a different corridor and she pointed out the correct door at the end. I entered, used the facilities and took my time before leaving. I was hoping that the woman would go back to whatever else she was doing, and that I wouldn't run into Jackie on the way out. As I left I scanned up and down the hallway and saw nobody. I strode over to the main area, determined to walk out confidently to avoid any further interruptions. However I was not that lucky.

"There you are," Jackie commented as I rounded the corner, "let's go over the statement now." At that moment I thought about just running out, and ending the charade. It was tempting but before I could come to a decision I found myself back in Jackie's office with her closing the door behind us.

"Time for an explanation," she told me as she sat down. I was about to protest my innocence when she brought what looked like a small recording device out from her bag and set it on the table, pressing the play button. I heard my conversation with Tony in its entirety, she must have recorded us in the interview room.

"I knew something was off about you, and the suspect's reaction when you came in confirmed it. I only wish I had not returned to the room so soon, the recording was starting to get interesting," Jackie said. I could only stare at her. She was sharper than I expected, and had easily exposed me. I was at a crossroads; should I confide in her and speak the truth, or say anything that came to mind to throw her off and give me an opportunity to leave without causing a scene. The choice was easier than I anticipated. I'm still not sure if I believed she was trustworthy, or I doubted my ability to fool her, but off I went, trusting her.

"Can I trust you?" I asked, "can you keep whatever I say in complete confidence?"

"Absolutely," she replied. I did feel at the time that she was telling the truth, and I believed she might even be able to help me. Again it was purely my instincts at work, as I had nothing concrete to base it on.

"You remember the articles you have recently written, about the Vale Club fire, the train disaster, the markets accident and that man we visited today, Tony?" I asked her.

"Yes," she replied, "What about them?"

"I've been following their coverage, because the Markus you overheard us talking about orchestrated them all," I replied in a matter of fact way. I expected her to be surprised but she seems unfazed by the sugges-tion. I guess as a reporter she had heard her fair share of outlandish stories and crazy claims.

"Who is Alexis then?"

"Alexis is the daughter of the man killed at the Vale Club. She wanted revenge but has since been captured by Markus."

"There's more you aren't telling me."

"Yes, but that's all you need to know to understand. If you help me, I could tell you more. But there's no room for a story on this, you would get nothing out of it," I explained. I hoped she would help, but still would have been happy if she just let me be, and wrote it all off as insanity.

"You don't know me very well, there's no way I could walk away from this. From a professional standpoint proving the truth of your story is too enticing to pass up, even if I can't report it. I'm pretty good at reading people, and the reaction of that guy at the police station when he saw you was unmistakable. That lends some credibility to what you have said. You also seem to believe what you are telling me, so I really think that there could be something to this."

"What about your editor and this statement we worked on today?"

"He doesn't care about that, it was more for my interest. I was stalling for time when we got here so I could listen to that recording of your conversation. I even had my assistant loiter around and keep an eye out for you."

"You're more resourceful than I gave you credit," I admitted grudgingly. "So where do we start?" I asked.

"Your main lead to this man named Markus is the people he has already targeted, and if there's something I excel at, it is finding the links between people," Jackie explained with confidence, "if you give me some names I can find the connection between them. Once we have that we link should have a shortlist of people who could be Markus." I can't really adequately explain how much that lifted my spirits. I didn't doubt for a second that she could do it either.

"Don't get too carried away though, these things generally take time. If what you've said about Markus is true he will have made an effort to hide himself and any information that can lead back to him," Jackie cautioned. I took a sip of my coffee and resisted the urge to spit it out immediately. The taste was terrible and it was almost cold. Coffee was definitely off the list. Jackie noticed the expression on my face and laughed.

"I like my coffee extra strong with no milk or sugar," she explained while still chuckling. We discussed her approach in more detail, it required me to write down all the names I knew and what details I could add about them. Based on that information we compiled a chart with a basic hierarchy and some notes about each person. Markus was at the top of course, but I couldn't help but notice the glaring gaps where I had left out important people. I had still kept a few cards close to my chest, I couldn't completely trust this woman so soon.

"I feel like we're already making good progress," I commented while looking over the chart.

"Where do you fit in?" she said. I felt like she had read my mind, as I was thinking the same thing.

"Depends on who you ask," I answered cryptically. She posed no followup questions, much to my relief.

"Who do we start with?"

"The big names," Jackie explained, "they will be the easiest to find information on. We have archives of the Gazette going back at least twenty years. Some of the people on this chart have been mentioned in articles I'm sure of it." She pointed at a number of names.

"Madison," I said.

"Sure, I trust you have a good reason for that choice. He may not be as easy as the others though," Jackie replied. I tried to think of a good angle of investigation to employ when she spoke up again.

"Have you met Markus? Have you seen his face? Could you pick him out of a photo?"

"Definitely," I answered.

"That will make things a lot easier. We may not need to find the main connection between them all, if we can get our hands on a photograph of him with one of these people." It made perfect sense, however the trick would be finding such a picture. I had a feeling that Markus would not have been so careless as to leave something like that around. Still I didn't abandon hope, a chance was a chance no matter how slim.

Jackie obtained some identification for me that said I was a research assistant working with her. That afternoon she showed me the archives and how to search the newspapers. They were stored on terminals that could be paged through, with images of each page of the paper.

The search system was rudimentary, and searchable keywords only existed if the employee who scanned in the paper created one. Our first effort was to use this search method to pull up any articles tagged with Madison. Only a few came up and they weren't even the person we were after.

Of course this made the search from then on like looking for a needle in a haystack. Every headline had to be appraised to see if it was notable. We couldn't even narrow down a specific period to search in. At least I could keep an eye out for anything else of interest while I dug through the articles. After a few hours neither of us had found anything of note.

"I'll show you the next haystack," Jackie said and walked over to another area of the archives. It was a large room filled with boxes and everything was coated with dust. Papers of all types were bursting from their containers, scattered all over the room.

"This is the miscellaneous storage area," she explained. "We keep notes, documents, photographs and other items related to our investigations and stories here." I looked around some more and sighed inwardly. You could spend years in this room and still not complete a thorough inventory of all its contents. There didn't seem to be any system in place at all. Yet a moment later it transformed for me into a bright shining beacon of hope. There could be anything here, nobody would bother to search this place to remove potentially damaging information.

"If you're lucky, this is the place you'll find what you need," Jackie commented. I agreed.

"You need to go back to your work don't you?" I said.

"Yeah, but I can shake a few sources to see if anything comes up. A name or place to focus our search on."

"Thanks, I really appreciate the effort."

"You can thank me if anything turns up." With that she left me with that giant room of potential. I picked up the nearest box and starting rifling through it. The only things of interest I discovered were some photographs of an orchestral concert in the local town hall, some notes for 'Mrs Price's Famous Plum Pudding' and a manual on how to change a tyre. The rest looked to be purchase receipts. I threw the box down in disgust, it had been a long day and I just didn't have the patience for a proper search.

As I left the building I realised just how late in the day it was, everyone else had already gone. Dusk was upon me when I reached the street and night was steadily creeping in. I hailed a taxi and travelled back to the hotel I stayed at previously. My mind was on my next move, how was I to approach this new avenue. Through Jackie I now had a possible link to Markus, buried somewhere in those archives. What weighed on me though, was time. How much time could I afford to spend on what might be a completely fruitless endeavour. With each day that passed the chance that Alexis was still alive diminished.

I came up with an answer. I would devote three days to the archives to try to find a lead. If nothing turned up in that time I would move on to something else. Perhaps in those days I could get some input from Jackie to either help my search, or provide something else to chase up separately. I'm not sure how I chose three days, but I thought that any longer and I would start wasting my time, as my focus would be naturally shifting to another lead. I still felt like I could not let her down, no matter what.

CHAPTER TEN

FINE DINING

Days passed and for the most part nothing of importance occurred. I merely ingested seemingly toxic amounts of dust as I sifted through the archives in the Ganford Gazette. The quiet, isolation and boredom of the task really got to me. I just wanted to go do something else, and feel like I was making some kind of progress. Even some basic human interaction would have been nice. Jackie was no help at all, keeping entirely to herself and not even checking in on me.

I was very close to abandoning the task, but each time I considered it, I paused and thought over all the time I had already spent on it. To quit with no result after all that effort was unacceptable. So for every time that almost quit I redoubled my intensity and searched even harder. Always at these times, Alexis was in my thoughts. How much had she suffered already? She deserved better. I remembered my promise to myself that I would set things right.

So after days of monotonous toiling I found a lead. It was a photo with Markus in it. But it wasn't the perfect lead I had hoped for. What I had was a picture, yet still lacked a name to go with it. But every small piece is required to complete a puzzle. The photograph in question was of a restaurant opening and Markus was one of the customers. The name of the restaurant and the date were written on the back of the photo. That made the photo a few years old, and in all likelihood the trail was already cold. Still there was a chance that Markus was a regular customer, or that the owners might still recognise him from the photo. I decided to go there the next day for lunch. I also thought it prudent to withhold the discovery from Jackie for the time being.

I bumped into Jackie on my way out of the Gazette building. She was on her way home, and an idea formed in my head.

"I need a break from this, are you free for lunch tomorrow?" I said.

"Sure what did you have in mind?"

"How about Astriana's? Meet you here at twelve and we'll head over together?"

"Sounds great as long as you're paying, I can't afford to eat at a place like that on my salary," Jackie joked.

"Yeah I have it covered, see you then."

With that the plan was set in motion. I rang the restaurant and booked a table for the next day, with the name Will Denton. I made a few more calls the next morning enquiring about the restaurant. It was run by a man named Albert Steyarch who was also the original owner. The name didn't ring any bells but I could always ask Jackie casually if she knew anything about him.

I met her just before midday outside the Gazette building and we hopped into a cab to get to the restaurant.

"Taking me in a taxi to an expensive restaurant for lunch, you seem to have money to spare," Jackie commented.

"I've found myself in a lucrative cash based business," I replied.

"Are diamonds next?" Jackie asked with a grin on her face. I could only look on in puzzlement before asking her a question in return.

"Do you know much about Astriana's?"

"I've never been there, just heard of its good reputation," she answered.

"I've heard similar things, I wonder what the owner's story is?"

"Apparently it was his dream to open a restaurant, but he could never afford it until he came into some money a few years back. I think the paper did a story on it, a brief public interest piece."

"You weren't lucky enough to get invited?"

"No, Joan the food critic was the only one to go. No fancy invitations for me."

"So you only cover disasters?"

"In theory no, but lately it seems that way. I've built my career around serious stories and that's all I seem to get. Not that I mind, I like it that way. It's just that I don't make as many friends that way."

"I guess if you are doing your job properly you will be uncovering things people don't want unearthed," I mused. We didn't talk much more on the trip there, and none of it was worth recording.

Once we arrived I saw just how extravagant the restaurant was. Either the photo had not done it justice, or it had been significantly renovated in the following years. It was perched atop a modest hill and you had to drive up a winding driveway to access the place. The building itself was surrounded by lush gardens but all the plants were rather short. My guess was that they wanted to keep the view unspoiled. The main building supported this idea, since the exterior was almost entirely glass panels giving the restaurant a feeling reminiscent of a fish tank. Inside I could see a bar, chairs and tables and a grand piano in the corner. The place seemed about half full. In the centre was a giant chandelier hanging from the ceiling. Before I could take more in I felt Jackie nudging me with her elbow.

"Right let's go in," I said. We walked over to the entrance and were met by a rather short middle-aged woman, with her hair tied up in a bun, behind a compact counter.

"Reservation?" she asked.

"Will Denton, twelve fifteen," I replied.

"Right, table for two, please follow me," she requested as she walked off. We were led to a corner table along the far wall that had a good view of the rest of the restaurant.

"Will Denton? Did you use your real first name when meeting me?" Jackie asked once we were seated. I just shrugged my shoulders, letting her believe it. She laughed.

"How naïve of you. Why are we seated over here?"

"I don't like being in the spotlight, plus I like how we have a view of the rest of the room."

"Don't want to be seen with me huh?" Jackie asked jokingly. When I didn't answer she asked another question.

"Why come to a place like this if not to have everyone know?"

"You drink wine?" I said. I wasn't sure if it was something I myself enjoyed, but it was a key part of my plan.

"Yes, but I prefer red," she replied. I caught the attention of one of the waiters and he came over promptly.

"Bring us your best bottle of red," I asked.

"Certainly sir, one moment," he replied courteously and sped off towards the kitchen.

"Are you trying to impress me?" Jackie asked.

"Why come to a place like this and not have the best?" I countered. She seemed satisfied by the answer. The wine arrived promptly. The waiter poured a little into my glass so that I could taste it. I drank it slowly gauging the flavour. I didn't care much for it, well truth be told I thought it horrible.

"Very good," I commented and he nodded, filling both our glasses. Jackie had a small sip from her glass.

"Wow I've never had anything like this before, it's fantastic." I was glad she liked it, as it would be easier to finish the bottle that way. I wanted to attract the attention of the owner by being a generous and well-paying customer.

"Entrées?" I asked.

"I'm not sure."

"No need to hesitate, I'm going all out on this meal. Half of it is a thank you for your help so far, half is that I needed to get out of those archives and take my mind off it." In my head I thought about how it was also to follow up the lead I had.

"You may regret those words," Jackie laughed and had a second look at the menu, this time much more intently. I had no idea what was in the food she ordered, and she even had several changes for the chefs to make. Judging by my dislike of the wine and the coffee that she loved, I avoided the things she had chosen and opted for what seemed like the simplest food available. While we waited I asked her about how and why she became a journalist.

"It's definitely not for the money, it's a passion of mine." she began to explain. "To me there's so many interesting stories in the world. They say that truth is stranger than fiction and I couldn't agree more. I think I became a journalist because I wanted to seek out those stories and share them with everyone." It made sense to me, and it also helped explain why she was helping me. Although my own story was one that she could not share.

"What exactly do you do?" she asked. I should have seen the question coming and had something prepared, but I didn't know how to reply.

"That's a good question, it's hard to describe."

"Try me, I'm sure I'll get it. I'm not going to report you to the police if you're worried about that." Part of the problem was that I wasn't sure myself what it is I did. What was it I did for Markus? Was I an assassin? What did I do before this whole mess began? I went out on a limb to gauge her reaction with what I thought was fairly accurate but not too detailed.

"Think of me as an agent of sorts, on a freelance basis," I replied.

"What like a spy? Give me a break if you are a spy you're terrible at it." I smiled at her, how right she was.

"That's my story and I'm sticking with it." I was rescued from any further probing as our entrées arrived. Hers had a rather pungent odour that offended my nose immediately. I felt that my decision to avoid her food choices was rather wise. The conversation died down a little while we ate and I used the opportunity to scan the room for anything of note. None of the patrons seemed familiar or particularly suspicious. This additional scanning of the venue revealed a second level that I had not noticed before. There was a small staircase leading up there and it only covered maybe one fifth of the floor space of the restaurant. I guess it was like an indoor balcony or viewing platform. It must have been reserved for special guests or something similar.

I continued to force down the wine and Jackie was happy enough to match my pace. When the waiter came to clear away our entrées I requested another bottle.

"I'm sorry sir we only have one other bottle of that particular vintage, and I believe the owner wishes to hold on to it," he explained.

"That is understandable, however I'm sure we can come to some arrangement. Can you call him over?" The waiter seemed apprehensive and not particularly willing so I slipped him a one hundred-dollar note and he promised to see what he could do.

"No need to be silly, we can just have something else," Jackie remarked.

"It's a matter of principle," I explained, "besides, money is just a tool to get what you want."

The extra money I gave the waiter must have greased the wheels appropriately because he returned soon after with a well-dressed older man with thinning hair. He was introduced to us as the owner of the restaurant, Albert Steyarch. He seemed familiar to me in some way, and while we were making small talk about the wine it hit me. I had seen him somewhere before, I just had to place it. He finally offered to sell me the last bottle at twice the original price. I think he had hoped to scare me off with the amount, but I agreed and he walked away with the waiter.

The owner himself came back with the bottle and placed it on the table. He gave me a strange look, that I could not decipher. At that moment I remembered where I recognised him from, he was at the Charity Ball I had attended before.

"Here for some house cleaning? You are certainly quite thorough," he remarked softly. I was at first confused, then it all clicked. He must have worked out that I had a connection to Markus and thought I was here to kill him. Out of the corner of my eye I noticed some armed guards come in through a door at the back of the restaurant. I had to act fast or else Jackie would be caught in the crossfire. I put my right foot under the main table support leg and with both my hands underneath the table I flipped it over towards Albert so that it was propped up like cover. He jumped back, startled and his guards opened fire thinking their employer was under attack. I grabbed Jackie and pulled her down to the ground as the bullets ricocheted around us, many striking into the table we were now crouched behind.

"Got a lighter?" I asked Jackie. Somehow she heard me over the noise and nervously fumbled a lighter out of her handbag. I grabbed the table-cloth and dragged it closer. It had been soaked in oil from a lamp fitting in the centre that had tipped over. I lit one corner of the cloth then draped it over the table. Fueled by the oil the thin cloth burned quite nicely, and with the fire came smoke. The gunfire had ceased and the guards were co-ordinating themselves to try to take control of the situation. I signalled to Jackie to follow me and we crawled along behind other tables hoping they were distracted by the small fire and protecting Albert. By this stage most of the other customers had already ran out of the building in a mad panic.

My plan was working, as the smoke helped distract them and cause confusion. We made it to a door that led outside the restaurant and I urged Jackie to go through it. She did so quickly and quietly but I did not follow her. I had to get to Albert, to find a better lead. I reached up to the table I was crouched behind, and felt around until I found a wine glass. I popped my head up and took stock of the situation. The guards were around the fire attempting to put it out, so I wouldn't have much time. I aimed at the far opposite corner of the room and hurled the glass as hard as I could. It smashed with a spectacular sound and two of the guards went over to investigate while the third continued focusing on the fire.

I used this opportunity to dash while crouched to the stairs leading to the small upper area in order to get a better look over the scene. As I ran I braced myself for the inevitable bullets riddling my back as I was shot to death, but they did not come. I had somehow made it upstairs undetected. Therefore my good fortune allowed me to peek out across the restaurant floor and assess the situation from up high. The three guards were standing together talking, having successfully put out the small fire I had set. Albert was lying on his side on the ground, a few paces away with his back to me. I wasn't sure if he was injured or not. It was at this point I noticed that all three of the hired henchmen were directly underneath the grand chandelier. If I could find a way to bring it down quickly they would have no chance to react and would be trapped under it.

The chandelier looked like it was secured to the roof with metal cabling, I would not be able to sever that cable with the tools and time available to me. My options were to either dislodge the cables from the ceiling causing the chandelier to fall, or somehow applying enough weight to it so that it quickly collapsed. Of course neither of these alternatives seemed practical, but the opportunity just seemed too good to pass up. I looked around at my surroundings, hoping that a solution would leap out at me. I then noticed the metal catch that connected the cabling to the chandelier itself. It seemed trivial to unhook the catch and send the chandelier crashing down, but I would have to be standing on it to do so. At least in that scenario my weight would help dislodge it once it was unhooked. The next obstacle was getting myself onto the chandelier, as it was too far to jump even from my elevated position. I gazed up at the ceiling and saw cute little lights strung along the entire length above me. If I detached the lights at one end the remaining cabling might support my weight. I had no other ideas and time was fleeting so I went with that option.

So, throwing good sense and caution aside, I stood up on a table and ripped the string of lights out of their fastenings. I now had a length of cable with small lights attached at regular intervals to swing myself across, as one end was still attached to the ceiling at the opposite end of the room. There was no time to second guess my plan, I just had to go for it. Grabbing the cable I climbed up onto the small railing overlooking the restaurant and steadied myself. I leapt forward still tightly grasping the cable and swung out towards the chandelier. As I travelled I felt the cable giving way, the force of my movement must have been loosening or removing the bindings that still held it to the ceiling. I let go of the cable and reached out for the chandelier. I managed to get some decent hand holds along the top, but most of my body was hanging over the edge. I wasn't sure how much noise I had made so I had to be quick before I was spotted.

I hauled myself up onto the chandelier quickly and stumbled over to the catch I had to release. My fingers were slick with sweat and I needlessly fumbled with it. It felt like I spent an age trying to unlock it. Suddenly I had succeeded without realising and the chandelier began crashing to the ground. I didn't want to be a part of the wreck it would become, so I dived off having the presence of mind to do a roll as I landed. Of course I overshot the mark with my maneuver and hit my head against the nearest wall. Swearing under my breath I stood up and surveyed the damage. Either I was very lucky or very quick because I had managed to trap all three guards under a pile of chandelier rubble. I had probably overdone it though, they didn't seem in good shape.

I saw Albert still lying unmoving on the ground not far away, so I ran over to see how he was.

"Those damn bastards shot me," he groaned as I turned him over. Once he saw my face his expression changed considerably.

"You! What do you want? Going to finish me off?"

"I'm not sure what you know about me, but I'm looking for information." I pulled out the photograph and showed it to him.

"Do you have a name for this man?" I asked and pointed out Markus. He appeared to recognise the face but looked away saying nothing.

"I need to find him, and make him accountable for his actions." Albert drew in a long ragged breath and then coughed weakly.

"Very well, I doubt I will survive this anyway. That man, is called Martin Hintle."

"Is there anything I can do for you? I'll get a doctor."

"No. Go do what you must. I gave you what you needed, make sure you don't waste it." So I left as quickly as I could. There was a crowd of curious people amassing outside. I slipped into it and through it, emerging at the street. Jackie was around the corner waiting for me.

"Did you kill that man? I saw your whole stunt in there."

"Of course not, I went to see if he needed help." She slapped me hard across the face.

"I know when I'm being played, you had better start explaining." I handed her the photograph. I could see her piecing it together in her head.

"Which one is he?"

"The bald one. Albert said his name was Martin Hintle." She slapped me again, even harder.

"That one was for withholding a lead. The first was for putting me in that situation," she explained crossly.

"Let's get out of here," I suggested and flagged down a taxi. I directed the driver to take us to the Gazette. Jackie and I didn't speak at all during the trip. When we arrived I didn't know what to say, but Jackie spoke up first.

"Give me your Gazette security pass," she demanded and stuck her hand out. I started to protest but saw the look on her face and didn't bother. I handed it over and she left without a word. Perhaps I should have trusted her more, but it was too late. Curiously she didn't ask for the photo back, so maybe she didn't hate me too much.

I walked the streets a little, pondering my next move. I grabbed something to eat and headed back to my hotel. I didn't have any great ideas and thought that recording the day's events would help. So here I am, with an account of how I recklessly obtained the name I needed. Jackie would definitely be a big help in my current situation, but I have to go it alone. The fresh memory of her slap just reminded me of that. Thinking it through logically I need to find any premises associated with this Martin Hintle and investigate them. I may recognise one or two, I may even find Alexis in one of them, or the man himself. I don't know what I'm going to do if I do find him. To be honest I don't want to think about it. I'm not a violent person at heart, I just want to stop him and rescue Alexis.

Tomorrow the search begins anew. I feel like I'm so close now, there's just a bit further to go. I have come so far already, since that first entry. I'm surprised by how well I have just adjusted to the circumstances and made things happen. That in itself is certainly a piece of puzzle, to be pondered at another time. However at the same time I'm a little worried too. I have adapted too well. What does that say about me?

RESTAURANT OWNER GUNNED DOWN DURING BIZARRE LUNCHTIME ATTACK

By Jacqueline Somers

Albert Steyarch died yesterday after sustaining multiple gunshot wounds in a freakish shootout at his exclusive restaurant. The police believe he died from friendly fire from his own security team during the incident.

The tragedy was reported to have begun when an unruly customer overturned a table and threatened the owner. The security team were quick to respond in defense of the owner and were on the scene in moments. A shootout began between the security team and the perpetrator and the owner Albert was caught in the crossfire.

Police arrived at the restaurant to find the security team trapped underneath a collapsed chandelier. The security team are being held in custody while they are questioned. No other people were injured.

The restaurant, Astriana's, was named after the owner's wife who died giving birth to his daughter. This is the only recorded incidence of violence in the restaurant since it opened four years.

BOATING ACCIDENT

I spent the following day thinking of ways to find out about a person from only a name and a face. The obvious options were large common databases like a motor vehicle registry or police records. However for good reason they are not accessible by the public. Another option would be to hire a private detective to do an investigation. But it would take time and money and I didn't want to rely on someone else.

I didn't feel like pushing my luck and trying to infiltrate the police station again. Nor did I want to bring anyone else into the situation. I felt the best option was the vehicle registry. I could pretend I wanted to get in touch with a distant relative and try to bribe a staff member. The risk wouldn't be too bad either, if I played it casual the employee would probably just tell me to leave quietly if they weren't interested. Provided of course that they believed my story.

With a plan settled on I sought out the vehicle registry in the central business district. Conveniently it wasn't that far from the gazette so I knew the area fairly well. I found the registry without too much difficulty, as it was located in a large building with an extensive parking lot that stood out from the rest. As I walked closer, I felt someone tap me on the shoulder three times.

"Come with me Mr. Denton, I have some information for you," a man said as I turned around. He was well dressed and appeared in his early twenties. A man knowing me by name, appearing at that exact location and under those circumstances was no accident. The question then was whether I should go with him. As far as I could tell there was equal chance for it to be a trap, or a friend waiting. Still, I came to the conclusion that who it was did not matter really, they were involved in some manner and my meeting them would only further unravel things.

"Certainly," I said confidently and followed the man's lead. We walked for close to ten minutes and entered a small dingy café on a quiet side street. The man stopped at the entrance and signalled for me to enter. My eyes took a second to adjust to the darker interior and I saw a woman seated at a table in the back left hand corner. I walked over wondering who it was.

"You're certainly predictable," the woman said as I approached. I recognised the voice instantly.

"This is a surprise Jackie," I said as I sat down opposite her.

"I knew you would make a move today, and felt confident that you would not try the police station again. So I had a few key places watched, and well you turned up at the one I had my money on."

"You went to a lot of effort, I'm flattered."

"This isn't about you, I did some digging around and Alexis Morgan really is the daughter of the owner of the Vale Club, and hasn't been seen by her neighbour for at least a week. That much of what you told me is true."

"Of course it is, why would I lie about that?"

"That is why I'm helping you, for her sake. It doesn't mean you are forgiven for the stunt you pulled."

"Sounds reasonable," I said wondering just how much help she was willing to provide.

"I tracked down several addresses for Martin Hintle, owned by different companies," she explained, and handed me a sheet of paper. I scanned the list, looking for something that stuck out.

"This is the right list," I commented while tapping the page. "The third entry is a safe house I've been to." I handed the paper back to Jackie.

"I don't know these areas that well, which ones are in an industrial area on the way from the Vale Club to that third location?" I asked.

"Hmm," she pondered while skimming over the list, "there's only really one that fits that description."

"Great I'll go check it out."

"Not by yourself, this is my information remember."

"You saw what happened last time I did some investigating, I've learnt my lesson."

"I'll stay in the car this time, since I know what I'm getting myself into." I felt elated, I had what was most likely the location of the warehouse that Markus met me in that first night. Even if the place was deserted there would be clues pointing to his current whereabouts. I was also pleased that I hadn't entirely alienated Jackie. She was still angry with me, and rightfully so, but her help made things so much easier. I doubt I would have been able to compile such a comprehensive list, and so quickly.

She had the man with us drive and as the trip progressed I began to recognise streets and the odd building. I became more and more convinced that the place we were heading to was the right location. I felt excitement, but at the same time anxiety. How would I handle the situation if Markus was there? What if Alexis was there? I decided to take a stealthy approach since I had the advantage. Markus wouldn't be expecting me to make another appearance at the warehouse.

"Stop the car," I requested and the driver readily complied. I could see the warehouse a block ahead, there was no doubt about it.

"Is this it?" Jackie asked. I nodded and kept my focus on the building. I couldn't tell if there was any activity inside the building from where we had stopped, but at the very least there were no vehicles parked outside.

"Stay here, I'll go and take a look inside. If I'm not back in half an hour then leave." I left the car and casually crossed the road walking towards the warehouse. I noticed a fire escape on the side of the building but the ladder closest to the ground wasn't extended. However there was a dumpster nearby, and it looked like it was the right height. I strolled across the driveway like I belonged there and walked past the boxes and other junk until I was at the dumpster. I glanced back at the road and saw that nobody was around, so I climbed up onto the dumpster and tugged at the fire escape ladder with one arm, hoping to deploy it with minimal noise.

Of course it clanged down noisily and I felt incredibly self-conscious, standing there on the dumpster next to the source of the commotion. Up I climbed, along the combination of stairs and ladders until I reached the roof. There was a roof access door, a few vents and turbines but nothing else of note. I headed straight for the door and gave it a gentle tug and it opened easily, it wasn't even locked.

I entered the building and quickly headed down the stairs, while still keeping quiet. I wanted to be in and out quickly to meet the deadline I gave Jackie, and also decrease the chance of someone arriving while I was inside. At the same time I didn't want to signpost myself any more than I had already. I came to a pair of double doors, no doubt the top-level of the warehouse. I stepped through and found myself on a square walkway around the edge of the interior. It was overlooking the primary storage area, filled with boxes and crates. From that position it looked perfectly normal. I couldn't see any staff working though. Nothing else was of interest so I went back to the stairwell and descended to the main level.

I arrived at the next set of double doors and checked my watch, I had fifteen minutes left. I gently pushed through the doors and found myself in the main area. I walked through a few rows of boxes until I spotted an open box on the ground. I looked inside and saw what appeared to be spare parts of some kind. Continuing until I had completed a lap of the area brought nothing else to my attention. As I neared the staircase I noticed a small exit leading into another room.

I walked up to the corner of the doorway and peered into the room. It looked empty and I could see no signs of electronic surveillance. I entered the room quietly and looked around. It seemed vaguely familiar, but plain. There were a few tables, boxes, shelves and copious amounts of paper. However when I saw the stairs down, I had a moment of recognition. I felt sure that down those stairs was the room where I met Markus.

I nervously continued down trying to make as little noise as possible. I couldn't hear anything coming from the room but didn't want to take any chances. I came to a closed wooden door with no lock on it. I slowly turned the handle and opened it extremely slowly. The room beyond it was dark and I couldn't really make anything out. There was no more time for stealth and little opportunity for it, so I found a light switch nearby and flicked it on. The lights flickered brightly before staying on and my earlier suspicions was right: this was indeed the room where I had met Markus.

There was nobody inside, so I began my search for information. The warehouse might have been abandoned directly after that night for all I knew, so I had to be thorough. The room was rather bare so my first thought was that my discovery was fruitless. I checked drawers, shelves, tables and even the waste paper baskets. Nothing turned up. My frustration was steadily building and I was inwardly berating myself for thinking this plan would work. Of course Markus was too careful to leave anything behind in places that he had exposed to others. I was too slow to follow his trail and a vacant room was the result.

I walked over to what was his desk and dropped into the chair, dejected. It was then I noticed one small piece of thin paper sitting there on the surface. I unfolded it and read the contents, it appeared to be a repair bill for a boat, named The Wayward Soul. Was this an oversight or an invitation? I took it with me and left the building. Jackie was visibly concerned when I returned, I had exceeded my self-imposed time limit, but not by much.

"Find anything?" she asked.

"Only this," I replied pulling out the ship bill and handing it to her. "It was left on a desk in a room which was otherwise completely cleaned out."

"You think he left it for you?"

"It's quite possible, you know it wouldn't be a huge step to assume I was tracking him based on the restaurant incident. This could be his way of suggesting a meeting."

"Why would he meet you if he thinks you are after him?"

"I have something he wants." This elicited a sideways glance from Jackie but she didn't say anything. I thought back to my growing collection of artifacts. As far as I knew it was now the largest collection, although it was safe to assume that Markus had the rest or knew where they were. It was logical that he would only go after the larger collection that Madison had assembled if he was close to attaining the rest. I asked Jackie if she had any contacts that could look up boats and their registration and she explained that after a quick stop at her office she could confirm its owner and where it was berthed.

We stopped off outside the Gazette and I waited in the car, idly watching the traffic and pedestrians. My mind wandered and I began to think about what the people I watched worried about. Were they also plagued with the same questions of identity, purpose and how they fit into the world? Or were they just caught up in their lives, too busy with their daily routine and responsibilities. Was I just different? Maybe my thoughts were not just a result of my situation, but also of my character.

True to her boast Jackie emerged from the Gazette after about fifteen minutes. I could tell by the way she walked that she had succeeded. The confident satisfaction of her stride was hard to miss.

"Mission accomplished?" I asked.

"Affirmative. The vessel is registered to a Martin Hintle at the Seafirth Marina," she replied.

"Great now I.."

"That's not all, the ship is the venue for a party tonight to welcome the new chairman of the Marchilde Foundation."

"And you're covering the story?"

"And I don't want to go alone, so you can tag along." So it was settled, and I was heading to another Foundation event. I hoped it would go better than the last.

I went back to my hotel room and found a good suit to wear to the party. I checked the artifacts and they were all present and accounted for. I decided to take one along as a bargaining tool just in case. If I had learned one thing from my trials, it was that nothing ever went to plan. A plan is but a loose framework to use to accomplish your goals. The world is too fluid to force into a rigid shape. Quite frankly I think I would be disappointed if everything went exactly as I had predicted.

I met Jackie at the marina and although I was there right on time she was already waiting. Behind her was The Wayward Soul, and it was bigger than I expected. It consisted of multiple levels and was brimming with people. A casual glance at them confirmed that I was dressed appropriately.

"You really know how to show a girl a good time," Jackie commented as I was looking over the ship.

"I'm sorry it's a bit bigger than I expected. I should have tried to get my hands on some schematics beforehand," I said in reply. I looked at her and she didn't seem upset. She just smiled at me, as one does at a foolish child.

We walked down to the end of the dock, Jackie showed her invitation and we boarded the vessel. Uniformed sailors directed us to the top-level, which was a large viewing platform. The bulk of the guests seemed to be up there. Jackie and I made our way up and over to the edge, looking off into the ocean. After a few minutes I turned and leaned back against the railing, scanning the crowd for any familiar faces. A waiter approached with a tray offering us champagne. We both accepted and I slowly sipped it while continuing to watch those aboard.

"See anyone?" Jackie asked.

"Not yet, I doubt Markus will appear amongst the guests. Still it doesn't hurt to keep an eye out." As I finished my sentence a low rumbling was audible and steadily grew in volume. The ship lurched forwards and them smoothly began to pull away from the dock. A group of musicians came upstairs and walked down to the bow where they began to set up. The music started shortly after but no formal announcements were made. I decided to bide my time upstairs with the crowd and not make any moves until I had more information. I needed something concrete to go on.

Jackie and I slowly worked our way around the top deck getting a good look at the other guests and assessing what security personnel were around. We were discussing our thoughts on the how the rest of the night would proceed when I saw something that stopped me mid-sentence. I asked Jackie to not follow, and I walked over to the bow to a small section besides the musicians. I took another look to make sure. There was no mistaking it, it was Alexis. She was looking off into the distance with her back to the crowd, leaning over the railing.

I felt a powerful rush of relief, seeing her alive. I almost ran over, but stopped myself and looked closer at her surroundings. There were some men nearby who were clearly her minders, but I felt it was safe to approach. I slowly walked up until I was right behind her.

"Not enjoying the party?" I asked.

"You should not have come," she replied without turning around.

"I received an invitation, how could I not come? Seeing you here has made the trip worthwhile."

"He is intrigued by you and is playing along, but it will not last. What do you hope to accomplish?"

"I've already explained myself to you and I'm not one to go back on my word." As soon as I said that she turned to face me. She looked exhausted and sleep deprived and at the sight of her face I lost whatever words I was going to say next. Most of all though, she radiated a deep sadness. I felt as though she was drained and the rage driving her had faded.

"I don't know how much longer I can hold on," Alexis said, and I just wanted to reach out and take her away from it all. Since I became involved her world had begun its decline and I was the main cause of it all. Why did she have to suffer for my mistakes?

"This ends tonight," I declared while walking away, I purposefully did not look back. I didn't want to see the expression on her face. I walked right past Jackie without acknowledging her and went back towards the middle of the boat. I was seething with a quiet rage but it didn't overcome me. I just had no patience for any niceties or distractions. I was completely focused on a single task: to find Markus on the boat and force Alexis's freedom. Woe betide anyone who stood in my way.

I marched downstairs, preparing in my head the excuse of using the bathroom but quickly ducked into a roped off section. I picked a corridor at random and walked down it. At each turn I took the option that seemed more lavish and decorated. After a few minutes of wandering a man was standing in my way guarding a doorway behind him.

"This is a restricted area sir, I'll call for someone to escort you out," the man said as I approached. However I didn't give him a chance. I quickly darted forward and grabbed the arm he was using to reach for a radio and yanked it as I spun him around. With a rough shove in the back he was now pinned against the wall and defenceless.

"Is the master suite through those doors?" I asked politely. He responded by spitting on one of my shoes. I kicked him hard in the back of his knee and he slumped to the floor. I repeated my question a little less politely and he simply nodded in reply. I saw a handgun poking out from the back of his pants, so I retrieved it and hit him squarely in the back of the head with the butt. He crumpled completely and lay unconscious on the ground. I checked to see if the gun was loaded, as if by instinct, and took off the safety. Weapon in hand I walked through the doorway into a richly carpeted area that was markedly different from the rest of the ship.

Elaborate paintings adorned the walls and gold leaf covered the ceiling. The occasional marble bust was on display in the hallways. I found myself in what seemed like a reception chamber and two suited men were standing there, alert and at attention. Once they saw me they reached for weapons and my arm moved as if of its own volition. It swung up with the gun, fired, swung over and fired again. Both men slumped to the ground and rolled over facing me. Each had a bullet hole squarely between his eyes. I should have been shocked, horrified and terrified. Yet no emotions touched me. I noticed a door behind them and walked over to it, carefully stepping around their bodies.

Effortlessly I pushed the door open and found myself in an extremely ornately decorated office. It made the hallways and rooms I had just been through seem like servants quarters. Sitting behind a giant desk was a bald man wearing a white suit. He glanced up at me and I recognised him instantly.

"I see you got my invitation," he commented casually and then focused again on the papers before him. I stood there, watching and waiting. Now that I was before Markus, I didn't know what to do. I had been running on instinct and now that I had made it, I was unsure of how to proceed. After a minute he shuffled the papers he had, put them into a drawer and leaned back in his chair looking at me thoughtfully.

"Well since you went to the trouble of coming here, I assume you have something to say," he said completely calmly.

"The way you are treating Alexis is unacceptable. Release her," I demanded.

"That didn't sound like a request. What happens if I don't comply?" he asked.

"You won't live to regret the decision," I said simply. It wasn't rage, it was cold determination. I felt incredibly detached and a part of me was wondering at what I was doing.

"You dare to threaten me?" He asked incredulously.

"You are but a man, Markus," I replied. He laughed out loud in response.

"I've given you far too much credit, it seems that you still know nothing. The girl is in my possession because she's one of the few who has seen Markus's face," he told me while snarling in disdain. As his words sank in I realised what they truly meant. I had made a mistake in assuming that this man was Markus. He was important no doubt, but I was foolish for thinking that Markus would deal with me himself.

"The girl only lives because of the valuable information she has and at Markus's whim. Otherwise she would have already been disposed of. However if she doesn't comply soon, I'm afraid our patience will have completely run out." I was lost, and felt out of my depth. I absent-mindedly put my left hand in my pocket and touched something cold and metallic. It was the artifact that I brought with me. It gave me an idea.

"I have an artifact with me. Did you know that they react when they are near each other?" I asked him. With a puzzled look he reached into his suit jacket pocket and I simultaneously raised my weapon and shot him in the shoulder. He fell down in pain clutching the wound. I walked across to where he lay and stood over him. He looked up at me in surprise and anger. I shoved his arm aside roughly and reached for his artifact. It was the gun that I had given to his henchmen after the charity ball.

"If you had collected more than one then you would have known I was lying. Thanks for adding to my collection though," I told him in a mocking fashion. He was absolutely livid, and so angry that I think he could not even utter a response. I knew I was pushing my luck, but hoped that since Markus wanted information from Alexis, then her life was safe for the time being. That, of course, was if I couldn't rescue her on my way out.

I left the room and made my way back to the upper decks as quickly as possible. I didn't have the time to really think about what had just occurred I just knew that I had to find Alexis and get us both off the boat as soon as possible. Strangely I encountered no resistance while in the restricted area and reached the common areas un-scathed. Hoping to avoid undue attention I put away the gun and slowed down to a regular walk. Each corner loomed with potential danger, yet I pretended all was well. I walked upstairs and found the main deck just as I had left it, as though the events that had just transpired were still unknown. Jackie spotted me and started to walk over but I shook my head and she stopped, con-fused.

I scanned the crowd for Alexis, but could not see her. I increased my speed to a fast walk, almost a jog and sped over to where I saw her last. She was gone. I spun around in a panic, looking for any trace of her. I cursed myself for not searching for her downstairs while mak-ing my way topside. I looked over the deck, and realised that if she had been taken back, it had to be somewhere below. I had a choice: leave while I had the chance or go back to look for her. No matter how I analysed it, I kept coming back to the one choice – leave. It was the logical option. Yet I could not.

I pushed my way back through the crowd in a direct line to the stairs down. Nobody challenged me as I once again entered the restricted area. I had another choice ahead of me, to travel towards the quarters of Martin Hintle or away from them. Would he have kept Alexis close by or not? I decided to try the opposite direction as I hadn't travelled through there yet.

I passed through some food preparation areas and storerooms, finding myself in a more sparsely decorated section with various cabins. I must have been in the crew quarters. I drew the pistol and walked up to the first door, determined to try them all. I tried the handle on the door, and it wasn't locked. I slowly opened the latch then burst through. The small room contained only a bed, a bedside table and a closet. There was nobody inside.

Each room I opened was the same, each empty and seemingly undisturbed as if nobody had slept there in a long time. I came to the last door, however my energy was mostly spent and I just carelessly shoved it open and strolled inside. I was greeted with a fist to the face and a large muscled man standing over me. That was just my luck. As I went to aim my weapon he stamped down on my hand and kicked it away. I rolled away and got up as quickly as possible. I was just in time to lean back and avoid the next blow. I caught his arm as it went by and twisted it roughly before shoving it back into him with as much force as I could muster. He cried out in pain and staggered back. I advanced and as he looked up I leaned forward and smashed him in the head with my own. Whilst quite effective, he dropped like a sack of stones, it hurt me a lot. Nursing my head with one hand I walked into the room and looked around to see what all the fuss was about.

The room was a bit bigger than the rest but similarly furnished. The main difference here was that Alexis lay upon the bed, partially clothed. I felt sick to my stomach looking at her, she was covered in bruises. I kicked the unconscious man at my feet again for good measure.

"Let's get you out of here," I said then left the room to retrieve my gun. I checked the corridor and nobody seemed to be coming. When I re-entered the room Alexis had put on a robe but still appeared visibly shaken.

"Are you OK?" I asked.

"No, but give me the gun and follow my lead," she replied. I handed it over and while she checked it her eyes lit up in a way that frightened me. She scanned the corridor and then took off at a pace I was not expecting. Perhaps she was running on adrenalin.

"We're probably a fair way from the mainland but there's some emergency boats accessible from down here," she explained as we went. She moved with purpose, it seemed as though she had memorised the way. I was happy to follow, I had spent enough time wandering the corridors aimlessly already.

We proceeded through an exit and found ourselves on the outer walkway that went around the edge of the ship. Attached to the side of the vessel, just below us, were the emergency boats. Alexis released a nearby lever and the nearest boat fell down to the ocean. All we had to do was climb down and paddle away to safety. There was no way they would be able to track us once we left. I felt this strange prickling sensation in my back, as if someone was watching and I turned to see a suited man aiming a handgun at Alexis. His face tensed up slightly and I shoved her down. The man fired but he had not adjusted his aim in time and the bullet sped past harmlessly. I stood over her hoping to block the next one. The second shot pierced me so suddenly I didn't feel it at first. I slumped down and stared incredulously at the wound, and then the blood on my hand. I heard two more shots ring out and a woman yelling at me.

I climbed down the stairs somehow and fell into the boat. I could see activity on The Wayward Soul, and the lights slowly becoming dimmer and dimmer. My awareness was slipping and we were getting further and further away. Eventually everything became black.

DRAMATIC SHOOT-OUT ON LUXURY SHIP

By Jacqueline Somers

Last night shots were fired on the luxury cruise ship The Wayward Soul during a function. Two men have been confirmed dead and another has been injured. The perpetrators fled on an emergency boat and are still at large. Police have declined to comment on the investigation. The ship was privately owned and the invitation only party was to celebrate the inauguration of the new chairman of the Marchilde Foundation. Only days ago the previous chairman was killed during a charity ball.

According to early reports the shooting began in the lower deck culminating with security forces firing on the perpetrators as they attempted to escape. No guests were harmed and all were safely returned to the Seafirth Marina once the shooting ceased. Representatives of the Marchilde Foundation were contacted for comment but have not yet responded.

CHAPTER TWELVE

DUTY OF CARE

I awoke to a feeling of nothing and a sea of white. As my eyes adjusted I noticed that I was in a bed in a plain white room. I tried to sit up but my body resisted. In a panic I moved my fingers and toes and they worked. Concentrating was difficult for some reason, like there was a fluffy blanket stuffed in my head making every-thing harder. However I did notice one thing of importance: a strap across my chest constraining my movement. That explained my difficulty in sitting up. Wherever I was, I was expected to stay.

Moments later a raven haired middle-aged woman in a white uniform entered the room.

"Ah, you are awake, Mr Masters," she said. I looked at her quizzically then realised that I had identification with that name in my wallet from when I went to the charity ball.

"Where am I?"

"You're in the hospital of course. You almost died from a gunshot wound to the chest."

"Why am I strapped into the bed?"

"You were thrashing around in your sleep, and we didn't want you reopening the wound." The explanation seemed plausible but for some reason I was not completely convinced. I watched her carefully as she glided around the room checking various machines and charts.

"How long do I have to stay here?" I said.

"Until the doctor clears you. Usually it takes a week or two." Regardless of their intentions I knew I couldn't wait around for that long. I simply nodded without questioning her answer and watched her complete her duties. Within a minute she had left and I was alone again.

I took stock of my situation. I was wounded, but alive. Alexis was presumably also alive since I was the one that had been shot and I had survived. My possessions were of greater concern. They had my wallet, but what else? I had two artifacts on my person, not to mention the hotel room key which led to the rest of my collection. I had to return as soon as possible and see if they were safe. It wasn't clear how much time had already passed since that night. I berated myself for not asking the nurse more questions.

I resolved to break out at the earliest convenience. I did not think it risky or unwise, I just knew that I was alive and would do whatever was necessary to keep moving forward. I did not have time to waste lying around. The hours until the next nurse turned up seemed like an entire age.

"Where are my things?" I said to the nurse, trying to be as calm as possible.

"Everything you had with you is in that cupboard in the corner," the nurse said simply. She continued checking the same things that the previous one had, only this time she paused before leaving.

"It looks like you are due for some more pain relief," she said. My dulled senses suddenly made perfect sense. The fact that I hadn't realised I was drugged was all the more problematic.

"Can I try a spell without it?" I asked.

"Don't be silly, you'll never be able to rest otherwise. That's the best case scenario, most likely you'll just be in agony," she replied.

"I can't relax doped up like this, it puts me on edge. Just let me try it."

"If I don't give this to you now, when your current dose wears off it'll be hours before someone else comes by."

"That's a risk I'm willing to take, I just need to see how I am without it."

"Fine, if you insist," she said and promptly left. I could feel the fog slowly lifting from my mind. However as it receded the pain began and intensified. The nurse was completely correct and for a moment I wholeheartedly regretted my decision. However the die was cast, so I had to continue on with my plan.

It was easier said than done. My entire chest was aflame and it felt like the pain was pulsing with a life of its own. I was still strapped into the bed. I examined the straps more closely and noticed that they were just cloth and their primary purpose was not for violent restraint. My guess was that they didn't want to cause me any more injuries. With considerable effort I was able to wiggle one arm out from underneath them and lay it on my chest in the open. I rested for a few minutes in that position then repeated the feat with my other arm. The sense of accomplishment I felt even rose above the pain, for a short while.

Now that I had use of my arms, the next step was to free myself from the straps. I didn't feel that brute strength would be the suitable approach in this instance. I decided that my best chance would be locating where the straps were secured and trying to loosen or remove them. With my right arm I reached down the side of the bed carefully, feeling along the strap to see where it went. I rounded the mattress and began to feel underneath it from that side, finding nothing promising. Catching my breath for a minute I retracted my arm and did the same on the left side with my other arm. As I inched down I had a worrying thought that perhaps I might not find anything within arm's reach. Just as that worry peaked I felt something metallic. I methodically felt all around the smooth metal, and deduced that it was a clasp. Lady Luck was smiling on me.

From what the nurse had said I had a few hours to myself, so time was also on my side. The last thing I wanted to do was unnecessarily injure myself during my escape attempt. I explored the metal clasp carefully and deduced it was a simple buckle type. However I had to figure out how to open it with only one hand and no visual reference. I closed my eyes and concentrated. I followed the cloth, pictured it in my mind and tugged at that I thought was the main loop. I shifted the buckle slightly and felt the tension in the strap lessen. It was a huge relief to discover that I was on the right track. Within minutes I had the strap loosened enough that I could sit up relatively comfortably.

I pushed the strap down and revelled in my new freedom. The pain flared even worse, something I didn't think possible. The surprising thing though was that I was able to push it away. My resolve hardened and I knew within that nothing would be able to stop me. I didn't become reckless though, and took my time moving myself so that I was sitting on the edge of the bed. Gingerly I put weight on one foot, and then the other, standing up with less trouble than I expected. I still felt incredibly weak though and a little unsteady on my feet. I shuffled over to the cupboard and opened it. As expected, my clothes and things were inside.

I dressed myself and felt better, and it was surprising the difference that it made. I checked my pockets and my wallet was there, but no artifacts. A further inspection of the wallet showed that it still contained all the money I had left in there. That seemed puzzling, but I didn't have the time or mental faculties to question it. I left the room and found myself in a long white corridor. I didn't see any obvious signs or directions so I turned right and starting walking.

I picked up the pace a little and felt a sharp pain in my chest. Stopping to inspect myself I didn't see any blood but felt that I should be careful nonetheless. I had paused outside what appeared to be a storage closet, so I ducked inside to see what they had. Shelves and shelves of medical supplies were in there, as well as some nondescript white cloth bags. I grabbed bandages, syringes, bottles of various kinds and other things that I couldn't name but knew what they were for. By now I had learnt enough to realise that when my instincts kicked in to just go along with them. Part of me knew what I was doing, in some strange way.

Once the bag was filled I expertly wrapped another bandage over the dressing on my wound, and then continued on. I walked past many rooms, all full of patients. Ahead I spotted two nurses chatting at a desk at the junction of two other corridors. I didn't want a confrontation in case they either recognised me or noticed the bulging bag of medical supplies I was carrying. Doubling back I entered the nearest room which had four beds in it. All were older men who were asleep. Each man had a machine or two plugged into him, whirring softly in the otherwise silent room. That would be my diversion.

I unplugged one of the machines from the power point and pressed a giant red button above the next man's bed. That would seize the nurses' attention, I just had to get across the hallway to another room before they responded. I rushed through to the nearest room opposite me, my haste causing each step to be more agonising than the last. Within seconds I heard a loud alarm sounding from the room I had just left. It was followed shortly by approaching voices and the clap of hurried footsteps. As they entered the room I stepped back into the corridor and walked ahead as quickly and quietly as I was able.

I turned left as I passed the nurse station and noticed an elevator at the end of the hallway. That was my salvation. As I walked towards it, I almost tripped over something left carelessly on the ground. It was a wheelchair. Getting off my feet seemed like a good idea, so I sat myself in it, placed the bag of supplies on my lap and started wheeling myself over to my exit strategy. It was nice to be off my feet, but my arms soon tired just from the act of getting myself to the end of the corridor. Thankfully the elevator buttons were at a reasonable height so I pressed the down call button without needing to leave the chair.

As I waited I examined the bag I had more closely. With a little maneuvering I was able to better arrange the supplies within and seal it so that I looked less suspicious. In my head I ran over my story, I was getting discharged today but nobody was meeting me. The bright tone of the lift arriving broke my train of the thought and as the doors opened inside was a man who looked like a doctor. I nodded to him confidently and then wheeled myself in.

"What floor?" the man asked helpfully.

"Ground floor please," I replied. He pressed the button for me and said nothing further. The trip down was slow, as it stopped at every floor even though some had nobody waiting. People entered and left as the elevator descended and finally when I reached the ground floor I was by myself once more. I rolled out into an incredibly busy foyer filled with all types of people ranging from the picture of health to death walking. Feeling at ease, I approached the doors to leave.

"Wait sir!" a voice called out and I heard footsteps rushing over to my location. I braced myself for a confrontation as I stopped.

"You will have to leave that here," a woman said, gesturing at my wheelchair. Immense feelings of relief overwhelmed me as I chuckled and stepped out of the chair. The woman smiled apologetically and wheeled it away as I walked out into freedom. I heard some sort of commotion behind me, so to be safe I walked around the corner from the main hospital exit and kept an eye out for any trouble.

"The man just left, I took a wheelchair from him", I heard a woman say as two tall well-built men all in white walked through the main doors.

"He can't have gotten far," one man said to the other.

"They'll have our hides if we don't get him back", the other replied. The two men dashed off towards the main road to begin their search. I didn't feel up to taking them on, so I looked around for a way to exit discreetly. To the back of the complex I spotted a wire link fence with dumpsters up against it. It seemed a desperate measure, climbing over a fence in my condition, but my desire to not return to that hospital was incredibly strong. So I found myself walking over to the fence before I had even decided on that course of action.

I occasionally stopped and checked behind me while I walked, however each time I looked there was nobody around. However that didn't stop me from checking again soon after. The dumpsters were both open and I caught a strong whiff of their putrefying contents as I reached over to close the lids. I gingerly tossed my bag onto the top of one of the dumpsters and clambered up to stand on it, a brutal stinging pain was my reward for the effort. Even standing at my full height I was still only halfway up the fence. Upon closer inspection I also noticed barbed wire at the top. This idea of mine had begun to appear even worse.

I removed my jacket and threw it carefully up onto the fence. It landed right at the top, straddling both sides of the fence and covering a small section of the barbed wire. I was immensely relieved that it worked, but also conscious that had I missed I would have lost the jacket for no gain. Next was the bag. I put more effort into that throw to ensure it went all the way over, grunting involuntarily with the strain. It was only me left in the confines of the hospital grounds.

I gritted my teeth for the explosion of pain to come and reached up, grabbing the fence with my hands to begin my ascent. The first movement was everything I expected but the pain soon dulled. What worried me more was the sensation of fluid dripping all over my chest. I could only hope it was sweat and not my wounds reopening. After what seemed like an eternity I reached the top and was within reach of my jacket. I paused for a brief rest then placed my hands carefully on it and vaulted myself over, gaining a foothold on the other side. The pain flared again but I ignored it and climbed down a small distance. I had enough presence of mind to remember my jacket, so I reached up to grab it and throw it down onto the ground below.

The way down was easier, but more stressful since the potential fall was twice as bad. It was with great relief and accomplishment that my feet touched the ground. I checked my bandages and everything looked fine, my fears of having bled everywhere were unfounded. Putting on my jacket and picking up my bag, I looked around to see where I had gotten myself. I was in an empty lot, surrounded by dingy back alleys and old buildings with the occasional graffiti. I wandered the streets at random, slowly working my way back to where I thought the main road was. I didn't want to pop up right in front of the hospital and negate all the fence climbing effort. Once I was free there would only one thing on my mind: returning to the hotel and securing the artifacts.

After roughly twenty minutes I found myself back on a main road with a healthy flow of traffic. I hailed a cab and directed the driver to take me to my hotel. He indicated that the trip would take over an hour, and wanted to see proof that I had enough cash with me. I dug through my pockets to get to my money, and showed him I had plenty. However that act triggered my memory, in particular the fact that both the artifacts I had carried with me were gone. In addition to that, I didn't have my room key. A flash of anger swept over me, but I managed to suppress it. With my escape now completed, the realisation that I was already down two artifacts made reaching the others to be of the utmost importance. I had no idea if they were still secure. The taxi could not drive fast enough to satisfy my sense of urgency.

I practically ran out of the taxi when it dropped me off, although composed myself enough not to draw attention when I entered the building. I walked confidently up to the reception area and waited patiently while the woman at the desk talked on the phone. I only listened enough to determine that it was a work call. As impatient as I felt, I needed a result and would not risk a problem by unnecessarily harassing the hotel staff.

"Sorry for the delay sir, how can I help you?" she asked politely.

"I've lost my room key", I explained.

"Not a problem, please show me some identification and tell me your room number."

"315," I replied calmly while I retrieved my fake ID. She glanced at it briefly, and then turned her attention back to the computer screen in front of her.

"There's a note here.." she said, trailing off before walking over to the rows of latticed squares behind her full of keys. She came back with the room key and a plain white envelope.

"It seems as though your wife returned the key Mr Masters and left this for you", the girl said as she handed over the envelope and key. I nodded while thanking her and walked off in a daze towards the elevators. As curious as I was about the note and the mysterious woman who had left it, I needed to check on the artifacts first. I proceeded directly to my room, opened the door and closed it quickly and headed straight to the room safe. It was still locked. I input the code nervously and swung open the door as soon as the lock clanked open. It was empty.

I stepped back with surprise and found myself sitting on the bed. Without thinking I had opened the note and started reading it. It said the following:

Sorry, I took the liberty of securing your collection while you were indisposed.

Let me take care of it from here.

I forgive you.

- A

A rush of conflicting emotions hit me. The note had to have been from Alexis, and that meant she forgave me for my actions. But at the same time she had taken from me the very objects that were instrumental in solving this mystery, and therefore my chance at redemption. And she was doing it alone, without my help. However, had I already redeemed myself by saving her from the ship? What was her plan? I thought back to what Martin had said before I shot him - 'The girl only lives because of the valuable information she has.' That could only mean one thing, that she knew the secret of the artifacts and wanted to use them against Markus.

I was despondent. I should have been joyous, given the circumstances. It just didn't feel right, that the job was unfinished and she was out of the picture. Logically it was another opportunity to walk away. I had done what was right and gone above and beyond to try to set things right. It wasn't my fight, not originally. Things seemed to go deeper than any involvement I had. But I couldn't just let go. I lay back on the bed, the strain of the day and my injuries suddenly coming to the surface. I struggled against sleep, trying to think of my next move and where Alexis would have gone. Then I real-ised that I was right back where I had spent all the previous days – looking for Alexis. At least this time she was free. My last thought as I drifted off was: 'I should be with you'.

CHAPTER THIRTEEN

EXHIBITIONIST

My first thoughts were of her, they rose above the intense pain assaulting every part of my body. With great effort I dragged myself over to my bag of medical supplies and took some painkillers. As they took effect I cleaned myself up, redressed my wound and made myself presentable. As necessary as these steps were, they were just diversionary. I didn't want to think of what to do next. I had a place to start though, or rather a person: Jackie.

Within the hour I was sitting on her chair, in her office, wondering where she was. My impatience got the better of me, and I started rifling through her papers in an attempt to work out where she had gone.

"You look half dead," Jackie said as she walked in, looking both surprised and annoyed.

"Getting shot will do that to you," I said sarcastically.

"Make yourself at home."

"I saved her."

"Let's go grab a coffee and you can fill me in." I thought back to the last time I had coffee with Jackie, steeled myself and followed her.

Jackie studied me closely as I sipped my hot chocolate. We were seated in the café across the road from the Gazette. She had not said a single word as I explained the events after I had last seen her.

"Is something wrong?" I asked.

"I should be asking you that," she replied. "You seem a bit lost."

"I'm just pondering my next move."

"No need to ponder, we just pick up the trail. Have you got an address for her? Chances are she went back there."

"I know of a place," I said, thinking back to the safe house where Alexis had taken me. I still remembered how to get back there.

"Let's go!" Jackie exclaimed, rising from her chair suddenly.

"Are you sure? I've brought you enough trouble already. I only came today to let you know what happened."

"You're alright Will," she commented while giving me a strange, somewhat approving look, and then left. I followed her closely, feeling a little puzzled by the exchange but thankful for her help. I just hoped I could keep her out of trouble.

The trip to Alexis's safe house wasn't as quick as expected, my memory of the route was not perfect and required a few readjustments. I also found the pain from my wounds making it hard to think clearly. However once we arrived there, all my doubts were swept away. I left the car confidently, and strode up the front door, turning the handle. It was locked.

"No key?" Jackie said. I looked her up and down, closely before remarking.

"No. Have you got any hair clips or jewellery I can use?"

"How about these instead?" Jackie said, as she reached into her handbag and pulled out some lock-picking tools. I chuckled and shook my head, not even regretting the pain the laugh had caused me.

"I won't ask."

"Sometimes the stories need help getting out." I made short work of the lock and opened the door carefully. I expected the dank shut up smell that I had encountered when entering the safe house assigned to me, but it was not present. Jackie noticed it as well.

"She's been here recently," Jackie commented as we walked in and closed the door behind us. The place was a lot different than I remembered. Pages of drawings and notes were everywhere, on the walls, on the floor, on any flat surface. I picked one up and examined it, at first it made no sense then I saw a rough drawing that looked exactly like one of the artifacts. I immediately thought of the manifest that I had inadvertently destroyed in the train incident. Alexis must have been recreating it, only this time using both her memory and the set of artifacts she now had.

"What is this all this?" Jackie asked.

"These artifacts are at the heart of everything. The notes must lead to where Alexis went next," I said. Jackie didn't need any further encouragement and grabbed a stack of papers. I followed her example, making an effort to sort the notes into some kind of order.

We arranged the papers into piles based on which artifact they were referring to. In addition to that we also had a general pile which outlined the history of the artifacts. I had to wonder if Alexis always had access to such information, because what she had noted down seemed a lot more in-depth and concrete than what I had managed to extract from the man in the market stall. However, he had just been stalling for time so perhaps I didn't scratch the surface of what he knew.

From the information we had read through, it seemed as though the artifacts, when combined correctly, deliver a message. The content of this message however, seemed to mean different things to each of the different sources Alexis had noted down. It ranged from secret potions and recipes, to locations of lost treasures, truth or even the power of miracles. The one constant though, was that you needed a separate codex to help assemble the artifacts and decipher the message. Alexis believed that Markus had the codex, and that explained his obsession with gathering them all.

The other useful information that came to light was the number of artifacts. Every reference we could find pointed to the same number: twelve. I had eight in my possession until my hospital visit. The question remained, how many did Markus have? Aside from that, despite the usefulness of the information we had gathered from the safe house, we were no closer to finding Alexis's next move. She could well be on her way to meet Markus.

"Hold on a minute, there's something missing," Jackie said excitedly.

"What do you mean?" I asked with interest.

"These notes are too methodical and detailed. Yet they only detail eight of the artifacts. Why do you think that is? Isn't it odd that there's no mention of any of the others?"

"Until recently I had eight in my possession, that can't be a coincidence."

"Are they the eight mentioned in detail?" Jackie said. I examined the pages she selected carefully.

"Yes. So you think that the missing ones are not absent due to lack of information, but because Alexis is tracking them down? These pages have been left behind because they are no longer required."

"Definitely. We just need to find any reference to an artifact not mentioned in these detailed pages and we may have a lead on where she went next." I nodded and refocused my search. Hours passed and my eyes grew tired from the strain. It was now late in the evening and we had spent the better part of the day collecting notes, sorting them and summarising them. My eyelids started to close of their own accord, yet as they did one word was like a searing torch, burning away my tiredness – Dragon. I found the offending word, and the sentence it was contained in. Then the relevant paragraph and read it over and over. The significance of the word was on the tip of my tongue, on the edge of my mind yet just out of reach.

"That's it!" I cried out, exultant. The noise startled Jackie, who had dozed off. She looked at me with surprise and puzzlement

"One of the artifacts is a dragon," I explained.

"What's the significance of that?" she asked.

"Alexis and I visited a man looking for information. The code phrase used referred to a dragon, but the information we got was bad and that was when she was taken. At the time I thought we were just going to pick the man's brain, but I think now that Alexis knew he was a lead for the dragon artifact. If that's the case not only is she going to go back there and find out for sure, I'll bet she also wants revenge."

"Sounds like our best and only lead. Let's go pay him a visit tomorrow."

"I'm not sure if his market stall is open tomorrow."

"You going to let that stop you?"

"No."

"Goodnight Will," Jackie said softly, as she rose and walked to the nearby bedroom. I found the sofa bed, dragged the mattress onto the floor and slept within seconds of my head hitting the cushion I was using for a pillow.

The drive back to the markets brought back all the emotions I had felt the first time I went there with Alexis. Jackie was quiet on the way, as if she sensed that I needed my own space for a time. It was an overcast day, threatening to rain at any moment. The roads were slick with water, it must have rained overnight. I just couldn't focus on what mattered. Part of me didn't want to think of what I might do when I confronted the old antiques dealer again. Part of me was worried that maybe Alexis had already gotten to him first.

We walked slowly through the markets, due entirely to my pace. There weren't many people around and half the stalls were empty. The place seemed much more sombre this time around. I could see the stall I was heading for in the distance, and periodically caught a glimpse when I was trying not to look. I was really dreading the encounter that I knew was coming, the encounter that had to happen. I looked over at Jackie and she had a look that seemed to mirror my own, as if she understood. We had already been through a lot together, were we friends now?

As I neared the antiques stall I saw the young man working out front. His presence meant that I could use him to gain access to the rest of their shop and look for clues. I asked Jackie to go and strike up a conversation with the young man while I took a slightly longer route to avoid him seeing me. I watched as she approached him, then made my move deliberately and carefully. It worked perfectly and I managed to sidle right up to the stall without him noticing.

"Hello again," I said cheerfully, enjoying the frantic and panicked face he made as he recognised me. I took advantage of his surprise and walked closer.

"My friend here is armed and a relative of the woman who was taken last time I visited," I told the young man calmly and confidently. He visibly gulped and drew in his breath.

"What's your name?" I asked.

"Jeremy."

"So, Jeremy, how about you and I have a nice quiet chat, and if it goes well nothing messy will need to occur," I offered. Jackie gave him a wicked smile and he nodded furiously, directing me over to the hatch leading downstairs. Jackie remained at the main stall while I followed him down.

The room was in disarray and looked like a brawl had occurred. My gut said that Alexis had already stopped by.

"I see she's already paid you a visit," I said, hoping to confirm my suspicions.

"Yes," he said meekly.

"How's the old man?"

"Alive, barely."

"It could have gone much worse. Were you with them?"

"Yes."

"I just have one more question then. Where is the dragon artifact?'

"I don't know I swear," he said. I strode up to him, looked him straight in the eye and put one hand on his shoulder. He flinched visibly, then spoke hurriedly.

"Seriously, she worked him over so badly he could barely speak. Finally he whispered something to her then laughed before he passed out." I could tell that he was telling the truth, so I removed my hand and started looking over the room carefully.

"If there's anything here to help me, it would be in your best interests to remember it," I announced as I sorted through the debris in the room. I had no intention of harming Jeremy, however I wanted to remain imposing to give him doubts about trying anything.

"There's one thing, Mr MacFinley was quite excited by an upcoming museum exhibition," Jeremy offered nervously. It sounded like a slim clue, but potentially useful. I refocused my search of the small room, looking for coloured or glossy paper. I found some magazines on antiques, laundry receipts and a pamphlet of some kind. Turning over the pamphlet I noticed it was for a museum exhibition. A great scholar's collection was currently being displayed as a special exhibit. I scanned the pictures curiously, looking for anything that stood out. It was then I noticed something unmistakable.

"I've got what I need," I said as I folded the pamphlet and put it in my pocket.

"What happens now?" Jeremy asked.

"Get out now. Believe me, you don't want to be mixed up in this business," I advised him as I turned to leave. I climbed out and found Jackie waiting for me patiently. There were no thugs awaiting to take us away. I was relieved, but at the same time slightly disappointed. There would be no opportunity to make up for last time.

"Fancy a trip to the museum?" I asked as I removed the pamphlet from my pocket and handed it to her.

"This special exhibition hasn't started yet, we may be in luck," she replied.

"It's about time."

"I'll see what I can dig up."

I returned to Alexis's safe house and continued combing through her notes while Jackie looked into the museum exhibition. The meticulous nature of these notes seemed odd when I thought about it. In all my dealings with Alexis, she had acted based on instinct, emotion and impulse. Yet here was thorough research, and evidence of planning. Perhaps there was another side to her that I had not seen. Part of me hoped that I would look up and see her walk through the door to the safe house. It would be worth whatever anger she had at my intrusion.

Despite my diligence I didn't gain any further useful knowledge of the artifacts, although I did gain some more background information on them. They were at least hundreds of years old, yet seemed to be made from metalworking techniques that were more advanced than the style of that time. The true origin of them was unknown, but every source agreed that one man created the whole set. He was a great scholar, and the creation of the artifacts was his legacy. They spelt out his life's work. Of course just what that meant differed according to each expert. My musing was interrupted when I heard footsteps out the front, and the sound of the front door closing. The thought that it might be Alexis put me on edge, and my heart rate quickened considerably.

Attempting to be as quiet as possible, I snuck over and peeked around the corner to discover who had entered the house. Seeing that it was only Jackie I relaxed and walked out into the open.

"Oh you surprised me!" she called out as I approached.

"Can't be too careful," I said.

"You now owe me a nice dinner out, preferably one without gunfire."

"I can't make you any promises," I joked. "What did you find?"

"There's a special media presentation tonight before the exhibition opens to the public."

"You can get me in?"

"Naturally."

"Let's hear the details." Jackie explained how she had obtained media passes for herself and a male colleague, who just so happened to be sick. I could use his invitation to gain entry to the event, but from there I was on my own. It would be a much more intimate affair than the boating escapade, and she couldn't be connected with me if anything were to happen. Which it would if I achieved my objective of stealing the artifact.

I had to be careful though, because either Alexis or one of Markus's men could also be present, and trying for the same result. I studied the visitors' guide she had given me, which showed the layout of the museum and the exhibition itself. The dragon artifact was not a head-lining item, so I would need to look for it myself and then assess how to extract it with the least possible commotion. To that end I memorised the layout of the building and marked possible exits as well as what looked to be security areas. My instincts told me that knowing where the guards would be coming from was just as important as how to get out.

I searched the safe house further, looking for tools. It appeared as though Alexis either did not keep much there, or had cleaned it out when she left. However I got my hands on some lockpicks, a few simple cutting im-plements and one or two items that seemed strange but I knew would prove useful. The trick though, was getting them in. With my luck there would be a proper security checkpoint with metal detectors. I wondered if the job could be done with whatever I found inside, and almost settled on that approach before I had a flash of brilliance. Inspiration had come from my hospital escape this time. I asked Jackie, and she confirmed that the Gazette had a courtesy wheelchair and that it would most likely be let through the screening without incident.

So to that end I presented myself to the special exhibition dressed in my second best suit and sitting in a wheelchair with my collect of tools secured underneath. Strangely I was not nervous as I wheeled myself to the security checkpoint and was waved through with great courtesy from the staff. My plan had opened nicely, although being confined to the wheelchair did slow my movements.

The exhibition itself was a strange assortment of items. The collector that had assembled them seemed to have an eye for everything. There were snuff boxes, fine china, ancient weapons and armour and even clothing. The only central thread seemed to be the man who had collected them all. After a methodical search I found myself in the one corner of the exhibition that I had not yet explored, and had almost missed entirely. There, tucked away as almost an afterthought, was the dragon artifact. I wheeled myself over directly and examined it closely through the thick glass cabinet it was in. There was no doubt in my mind, it was definitely one of them.

"You have a good eye," a confident male voice commented. I turned and noticed a man approaching me and pointing at the artifact.

"It just caught my attention, it seems different from the rest," I said.

"Indeed it is quite a mystery this one. Feels out-of-place compared to the rest of the collection. We aren't entirely sure of its origins. Oh forgive me, I'm Andrew Bedford, the curator."

"What's it made of?"

"It's a peculiar metal alloy. We don't know for sure because we've been expressly forbidden to perform any tests on it."

"Have you ever seen anything else like it?"

'No, not at all. What an interesting question, I hadn't considered that maybe it wasn't a one-off piece." As pleasant and potentially informative as the curator was, I didn't want to bring more attention to the artifact than absolutely necessary. I needed some time and space to come up with a plan.

"Do you have an accessible bathroom nearby?"

"Of course sir, just go through this doorway and turn right. You can't miss it."

"Thank you for your assistance," I told him and followed his directions. As soon as I was inside the small bathroom I locked the door and stood up immediately. Although I had not been sitting down long, it still felt great to stretch my legs. I reached down under the chair and removed my tools, evenly distributing them throughout my pockets. I paused and reviewed the layout of the museum in my mind, focusing on my location and what was nearby. There was an emergency exit at the opposite end of the hall just outside, and a dead-end around the corner. In my mind it was the only place to put an entrance to the secure area.

I withdrew some of my smaller lock-picking tools and some wire from my pockets and rigged the lock on the bathroom door so I could lock it from the outside. I took a deep breath, hoped for the best and walked out closing the door behind me. The hallway was empty and I couldn't hear anybody approaching. I used the opportunity to head to where I figured the secure area was. As expected I found a locked door with a sign labelling it as a restricted area. The door was secured by a thick mechanical lock and a metallic keypad.

I had seen this type of keypad before. Each key was an extruded metallic rectangle that visibly clicked in when pushed. The beauty of it was that the order of the key entry was not important, just that all the right keys were pushed and no others. I positioned myself to the left side of the door, so that if anybody came through I would be hidden by the open door. Keeping an eye on the nearby corridor I rifled through my tools and removed a small vial of powder. I applied it liberally to the keypad and saw that only a handful of keys had multiple strong fingerprints on them. I put my head up to the door and tried to listen for any sounds of movement on the other side. Once I was satisfied the coast was clear I entered the correct key combination.

The door clicked open and I pushed through confidently. A plain white-painted corridor extended out in front of me with concrete floors. I spotted a branching hallway off to the left side and headed towards it. As I crept closer I sidled up to the wall and peered around the corner to see where the alternate path lead. There was a room at the end that looked like a security monitoring room. That room would definitely have one or more people inside, so I decided to keep going. I followed the hallway I was in and saw that it branched around to the right at the end. I continued on, trying to make as little noise as possible.

The low humming of machinery was all that I could hear from my surroundings. Far from being reassuring, it made me feel like I was making way too much noise myself. Once I reached the end of the hallway I didn't stop to peer around and kept walking softly but confidently. There was another room at the end of this path, but it seemed different and less formal. I opened the door slowly and slid into the room as carefully as possible. I was standing on carpet, in what seemed like a recreation room of some description. There was a bathroom in the corner, an array of tables and chairs placed haphazardly around the place and many tall lockers against the walls. I headed over to the nearest locker that appeared to be unlocked and opened the door fully to inspect it. The locker was much bigger than I expected, and had only two shirts hanging inside as well as a jar of hair gel.

As I pondered my next move I heard footsteps echoing through the hallway outside. I stepped inside the locker, pulling the door closed behind me. It was cramped, but I fit inside and felt like I was fairly well hidden. I held my breath and strained my hearing to try to chart the person's movements in the room. The carpet made things harder, but the unknown person was not making any effort to be quiet. I deduced from what I heard that it was a man. It also sounded like he was approaching my position. My fears were founded when I noticed a presence right in front of the locker I was hiding in. My mind was racing, deciding whether I had concealed myself poorly or had the horrid luck of picking the wrong locker. However it mattered not, as I noticed the man reaching to open the locker. There was no time to think any further, I just reacted.

I kicked out fiercely and the locker door slammed into him hard, knocking him to the ground. I leapt out after him, and dropped to the ground with my elbow slamming into his chest. He grunted sharply then wheezed, struggling to regain his breath. I stood up and looked around the room, hoping to spot something of use in my situation. I noticed a thick roll of grey tape sitting on one of the tables and ran over to grab it. Walking back I pulled off a piece of tape, cutting it with my teeth, and placed it over his mouth so he could make no noise. Next I rolled him over onto his stomach and bound his hands and feet behind him.

The security guard was now disabled, but I couldn't just leave him in the middle of the room in case one of his colleagues stopped by. As I scanned the room looking for somewhere to hide him, my eyes rested on the locker that I had sprung out of. I chuckled to myself quietly and picked up the man, pushing him into the locker and closing the door securely. It was like we were trading places. Just before I left, I noticed that the security guard had dropped his pistol on the ground when I struck him. I retrieved it, checked that it was loaded and took it with me. Now I was armed, I felt like I could safely check out the security monitoring room. I retraced my steps and approached the monitoring room carefully with the gun drawn. I paused outside, took a deep breath then kicked the door open. As I burst through I swept my gun around, scanning the room for threats. It was empty. The man monitoring the security camera feeds must have been the one that I subdued.

I put down the gun and sat in front of the panels of monitors, watching the museum. Other than the guests viewing the exhibition I could only spot one other walking around. He appeared to be another security guard. I took note of each of the monitors until I discerned which one was closest to the entrance I had used to enter the security area. Until I saw the security guard on that screen, I was safe from discovery. I decided my best move was to wait until the guests left then go after the artifact.

I didn't have to wait long. After approximately half an hour the guests began to leave. The security guard had done a lap of the complex but not once looked like checking in. The time for me to move was approaching. As the last guest left, I saw the curator check in with the lone security guard before he also left. Finally it was only me and the security guard left in the museum, not counting the man I had already taken care of. I guessed that now was the time for the guards to swap over. The security guard's purposeful walk looked to confirm my guess. I only had to decide on how to deal with him when he arrived. Only one option came to mind, and with the time available to me I set my mind to it.

I picked the gun up once more and moved into a position in the corner where I would not be spotted by someone entering the room and could potentially move in behind them. I aimed the gun and waited. After a minute I heard footsteps just outside the room, and refocused my attention.

"Yo Johnson, it's your turn to do the rounds," the security guard called out jovially as he walked through the door.

"Stop right there, hands where I can see them!" I commanded. The guard was taken aback but complied and turned slowly to face me.

"What is this? Where's Johnson?" the guard asked.

"He's tied up. Walk slowly into the centre of the room," I instructed him. As he walked I circled around him while keeping my gun aimed at his head, and then moved closer. When I was close enough I changed the grip on my weapon and struck him with the butt on the back of the head. The guard fell down in a heap and all I could hear from him was slow regular breathing. I strode over to the security monitors and examined the system, looking for how they recorded the footage.

By following the cables I discovered that a series of rack mounted grey boxes looked to be where the recorded video was saved. I wanted to destroy the footage to ensure I didn't get too much unwanted attention. However I didn't seem to have the tools to easily and reliably trash the machines. Suddenly I had a brain wave. Amongst my tools was a strong rare earth magnet, and if the recordings were stored on magnetic disks then I could destroy or damage the data with it. I already felt like I had stayed too long in the museum, so decided to rely on that plan. Minutes later I decided that I had done enough and tried to access the recordings from one of the cameras through the system. It was not responding. For extra safety I pulled out all the cables.

I checked on the unconscious guard, then left the monitoring room. All I had left to do was take the artifact and make my escape. With any luck there would be no more interruptions. I walked through the security door and back into the museum proper. Wasting no time I made my way directly to where I had spotted the artifact earlier. With great relief I arrived at the spot and saw that it was still there. Not that I expected it to be gone, but I had learned by this point not to take anything for granted when it came to the artifacts. I examined the display case it was in, looking for an easy way to retrieve the dragon with minimal alarm. I could not find any obvious security measures protecting the artifact. Assuming that this particular item was not a focus of the exhibit, I settled on using a glass cutter to open the case.

Taking my time, I cut a large circle out of the top of the glass and lifted it off, leaving me with easy access to the dragon artifact. I reached in with my right hand, picked up the artifact and slowly removed it from the case. No alarms sounded, stillness reigned in the museum. I spent a minute looking over the artifact, passing it between my hands. The texture and weight of it felt familiar, and I found some strange engravings between some of the wing details. I didn't have any doubts as to its authenticity, but the examination of it cemented my opinion.

"Kindly hand that over," a male voice said behind me. I froze, trying to think of the best next move. I had carelessly left the gun I acquired back in the monitoring room. I didn't want to test my luck using the same move from back when I was on the markets rooftop, but perhaps a variation would suffice. I turned and tossed the artifact carefully to the figure in front of me. It had the intended effect. The man dropped the gun he was holding and focusing his entire attention on catching the artifact. I dashed forward without hesitation, charging him to the ground as he secured the artifact. It dropped out of his grasp and rolled away. In a swift motion he rolled over and drew something from his pants leg. Instinctively I raised up my arms to protect myself and caught his arm as he tried to plunge a knife through my chest. His blond hair and rough face were almost touching mine as he strained desperately to gain advantage. I could see the desperation in his eyes, which was almost certainly mirrored in mine. We both struggled for our lives, the deadly weapon slowly moving back and forth between us.

I knew that I could not die in those circumstances. I had unfinished business, questions that needed to be answered and someone to find. I found within myself a new strength, and almost effortlessly turned the knife against him. I saw it first in his face, then felt his body go limp as his life expired. My moment of triumph was short-lived, I just felt ill. I pushed his lifeless husk away and got up attempting to purge the event from my mind. However the image of his expression as he had died was burned into my memory. I picked up the artifact, placed it in my coat pocket and walked towards the nearest emergency exit.

I barely noticed the alarms sounding as I stepped outside. My mind was elsewhere. Once I was clear of the museum grounds I just walked and walked. I know not where I went, and an hour or two passed in a blur, a haze of nothing. I found myself outside a seedy hotel called the 'Pleasure Nest'. I paid for a room, signed in with a name I conjured up on the spot and went directly to the room. It was as dirty and plain as I had expected. I sat down on the bed and looked at my hands. Apart from a little dried blood they were fine, but they shook uncontrollably.

I peeled off my clothes and got into the shower, hoping that the steady stream of hot water would relax me and give me comfort. I made the mistake of looking down and seeing the river of red going down the drain. I had not even realised how much of that man's blood was on me. I felt faint, and unsteady on my feet. I stumbled out to the basin and threw up violently into it. Cleaning myself up as best I could, I staggered back to the bed and collapsed onto it. I had done terrible things before this moment, killed many people and injured others. In some way this act had brought everything to the forefront. All my actions so far took on a new significance. It was as if I had been cleverly fooling myself all along, not truly acknowledging my deeds. I had been dodging the weight behind them, only dealing with them in a theoretical and controlled manner. I wished desperately for sleep, and clung onto the hope that things would be different when I awoke. It was a foolish hope, but I let myself have it.

DARING MUSEUM ROBBERY BEFORE PUBLIC OPENING

By Jacqueline Somers

Last night an item was stolen from a special exhibition at the museum, set to open tomorrow. The item was identified as a metallic dragon figure. A man was also found stabbed to death at the scene, thought to be an accomplice of the thief who escaped.

The theft occurred outside normal hours, just after a special preview event showing off the collection to press and VIPs. Police suspect that one of the attendees may have a connection to the theft.

Strangely the item stolen was not noteworthy and much higher valued items were left untouched. Museum stuff are baffled as to the motives of the thieves and the targeted nature of the theft. Extra security has been added for the duration of the exhibition.

CHAPTER FOURTEEN

A HOUSE OF CLUBS

I felt no better the next day. The world had not rear-ranged itself to make everything better. The previous night had still happened, and the new perspective that came with it persisted. On top of that the pain from my injuries had resurfaced leaving me in multiple types of agony. My supply of the potent painkillers was running low. I called Jackie's office and asked her to meet me at Alexis' safe house. She was brief with her words over the phone and sounded strange.

When I arrived at the safe house she was standing out front. Wordlessly we entered and I started shuffling through the closest pile of notes.

"Are you going to tell me about what happened last night?" she asked finally.

"Everything was going smoothly, I made it back to the museum security area without incident. I encoun-tered two guards and disabled them. I even took out the cameras and recording equipment so that there wouldn't be any incriminating footage. But there was someone else there."

"Who was he?"

"I don't know, probably one of Markus's operatives. Alexis would have come herself, not sent someone. I'm not sure where he had hidden himself, but he was behind me as I took the artifact. I knocked away his gun and there was a struggle. He drew a knife, and then it came down to him or me." My words sounded hollow and emotionless, they didn't at all reflect my true feelings. Perhaps it was a self-defence mechanism.

"This needs to stop!" she declared.

"It won't stop until I find Markus and confront him. That's what Alexis is planning and she will be there sooner or later. I just need to be there when it happens," I replied.

"If that's the case there should be some information here regarding him and not just the artifacts," Jackie stated with confidence and walked around the house looking with a new purpose. I focused my effort on the stacks of notes we had previously discarded as irrelevant. I hated such tasks, but it was necessary. The problem was that each page had to be read properly to deduce if it had any relevant information or would be a useful reference.

At first everything seemed potentially important in some way, but soon I had found that I could easily discard certain notes once I had seen a few like them. The amount of notes was so substantial, it seemed completely unlike her. I decided to ask her about it when I met her next. It was very emphatically when and not if, I knew that we would meet again. The only uncertainly was the place and the circumstances in which we met.

I didn't see much of Jackie at that time, after her initial search of the place she left and returned a few hours later.

"I have a lead," she said simply.

"You're doing better than me, what is it?" I asked.

"A golf course and club. It seems to have some importance either as a place he owns or frequents."

"Sounds promising, but what should I be looking for? Do you have anything more specific?"

"Sorry no, you're on your own there. However if you can get a copy of their records there could be something to follow-up on."

"You're right, we could investigate the owners, and try cross referencing some of the member details with the other information we have."

"Here's the details, check it out tomorrow. You'll probably have to become a member," Jackie said as she handed me a slip of paper. I thanked her and she promptly left. It was clear that the death at the museum was having an effect on her too. It was a confronting event, and she probably didn't know how to think of me. I was suffering from the same problem.

What I couldn't understand was that my reaction to killing that man, who probably deserved it, was greater than all the other things I had already done. Although the link was not as clear to me, I was obviously instrumental in the train disaster that killed hundreds. However understanding or not understanding the feelings didn't seem to be as important, it wouldn't change them. I knew deep down that only through action and time would things improve. I looked again at the paper that Jackie had given me, not only did it have the name of the place I should visit but also a suggested dress code and information that I would need to have with me to become a member.

I hired a taxi and stopped by my hotel room, collected my things and checked out. Alexis knew of the place, and if she did then others could have as well. Next I visited my original safe house and took a selection of clothes and other items I thought would be useful. I needed to set myself up with a new place for my base of operations. My main concerns were security and privacy. I asked the taxi driver for some suggestions, and he mentioned somewhere right in the centre of the city that had maintained apartments that could be rented out on a monthly basis. That suited me fine, I didn't want anything too permanent.

The process of securing a place was actually quite simple and by nightfall I was settled and had paid for a month's rent in advance as well as a security deposit. My cash reserves were still fairly well stocked but I knew if things dragged on too long I would need a source of income. However that was not something I wished to think of. My future life, after Markus was dealt with, didn't really exist for me. If I found myself in that situation I would deal with it then. Once I had prepared for my day at the golf course, I tried to sleep. However I had trouble, my mind wandered and I could not stop thinking. What lay ahead, what had already happened and much more occupied my thoughts and stole my ability to rest.

The next day I did not feel rested, it was like I had not slept at all. My body ached and complained as I rose and prepared myself. Regardless of my desire to just sleep, I had a plan and a job to do and the Seaview Golf Course was my destination. I gathered my fake IDs, dressed appropriately and went on my way. I was familiar with the idea of golf, but couldn't remember ever playing or following it. However I didn't think that proficiency would be necessary in this case.

It was an overcast day with only the occasional pocket of blue sky poking out from the clouds. Thankfully it was not wet, as that would render the course itself off-limits and restrict my possibilities. As I arrived I got a good look at the course, it was expansive and impeccably maintained. The grass, trees and bushes were immaculately trimmed. The pools of water were perfectly still and serene. The care that had been taken in the maintenance of the course was beyond diligence, it reeked of perfection and money. Exactly the kind of place I expected Markus to be affiliated with.

The clubhouse itself was suitably impressive. The exterior was all white with large glass walls showing off the course to those inside, arch lined courtyards and bright and inviting gardens. A large tower rose in the middle of the building which would no doubt provide an excellent view of the entire course. I made a mental note to explore the tower when possible. I walked down the cobblestone path and through the great main doors into the clubhouse. The extravagance of the façade did not prepare me for the opulence of the interior. Luxurious carpets, hand crafted furniture and copious amounts of pristine marble were just some of the highlights. It appeared as though it was a place of great history yet at the same time maintained with modern sensibilities.

I spotted what looked like the reception desk which was staffed by a young man. I wandered over casually and waited patiently for his attention.

"Hello my name is Billy. How may I help you today sir?" he asked.

"I'd like to become a member of this club," I responded.

"That is a rather involved process, I take it you already have the sponsorship of one of our members?"

"Naturally," I said, feigning confidence. This was the one thing I had not been able to procure beforehand.

"May I have his name?" he asked.. I racked my brains for a suitable response, then had a fantastic idea which brought a smile to my face. I had a name, one closely connected to Markus. One that no doubt hated me with a passion after our recent encounter.

"Martin Hintle," I replied. Billy typed something and intently appraised the small monitor in front of him.

"Excellent sir, do you have the required paperwork with you?"

"I'm sorry no, at our last meeting I had to shoot through and attend to pressing business. I had hoped coming here would be sufficient."

"Sadly no, we still need the signed declaration from your sponsor. I'll go fetch the forms for you," Billy explained, then turned and walked through a door behind him. As I watched the door open and close I noticed that the room consisted of filing cabinets, records lying on tables and computers. That was where I needed to go. With Martin Hintle on their books his address would be available. Finding him would lead me to Markus. As I thought this through Billy returned with a stack of papers and briefly instructed me on how to fill them out. I thanked him for his time and strolled over to one of the chairs that littered the lobby.

Pretending to peruse the papers further I scanned the room devising my next move. What I needed was five minutes uninterrupted in the records room to get as much as possible. That would be nigh on impossible if the only entrance was through the reception area. I had to find another way in. As I didn't know the layout of the clubhouse I would need to do some exploring while staying under the radar. That wouldn't be easy since I wasn't a member.

I ruled out impersonating a member. Whilst possible, I didn't have the time or tools available to do it convincingly even if I managed to swipe someone else's credentials. The other main option I considered was to create a suitable diversion. With luck I could slip into the members' area while people's attention was elsewhere, and once there it was less likely I would be challenged by other members provided I acted appropriately. I felt that this was the most suitable and represented a good mix of potential success and only a little preparation required.

My next decision then was what diversion to use. It had to be something striking that drew everyone's attention without impeding my search for documents. I looked around the lobby for inspiration. What caught my attention was the small oil lamps littered around the place. They would provide some nice ambience at night, but of course were unlit during the day. A fire could work, but I would still need a source of ignition. I didn't carry a lighter with me as I didn't smoke, however others did. I observed the other people in the lobby more closely, and a plan formed.

I spotted an older man, probably in his fifties, sitting by himself and smoking in the corner. In close proximity to him was one of the lamps. I strode over and sat across from him, and enquired about the benefits of being a member and his experiences at the club. He seemed annoyed by my interruption but answered my questions politely. Nothing he said was of any particular use, but I felt that my conversation seemed both genuine enough and also not particularly noteworthy. Thanking him for his time I stood up and knocked over the nearby lamp in a manner that was carefully calculated yet appeared clumsy and accidental.

My aim was impeccable and the oil spilled out over his ash tray as he added another burning ember to it. A flame began but he didn't notice right away, being more concerned with the broken lamp and spillage. I stepped back hastily lest I be caught up in the growing blaze. I also wanted to ensure that I was near the members' area entrance when the commotion started. It didn't take long, in moments the lush carpet had begun to burn and the fire started to spread to furniture located nearby and some drapes. The man, who had unwittingly starting the blaze, thankfully retreated from the flames.

Cries of 'Fire' rang around the lobby and people started scurrying in all directions. Some were exiting the building, some were looking for a way to help, others were just observing the spectacle. I waited for an opportune moment and headed the other way, into the members area. I had not thought it possible, but the area I had just entered was even more ornate than the lobby. I considered where I was in location to the reception area and records room and tried to head in that direction. I continued on past change rooms, private bars and smoking lounges. When I passed a kitchen I stopped and regarded it more closely. I could see how the area around the kitchen that branched off was a little different, it was more utilitarian. I decided to see where it led.

My reasoning was that the less decorated area was not designed for guests and was more intended for staff. Thus it was also more likely to lead to staff only areas such as the records room that I wished to enter. I checked my watch, it had already been around five to ten minutes since I had escaped the lobby. Unless I had started something exceptionally dangerous it should have been mostly contained already. Whilst there would be some distraction and interest for a while afterwards, business would either halt completely or resume suitably normal interactions soon. Both of those situations would be problematic, either too many people or too few. No matter the way it turned out I wanted to complete my objective as quickly as possible.

I passed through a staff change room and into another corridor and found myself in front of a closed door. Given my bearing I was fairly confident that I was in the right place. I tried the handle and the door moved slightly, it wasn't locked. I listened carefully for sounds of activity inside, and when I heard nothing I quietly entered the room. It was bigger than I had expected from my glance earlier. I decided to begin my search with the computers, they had potentially more information and a portable drive would be easier to conceal than folders and papers.

I sat down at one of the terminals moved around the mouse to disable the screen saver. A login prompt appeared and I panicked for a minute. I hadn't prepared myself for this eventuality even though it was completely plausible, no it was actually completely likely. I took a deep breath, refocused myself and placed my hands above the keyboard. As if of their own volition my fingers started pressing keys and typing. Alternate terminal screens popped up, commands were typed and I realised that I was probing the system for access. Within thirty seconds I had bypassed the login and found myself sitting there with full access to the system.

I poked around trying to find a list of members or similar information. I checked my watch again, my self-imposed target of five minutes in the records room was almost up. Even though that limit was self-set and arbitrary, it meant that I felt like someone could burst through at a moment's notice. As I searched something caught my attention. It was a procedure document outlining how to perform a full system backup. It gave me a good idea. I scanned through the instructions, looking for where the backups were stored. It turned out they were using a manual tape system once a week and then would swap tapes around. The location of the archive machine was in that very room. I tore around the room at speed searching for it. It was nestled back in the corner. Just as I was about to open the tape input to check inside I noticed a plastic box next to it. The box was full of smaller boxes containing tapes and one was labelled with the previous week's date. I checked that the box was not empty, then shoved it in my pocket. Not a moment too soon either.

"Hey you, what are you doing back here?" Billy from reception called out. I didn't have a response to his query so I bolted out of the nearest door back into the staff area. As I ran I kept a look out for signs that would direct me to an exit. I spotted one, back tracked slightly and went down the corridor that it pointed to. As I reached what looked like my doorway to safety, a large man with a pistol burst through it from outside and started to take aim. I turned sharply and entered a staircase to my left. I wasn't sure where it went but knew it would at least buy me some time before I got shot again. I could still feel the effects from the last time and wanted to avoid it happening again at all costs.

Up and up I ran. It started to dawn on me that there was only one place in this building that multiple sets of stairs could be leading to – the tower. I paused for a second to listen, and could hear footsteps below me. One man was in pursuit, if not others as well. That did not bode well for me. From what I could recall from seeing the tower, it didn't lend itself well as an exit. Most likely I would be trapped at the top. At least I'd get a nice outlook over the golf course. As soon as that thought crossed my mind, I reached the target of my fears. I was in a sandstone square viewing area at the peak of the tower with large window shaped gaps to peer out of. Thankfully they were not covered with mesh or grates. I took a moment to admire the view, then clambered out of one of the gaps and started to climb down the outside of the tower.

Due to its construction there were plentiful hand holds as I worked my way down to the roof. I heard some commotion above me in the tower. They were probably wondering where I went and how to follow. No doubt there would be a few willing to climb down while others raced outside to intercept me. I did not focus on that though, I just concentrated on getting myself down. It only took me a minute or two to reach the tiled roof. I could walk on it carefully without falling, but it was too high to just jump down to the ground. I looked around for another way.

There appeared to be a cable going down from the roof to a junction box halfway up a thick pole in the car park. If I climbed down it I would be too slow and po-tentially a sitting duck. I thought of using my jacket to slide down but didn't think it strong enough to handle the task. I saw an antenna on the roof that looked similar to what I needed. I carefully stepped over to the antenna, broke off a section of it and bent the end into a hook shape. I placed the hook over the cable and tested it. It seemed fairly stable and solid, and I didn't really have any other options jumping out at me. I pushed myself off and brought my legs in close, throwing my weight for-ward on my makeshift flying fox. The speed that I acquired was quite surprising, and so by the time that I had considered the chances of my contraption failing and sending me hurtling to the ground I was about to collide with the junction box. I let go of the hook and falling head first I put my hands out and rolled safely away. I heard shots behind me so I immediately stood back up and started running without losing any momentum.

I saw some golf carts ahead of me and ran straight to the nearest one. I jumped into the driver's seat, and noticed that the keys were in the ignition. The engine came to life with a gentle growl. I backed the cart up slightly then turned to ascertain where my pursuers were. They seemed to have the exits to the street fairly well covered, so I turned my attention to the golf course ahead of me. Perhaps I could lose them in there and sneak out later. The layout of the course was somehow ingrained in my memory after only the small look I took from the top of the tower. Recalling the layout gave me an idea, but I needed as much space between me and the security staff as possible to make it work.

I floored the golf cart and shakily steered it onto the course. I went straight up the fairway of the first hole, then turned sharply heading into the trees. Dodging trees and small bushes I popped out on the fourth hole. I continued along, looking behind me to see any signs of pursuit. There were none yet, I must have taken them by surprise by commandeering a cart and avoiding the road. I reached the green and ploughed on until I arrived at the seventh hole. Between the two holes was a large bridge. I examined the bridge closely as I drove along it, paying particular attention to the space below it. My suspicions were correct and my idea seemed like it would work.

The gap below the bridge was big enough to hide the golf cart fairly well. I just needed a way to get it down there without drawing too much attention. I noticed a natural incline leading down under the bridge. Under the bridge was a canal with a minimal amount of water covering the bottom. By adjusting my speed and using a bit of patience I was able to drive the cart into that canal. I followed it along until I found a nice hiding place between two major struts of the bridge. It would still be easily visible to anyone who came down looking for it, but I felt it should be good enough to go under the radar of those pursuing.

I stepped out of the cart and walked along the canal for a time. My plan was to swing around and emerge at the perimeter of the course in a place that was not as well guarded. It took close to half an hour to reach the edge of the block but my persistence was rewarded. Beyond a thick line of trees was a quiet residential side street. I walked out with great satisfaction. I had extracted from the club house all the data they had and done so without getting caught or injuring anyone else. I checked the tape to ensure there was no damage from my adventure, and it seemed fine. With great leisure I strolled down the street and the ones that connected to it, working my way towards a main road.

Once I felt that I was far enough I lunched at a café to celebrate my minor victory. As I ate I contemplated the possibilities of what I had secured. At a bare minimum I had to have obtained a usable address for Martin Hintle, one of Markus's top men. If I was luckier still, some more of Markus's associates would be detailed in the member list, although I may not know of them yet. It was even possible that Markus himself could be found by examining the data and connecting the right dots. However I had to temper my elation, as I would need assistance both reading and sifting through all the data. I didn't have the equipment to restore the tape backup to something readable, but I did know someone who probably did.

I took a taxi and went directly to Alexis' safe house. I looked through the place, and found no computer gear. As I searched, I had a thought. There had been no sign of Alexis since that night on the boat. She had left this safe house and never returned. There had to be a reason, one that didn't involve her being captured again. As I prepared to leave the house, I noticed someone approaching.

"I had a feeling that I would find you here," Jackie said as she entered.

"Mission successful," I replied and tossed the backup tape to her.

"You're lucky, I think this uses the same system as the one we have at the Gazette."

"I'm even luckier still, Martin Hintle is a member of that club."

"If that's the case the location of Markus himself, or more of his lieutenants could be in there."

"I was thinking the same thing."

"Leave it with me, I'll look over it tonight. Take this phone and keep it with you. I'll use it to call you when I have something so we don't have to keep guessing or pre-arranging meeting spots."

"Thanks," I replied and took the small phone off her. She promptly left and I examined the phone further, ensuring I was familiar with how it worked. I noticed that Jackie had programmed her number into it for my convenience.

I thought over what I should do next. Jackie would no doubt find another lead worth pursuing, but did I have to wait for her? There should still be another artifact or two to find. The question was though, did I need more of them? Surely even one would be enough to get Markus's attention. Although it was safe to say I already had his attention, if he had been the one to send that agent to the museum. The one that I had stabbed. Another pang of regret hit me, as though I had not suffered enough from that event. Merely recalling it brought back all the emotions, as fresh as if it had just happened.

There was something else though. It was a strange feeling. It was about Alexis. Not that that I wanted to find her, not even that I was worried about what she would do next. It was deeper than that, more inconsequential and yet more important. As you can imagine it was hard for me to put it into words, but I wanted to be with her purely for the sake of being with her. I wanted to try to make her laugh or smile, see those intense eyes of hers light up. It wasn't even about atonement any more, I cared for her. How foolish of me.

I murdered her father, killed one of her closest friends and destroyed their life's work. No explanations or excuses could change those facts. I should have felt nothing, tried to repay my debt and move on. There was no reason to invest in her, especially when there was nothing to gain. The best possible result was that she didn't kill me before I discovered the truth behind my past. Why was it then, that each day I had not heard from her was like an additional millstone dragging me down? Why did I harbour that small piece of hope within myself, that one day I would be with her and we would be happy, and pretend it was not there?

Those were the thoughts that occupied me as I aimlessly looked for another clue to follow in that safe house. My heart was not in it though, and after a time I fell asleep with a stack of papers in my hands.

BRAZEN THIEF ESCAPES WITH GOLF CART

By Jacqueline Somers

Yesterday an unidentified man broke into the records room of Seaview Golf Course and escaped with the use of a makeshift flying fox and stolen golf cart.

Club officials reported that the man used the chaos of a small fire to enter their records room and when confronted fled to the tower at the top of the club. Several witnesses on the scene confirmed that the man escaped capture by sliding down a cable at high speed similar to a flying fox.

The thief then stole a golf cart and ventured onto the course to make his escape. The golf cart is still unaccounted for.

CHAPTER FIFTEEN

THIRD HAND

Ghostly spectres drifted past me slowly as I walked along the train platform. They all watched me closely, accusatory looks directed at me. Whenever one passed too close I could hear a deep, despondent sigh carry through the air. I was not afraid, however I could feel their sadness sweeping over me. With every step I took on more.

The train wreck lay out before me. It's twisted and blackened shape was skirted with an eerie fog. I continued walking closer, reaching the end of the platform then going along the tracks. The closer I got, the thicker the spectres were. Their sighs were louder now, although I think that was just a matter of their number and the way they seemed to merge together. I kept moving.

I was at the front carriage of the train, looking into the driver's compartment. A ghostly version of the driver himself sat there, staring forward into oblivion. I stepped into the open doors of the carriage itself and found it populated with what seemed to be a representation of all the people who had been it. They too had an oddly transparent existence, but I felt a chill when I brushed past them as I walked. At first it was only a slight chill, almost a tickling touch. The sensation didn't change as I progressed through the carriage however, it was as if every touch was additive.

As I reached the end of the first carriage, I felt a sudden shiver ripple its way down my spine. I shook my shoulders to usher it away, and resumed walking. The next carriage seemed more densely packed with what I could only think of as shades of the deceased. The growing sense of cold continued in step with my progress, and by the time I arrived at the end of the next carriage it felt like an icy hand was gripping my right shoulder. I looked over hastily, but could see nothing. Steeling myself I pushed on further.

After progressing through another carriage my entire right arm felt deathly cold. Not only that, but it had a terrible weight, like it was dragging me down. At that point I felt afraid. My pace slowed considerably but I could not stop. I was driven to keep going. The next few carriages had the same effect on my left arm. Both my arms were causing me to stoop, and there was no feeling in them save for the cold. I had reached the carriage where I had left the train before the disaster occurred. I looked over at the doorway, instinctively. It was slightly open and a warm light poked its way through the gap. I shuffled over and placed my arms in the gap one above the other, trying to force the doors apart. A searing heat overcame me and some kind of force knocked me back to the opposite wall of the carriage.

I picked myself up and noticed that the doors were now completely sealed shut and had no hope of being opened. However the chill and weight from my arms was gone. I revelled in the new-found feeling in my fingers then resumed my walking. An idea slowly formed in my head, and then settled itself in such a way that I knew it was true. There was something waiting for me at the end of the train, in the last carriage. I just had to continue.

My strides were more confident, more powerful and faster. I shrugged off the ensuing chill as if it were nothing. The sadness was still with me, but it was accompanied by something else. I couldn't quite put a name to the feeling, that things would get better. That the future was still uncertain, which was actually good because it was not written yet. Rather than being sapped, I was getting stronger. I was practically running by the time I reached the final carriage. I passed through the final set of doors with enthusiasm, eager to see what lay beyond them. The last carriage was different from the rest of the others, and almost entirely empty. There was one figure standing in the middle, and I recognised him instantly. It was Elias, the blind man. However he wasn't wearing any dark glasses, and his eyes were yellow, glowing intensely.

Unsure of what to do I stood and observed. He seemed to be doing the same, and I found myself in some sort of bizarre stand-off. Those golden eyes of his seemed aflame and his stare unnerved me. I took a step forward involuntarily. I looked down at my feet, puzzled. I half expected to see a strange spectre of some kind moving them for me. Yet there was nothing unusual about them. Returning my gaze to Elias I saw that he too was closer. I decided to speed things along, and took another step forward. I kept an eye on him carefully, and he didn't move even the slightest amount, he just continued staring at me. I blinked and almost jumped back in fright when he appeared right in front of me. I reached out to touch him and time slowed to a crawl. I watched my arm go out in slow motion, yet was distracted by something else moving with much greater speed. I turned and looked just in time to see Elias' fist slam into my chest with immense force. I doubled over in pain.

The pain however, was nothing compared to the sight now before me. Elias' attack on me had created a black hole in my chest, and he was rushing into it in a wispy smoke like state. I could only look on in complete and utter disbelief. The whole experience only lasted seconds then every single fibre of my body felt like it was on fire and I blacked out. I awoke back on the train platform, lying down on a wooden seat. The pain was gone, and I sat up quickly. My right hand was clutching a page. The paper depicted a statue of a male figure and the words

'Templeton Higgins'. The page then faded from sight and I was blinded by a bright light.

I awoke to morning sunlight streaming through the nearby window and pooling on my face. It took me a moment to collect myself and work out what was happening, and then the recollection of the dream came back all at once. The strangeness of it was noteworthy, however the extreme vividness of the experience is what really struck me. Every moment of that dream was burned into my memory, unlike what I expected. Dreams usually fade leaving behind only fragments, and then the idea of fragments. Finally all but the essence of it is gone, and even that only remains in special cases. Yet even still not a detail from it has escaped me.

I came to the conclusion that the dream was important. Its origins were unknown, but my best guess was that some memory of mine was resurfacing in a dramatic way. Regardless, I had to act on it. I would find out by the day's end if there was anything behind the strange dream, and if it lead me to an artifact as I hoped. The statue of a man was to me an artifact, and the phrase 'Templeton Higgins' represented its location or owner. As I began to muse over what it could mean, a loud ringing startled me. I scrambled over to its source, and discovered that it was my phone.

"Hello," I answered.

"Will, I think I have something to go on from that data you gave me. I'll need another day or so to confirm though," Jackie said.

"Sounds great."

"Anything new from your end?"

"A slim lead. Does the phrase 'Templeton Higgins mean anything to you?"

"It doesn't sound like a proper name, maybe it's an alias. Street names perhaps?"

"Thanks, I'll see what I can find. Let me know as soon as you confirm that lead you mentioned."

"Sure thing, take care," Jackie replied and hung up.

I dressed and left, wondering to myself how best to investigate the strange lead from my dream. Jackie's experience and instincts were to be trusted, so I decided to start with her suggestions. I had no way to look up aliases, however street names seemed plausible. I stepped into a local newsagent to pick up a copy of the day's paper. I browsed through their other printed offerings and discovered many different magazines and publications. Towards the back there was also a section filled with books, with a small automotive subsection. Amongst these I found something titled 'Gregg Pec's Street Directory'.

I bought the street directory and paper and walked outside, sitting down on a nearby bench. I flicked through it, finding the index at the back with a list of streets. I started with the first word, Templeton and searched for it. Surprisingly I found one entry, a 'Templeton St'. I turned to the indicated page number and grid reference, finding it to be a reasonably long street. I needed something to narrow my search, if I was on the right track the word 'Higgins' had to be relevant somehow. I thought of people, businesses and landmarks. At that point I had an epiphany and muttered at myself for being so dense. Using the supplied ribbon to mark the page, I flipped back to the index and scanned it for any streets going by the name 'Higgins'. There was a 'Higgins Rd' located on the same page as the one I had marked. Once I looked up the exact reference I noticed that Higgins Rd was actually a cross street that intersected Templeton St. I had to be on to something, and what I was looking for was at the corner of those two streets. Well, one of the four possible corners.

The fact that I had discovered a location based on those two words appeared to be more than a coincidence, and that however I had gotten it, my information had checked out. I flagged down a taxi and gave the driver the address. As we drove I found myself tapping my foot impatiently and wringing my hands together. Since I finally had what seemed like a solid lead, I just couldn't wait any longer. I was bursting with anticipation, desperate to see where this latest inquiry would lead. It seemed to me that on the way, every set of lights was red and our progress was incredibly slow. At times I felt that getting out and walking would be faster, and only by exercising the full extent of my restraint did I remain inside the vehicle.

When the driver finally announced our arrival, I was taken aback. I think that in some way I actually believed we would never really make it there. I paid him and stumbled out of the cab awkwardly, steadying myself on the pavement and taking stock of the location. I could clearly see from the street signs that I was at the right intersection. I threw the street directory into a nearby bin and scanned each part of the intersection to see what it contained. Behind me was a convenience store, which seemed particularly unlikely to be useful. However since it was the closest and wishing to be thorough, I walked in and did a lap around the store. Nothing seemed out of the ordinary, and all the merchandise was a variety of useful consumables and junk food. I loitered around for a few minutes more to see if anything of interest occurred and left satisfied that whatever I wanted was not in that place.

I looked over at my three other options. One was a lighting store, another a jewellers and the last was a pawn shop. I decided that the lighting store had the least potential so I crossed the road to visit it next and eliminate it as an option. Upon entering I was stopped in my tracks by a curious sight: they had an exact replica of the chandelier I had used to my advantage in my restaurant escapade. Was that a coincidence too? I wandered the store, examining all their merchandise looking for any statuettes that would resemble the one from my dream. Whilst they had some statue shaped lamps and other decorations, there was nothing quite like what I wanted. I even engaged the owner in small talk and discussed the types of lights that passed through and what the strangest ones he had seen were. The conversation was enlightening but not in the way which I required.

The fruitlessness of my search so far spurred my impatience, and I selected the jewellers next. In my mind it had the greatest chance of being what I was looking for, both for the style of stock I expected them to have and also the similarity between their wares and that of the artifact expert from the markets. I crossed both streets and found myself standing before 'Alkoras'. After taking a moment to compose myself, I walked inside. There were a few people browsing, and two attendants minding the shop. One was a woman behind the counter serving a customer, while the other was a bored looking man. He looked over at me with disinterest and I avoided making eye contact. I slowly perused the various display cases within the store, but discovered that they didn't really have what I was expecting. The entire selection consisted of rings, necklaces, amulets and precious stones.

I approached the bored looking man and asked him about small statues, and where around here I could find some.

"That's an odd request," he replied, looking a little more animated.

"Can you think of a place? Are you sure there's nothing around here like that?" I pressed him.

"Definitely, we've never had anything of the sort. You'd have more luck with the pawn shop across the road."

"Thanks, you have been a great help," I told him, before leaving. The man seemed puzzled by my words and went back to his previous state of boredom and inactivity. I left the store, energised by the prospect of finding what I wanted in the pawn shop, but also annoyed that I had left it to last. The fact that he had confirmed the pawn shop as a likely place for such an item suggested that my search was not in vain. Had the traffic not been so thick and fast I would have darted across the road in my impatience, instead of waiting for the appropriate time to cross. The pawn shop occupying the last corner of the intersection was innocuously named 'Cash Traders' and looked fairly run down.

I crossed over and entered the shop without delay. A musty smell assaulted me as soon I stepped through the doors, and the lighting inside was quite poor. The place was empty save for a short bearded man behind a well secured counter, complete with bars. I ignored him and began to browse through the merchandise. The stock included odd electronic gear, musical instruments, televisions, sporting goods and many other random things. I found a corner which seemed full of more decorative items, some locked within a display cabinet. I saw crystal balls covered with dolphins, dragon statues and other bizarre combinations but nothing resembling an artifact, or the one that I was specifically looking for. Completing my tour of the store, I found that they had nothing at all matching my dream. I turned to leave, but didn't want to leave empty-handed.

"Excuse me," I asked the man behind the counter.

"Yes sir?" he replied.

"I have a bit of a strange request. I'm looking for a statue of a man. Do you have anything like that?"

"I believe so, but it hasn't been added to the floor stock yet. If you'll follow me to the back area?"

"Sure, lead the way," I replied. However I didn't trust the expression on the man's face when I had mentioned the statue. He emerged from behind the counter carrying a large collection of keys. Towards the back of the room there was a small door, which he opened with the keys and disappeared into. I followed closely behind. The back area was littered with shelves, cardboard boxes and the occasional oddity left lying around. The man expertly navigated his way through the haphazardly placed items at a great pace and I found it hard to keep up with him. It seemed strange to me that he so confidently remembered the location of a single item amongst all the sprawling chaos. Still, who was I to judge, that was the man's business after all. In the far corner of the second room we entered he stopped, lifting something out of a box and showing it to me. I walked closer and looked at the item properly. It was a statue of a man, but completely different to that which I had seen in my dream. It was ceramic, the man was armoured and the pose itself was not even remotely similar. I shook my head, and turned to leave. However something caught my eye and I moved in closer.

"Hang on a second, this one over here is perfect," I said excitedly. I heard the man approach but didn't hear the sound of him swinging the ceramic statue at my head. I certainly felt the impact though. Everything went black at that point.

I awoke, my hands and feet tied to a chair, in what seemed to be another back room of the pawn shop. The man from earlier was watching me from his own chair, a gun cradled in his arms. Seeing that I had awakened, he spoke.

"I had hoped that you were just a man, who by some coincidence had asked for the wrong kind of thing. However the odds of you coming here for that exact piece being a coincidence are suspiciously slim. I am holding that item for an important client who warned me of troublemakers. How did you find out about it?" he asked me.

"It came to me in a dream," I joked, knowing that he would not believe me. He did not seem impressed by my humour.

"I have no patience for games. Give me a name!" he demanded angrily. I didn't want him to shoot me out of anger, but had no suitable answer to give him. I went to speak, not knowing what to say, but instead swallowed and breathed in at the same time, resulting in a coughing fit. I had enough awareness to realise that the man had risen to check on me, and when I felt him close I swung my chair around quickly to take out his feet out from under him. Luckily he hit his head on something as he fell, and appeared to be out cold.

I struggled against the ropes holding me, but they weren't budging. My hands were bound together behind the chair, and each my feet was strapped to a chair leg. I looked left and right, searching for a way to cut myself free. I noticed behind me on a shelf a series of antiques, one of them a ship in a bottle. They were definitely of no use. On a small table near me was a hammer. It could be potentially used as a weapon if the man on the floor near me woke up. I thought about the logistics of attempting to use the hammer in my predicament and realised that it could potentially be quite useful. I shuffled my chair over and spun it so that I could grasp the hammer with one of my hands. With a little awkward manipulation I had the hammer clutched in both hands.

Using all of my concentration to avoid dropping the hammer I shuffled my way back to the shelf of antiques. I lined myself in front of the ship in a bottle as closely as possible, and tried to picture the relative position of my hands with the hammer. I only hoped that the glass was not too strong, due to the constricted nature of my hands. Propping up the hammer as best I could, I let it fall on the glass bottle. The hammer fell to the ground with a loud clanging. However it was also accompanied by the shriek of shattering glass. I turned my head quickly to admire my handiwork. The bottle was broken, and now had a few nice jagged edges. I just had to be careful.

Feeling my way slowly, and looking back when I could, I lined up my ropes with the biggest sharp edge of glass, and slowly moved my hands up and down as much as I could. The sounds of the rope being cut emboldened me and I increased my speed. It didn't last long as in my haste I slipped slightly and felt the glass dig into my skin. Cursing myself and trying not to notice the feeling of blood dripping down my hand, I lined up the bottle again and more carefully resumed cutting. Thankfully my new-found focus sped things along and within a minute or so I felt the ropes fall to the ground. I quickly whipped my arms back around to their natural positions and inspected my injury. It wasn't particularly deep, but was bleeding fairly steadily. I untied my feet and went in search of a way to treat the wound. I found a spare shirt in a chest of drawers elsewhere in the room, and used that to bind the wound and stem the blood flow.

With my freedom and injury taken care of, my next objective was the artifact. I found my way back to where I had spotted it earlier, but it was gone. Panic set in for a moment, but then I reasoned that the man had just moved it to somewhere else, and it had to still be in the building if he was waiting for me to awaken. That man was my key to finding the artifact. I jogged back to the room where I was held captive and found him still lying on the floor where I had left him. I lifted him roughly, and placed him in the chair that I had been sitting in. As I reached around to bind his hands I brushed up against something hard poking out of his jacket pocket. I reached in and plucked the item out. A great smile crept over my face when I saw what it was: the metallic male statue. Turning it over in my hands I knew that it was without doubt a legitimate artifact. I placed the statue inside my own jacket pocket.

I prepared to leave, and then a thought struck me. Why should I stop at getting the artifact? If this man was holding it for someone, there was a good chance that person was either Alexis or Markus. I would be happy finding a lead to either one of them. I felt that it was time to act smarter, that I had been relying too much on others for my leads, and my progress. Things had dragged on so long because I had not been active enough. I was determined to find out what this man knew. I bound him to the chair with the same ropes he had used on me, picked up his gun and sat in his chair, waiting. Our positions had reversed, I just had to prepare myself for the impending interrogation.

The sound of a door slamming broke my concentration. I stood up and listened closely. Male voices were arguing in the distance. One called out over and over, and then I heard another door slam, this time closer to my position. They had to be his colleagues, angry at his absence and coming to find him. I had to make a decision: stand and fight or flee with my spoils. My desire for further action was strong, but in the end was quelled by my prudence. The artifact in my possession was a powerful bargaining piece, and should not be risked in such a situation. In truth I also felt relief that I would be avoiding a situation in which I would most likely have to kill more people.

With my decision made, I rushed further back into the building looking for a rear exit. I tripped over some boxes and debris in my haste, but finding the door was simple. It was not locked and I left through it just in time to hear the angry voices cry out in what had to be their discovery of the man and the state I had left him in. Taking no chances I ran through a zigzag pattern of side streets and alleys to lose any potential pursuers. I paused briefly, checking my injury to ensure that it was not leaving a trail to follow, then made my way to where I thought the main road was. Within minutes I found one, cautiously peeking out from the alley to see if any suspicious people were waiting for me. Feeling that it was safe, I hailed a taxi and rode it back to my rented apartment.

Once inside I properly dressed my wound, and inspected the artifact more closely. I could not believe that my strange dream had resulted in such a clue, and in me finding another artifact. At this point I finally relaxed, and all my energy spilled away. The puzzle of that artifact, and my future plans had to be considered later. I hid the artifact in a safe place and then slept. I felt content again, in some part. I felt like I had achieved something once more, and more importantly, by my own hand. I was one step closer, I was back in the game. I just had to figure out the next move.

CHAPTER SIXTEEN

TERMINAL

The next morning I awoke refreshed and renewed. I idly flipped through some of Alexis' notes searching for another clue, however my real intention was to wait for a call from Jackie. When I had not heard from her by midday, I resolved to contact her myself. I dialled her number and called, hearing it ring over and over. I was just about to hang up when I noticed some kind of noise on the other end. It was followed by a harsh whisper.

"About time you called, I think I'm being tailed," Jackie said.

"I don't like the sound of that, where can I meet you?" I said.

"We must be careful. Come down to Anire Mall and call me when you arrive," Jackie said hurriedly and then hung up. The new development was exciting, but had me worried. On the one hand Jackie had clearly found something of importance, but that had also placed her in peril.

That or she incorrectly feared herself in danger, but I didn't take her for the type to scare easily.

I left immediately, hailed the nearest cab and directed the driver to take me to Anire Mall. As soon as I had left however I felt that I should have taken the artifact with me. I didn't want to go back for it though, I couldn't waste any time getting to Jackie. The trip was largely uneventful, but my concern for Jackie grew as time went on. Yet I was distracted from it momentarily when I caught sight of my destination.

Anire Mall was an enormous structure, roughly square in shape with large walls around the outside. There were only a few entrances, and as we passed through one I saw before me masses and masses of shops. There were even gardens, water features, children's play equipment and cinemas. I exited the taxi and wandered in amazement, wondering at both the sheer size of the place and the huge crowds of people. Jackie must have come here trying to lose herself in the flowing multitude. Remembering her instructions, I found a quiet corner and dialled her number.

"You made good time, excellent. Head to the south end of the mall and catch the next one-three-two bus," Jackie said quickly and quietly before hanging up. I put the phone away and headed further inside the monstrosity of a mall, trying to find my bearings. I found a map of the complex, found my position on it and looked for the bus terminals. Once I confirmed their location, I started walking in their direction. I found myself increasing my speed little by little. Soon I was jogging, and then flat-out running. I didn't know what prompted me so, I just knew I had to make haste. With expert footwork I dodged people in the way, in both directions. I weaved through groups of women laden with bags, kids holding balloons and old men taking their time.

With a thud I ran right into a larger man, and fell to the ground unceremoniously. I had been extremely careful in my route, and felt for sure that he had stepped out in front of me deliberately. As he stood over me, I looked up and saw the truth of my assumption on his face. As I stood up I saw him reach for something in his pocket, and I didn't wait to see what it was. I shoved him into a nearby man and bolted as quickly as I could. I continued on as fast as possible, not even turning back to see what was behind me. The sense of urgency I felt previously came on even stronger. If there were people here to stop me, what about Jackie? I kept my pace as best I could while still scanning ahead of me for more potential roadblocks.

Whether it was luck, or my careful avoidance of stationary groups I encountered no more obstacles. Within minutes I arrived at the bus terminals. I stopped for a moment to catch my breath, and looked around for directions on where to find the bus I was after. I consulted a few signs and timetables and saw that the stand I wanted was at the far end of the bus interchange. I broke into a run once more, and as I rounded the next corner I saw the bus numbered 132 sitting idle taking on passengers. I increased my speed further, spurred on by the presence of the bus.

As I dodged clumps of people I kept a close eye on the line of people snaking their way onto the bus. At first I believed that the rate of entry was slow enough to ensure that I would get on the bus with no trouble, however that was not the case. Whatever slowness or blockage existed when I first observed the passengers entering cleared promptly and before I knew it I could see nobody else queuing up to get on the bus. The bus doors remained open tantalisingly as I drew closer. Moments later I was right behind the bus itself. Victory was within my grasp. With a start the front doors closed and the engines huffed their way into life. I banged the side of the bus in frustration as it pulled away, and studied it desperately for any sign of Jackie. I saw her looking back at me, fear in her eyes. I could not look away until the bus had disappeared from sight.

I shook myself from the daze I was in, and called her phone.

"Sorry I couldn't risk waiting for the next one," Jackie answered.

"It's fine, where should I go next?" I said.

"This bus is not very direct and stops a lot. If you can get on another bus soon you'll get to Harrison St faster than I do and can then hop on this bus."

"I'll make it this time for sure."

"If you don't, meet me at the Central Interchange."

"Take care," I told Jackie before hanging up.

I stood still for half a minute, thinking through my next move while slowly scanning the bus interchange unsure of what I was after. In the middle I spotted what looked like a map with routes marked on it. I rushed over, almost stepping in front of an oncoming bus in my haste. I cursed myself under my breath and continued on my way.

I was right, it was a map with bus routes marked on it. The large map was behind glass, and the interchange I was currently in was clearly marked. I ran my finger over the surface, on the lookout for main streets that multiple bus routes intersected. From what Jackie had said, there were a few different buses that would get me to that same stop. I kept scanning the map over and over trying to find Harrison St, before realising that I had already located it with my hand, and was covering the street name. Three routes other than the one Jackie was on intersected at that spot, and according to the legend they were all from the same stand.

I scrambled over to the stand as quickly as possible. I was determined not to be late again. A similar situation unfolded before me, with a bus waiting at the stop and a line of people slowly entering. The events of just minutes ago played over in my head once again. However this time, whether due to greater luck or greater speed on my part, the outcome was different. Not only did I enter the bus with no fuss, but I had to wait for an age with nobody attempting to board at all. Then, just as we were about to leave a young man ran up to the bus and it stopped to let him on. I was infuriated that I was to be delayed by this person, aggravated that this bus driver was diligent enough to stop for the man, and also sympathetic for the man and glad that he made it. It was a strange mix of emotions. I absent-mindedly pulled out my phone and looked at it, wondering if I should call Jackie or not. It would be reassuring to talk to her more, and I thought that we could coordinate better if I knew how far she had travelled. Yet at the same time I thought that maybe she was keeping communication to a minimum for a good reason, and perhaps I should honour that.

"Do you know how long it takes to get to Lanesvale?" a voice next to me asked. I had not paid attention to where I sat when I got on the bus and looked over for the first time. The speaker was a young woman, with blonde hair arranged in thick clumpy strands and wearing loose brightly coloured clothing.

"No, I have no idea sorry."

"Oh that's alright, I was just curious," she said, before rifling through her cloth handbag. I went back to staring at my phone. I was both wondering what I should do next, and also feeling nervous about missing my stop.

"Do you know what those are made out of?" the young woman asked, pointing at my phone. I was unsure of how to respond, due to the strangeness of the question.

"I'm not sure, I guess some plastic and metal mainly," I answered.

"Aren't they amazing? I really wonder though what the screens are made out of!"

"I really couldn't tell you exactly."

"Have you been to Lanesvale before?"

"No, not that I can recall."

"I have some friends that live around there. But today I'm going to the bead store."

"Great," I said, trying to be polite but becoming increasingly puzzled and frustrated by her attempts at conversation. I looked out of the bus, trying to ascertain my location and felt that I was probably halfway to my destination.

"Do you know how electricity works?" the woman asked me.

"Yes," I said, then instantly regretted my answer. It would only lead to follow-up questions.

"Can you explain it to me?" she requested, exactly as I had feared. Surprisingly an explanation leapt into my head, in large amounts of detail. That would not do. I decided to avoid getting into the nitty-gritty.

"Obviously you know enough of how to use it. Explaining the theory behind it would take too long."

"Oh OK. You seem really smart. Did you go to university?"

"Yes."

"What did you study?" she inquired excitedly. I wondered why I answered yes to her previous question, given that I could not remember going to university. Still, I had said yes so I needed to give her an answer. I thought over my skills, and the perfect response sprung to mind.

"Engineering."

"Wow so you are smart! Don't you think it's crazy that everything is made up of atoms? Oh and molecules. So small that we can't see them, yet they're everywhere!" she commented. I wasn't sure how to respond. Before I could though, she spoke again.

"Oh look it's my stop. Was nice talking to you, thanks for answering all my questions," she chimed and then got off the bus. I sat back down and looked through the window to other side of the street and lo and behold there was a giant pink store with a sign that read 'BEADS'. As the bus pulled away I shook my head in amazement at the strangeness of the girl and idly read a nearby street sign to get my bearings. I was jolted wide awake by the realisation that I had gone too far. I pressed the button for the bus to stop, and rushed down to the rear doors waiting impatiently for the bus to slow down and let me out. Once the bus finally stopped and I stepped out, I looked around the street trying to figure out exactly how far extra I had travelled. By my reckoning I was only a block or two past the cross street I needed to get onto for the next bus. I settled into a jog down the road keeping an eye out for any oncoming buses. There was surprisingly little traffic, and none of the vehicles were buses. One block passed, and then the second. It looked like I was in the clear. I walked down Harrison St, a short distance, and found a bus stop com-

plete with a bench seat and small shelter. A quick perus-
al of the timetable confirmed that I was at the right stop,
and that a 132 bus was due any minute.

I sat down on the seat, and waited. My right leg was
moving nervously of its own accord, I just couldn't relax. Although all the available facts pointed out that I
was on time and everything should be fine, that didn't
help reassure me. In the back of my mind I thought
about all that could have gone wrong. The bus could
have been running early, it could have broken down
somewhere. The bus could even have been stopped by
whoever Jackie was running from. No matter how much
I tried to convince myself that each of those options was
silly and unrealistic, I couldn't put them out of my
thoughts.

It was with a great deal of relief, and a small measure
of trepidation that I saw the bus I expected come around
the corner towards me. I signalled for it to stop, and the
bus pulled up right in front of me. My doubts washed
away and I patiently waited for the front doors to open. I
stepped onto the bus confidently and looked around for
Jackie to ensure I had the right bus. I found her seated
near the front of the bus, and made eye contact. However
something was not right. She shook her head, put up two
fingers then motioned outside the bus with her head. I
looked back at her for confirmation, but she avoided my
gaze. I turned and apologised to the driver, mentioning
that I had picked the wrong bus and got off.

I noticed two men lurking behind the bus stop shelter as I returned to the street. They had to be the two figures who had spooked Jackie. According to our conversation, I had to catch the next bus and meet her at the Central Interchange. That meant that I had some time on my hands, so I decided to make contact with the two shady characters and see how they reacted. They had both just lit cigarettes and were talking to each other about something as they smoked. Both men were dressed in grey pinstripe suits with matching hats and expensive looking black shoes. Jackie was right to be suspicious, they looked like a pair of hired goons. I walked closer, a plan forming in my head.

"Can I get a light?" I asked as I approached. The man on the left looked at me carefully, then nodded slowly. He removed a metal lighter, flicked the cap off and held it in his hand. He didn't hand over the lighter, but watched me closely. I made a show of going through my pockets as if looking for something, and turned up nothing.

"Can you spot me one?" I asked, trying to be as disarming and sheepish as possible. The man on the right grunted and offered me a cigarette packet. I withdrew one, held it in two fingers and placed it against my lips. The man on the left moved his lighter closer and flicked it alight. I leaned in and lit the end of my cigarette. Taking a puff I drew the acrid smoke into my mouth, and then breathed it right back in the face of the man with the lighter. While the smoke distracted him, I flicked my lit cigarette into the face of his companion, hitting him expertly in the face. The second man cried out in pain and grasped his face in surprise. I used this opportunity to elbow the first man in the chin knocking him down. I then struck out with my right leg, kicking the remaining man squarely in the chest. He fell back into a seated position leaning against the wall behind him.

Ignoring the first man who appeared to be unconscious, I walked over and stood over his partner who was having trouble catching his breath.

"Nice move," he commented hoarsely.

"Start talking!" I demanded. The man managed to get out a small chuckle, before coughing.

"What makes you think I know anything?" he said   .

"I'll be the judge of whether you know anything or not," I said.

"Don't waste your time. Only the two of us were assigned to watch you. The others are on the girl. They must have her already."

"See, you've been quite helpful," I told the man and turned to leave. I had to get to the Central Interchange as quickly as possible. I sped around the corner and along the street to reach the main road, flagging the first available taxi. I promised the driver double what the meter reported if he made the trip extra quick. The screech of the tyres as we rapidly accelerated signalled his acceptance.

I racked my brains to try to figure out how I had been followed. Logic dictated that they couldn't have been following me long, or they would have already attempted to seize the artifact. My only conclusion was that they had been tailing Jackie and had split off to track me once I crossed their paths. What worried me was that others were not as delayed as the pair I had just encountered, and potentially right on Jackie's trail. I didn't even know how many were after her.

My next concern was how to find her when I arrived. She had not mentioned any details on where to meet. I couldn't rely on her being easy to spot, since she was trying to avoid attention. My only hope was that she found a good hiding spot and I could get to her first. Her caution and fear were completely warranted. I felt a terrible weight dragging on my chest, as I realised it was I who had put her at risk. I had never considered how real the danger would be to her if she unearthed anything that led to Markus. Alexis had clearly suffered while in Markus's custody, hardened as she was. I feared what would happen to Jackie if she were taken. For all her worldliness and bluster, she was not prepared for what they could do.

I put those thoughts from my mind and concentrated on my objective: finding Jackie and protecting her from those in her pursuit. At least the goons would be easy to spot, the suits on the two I had already encountered were quite distinctive. While I considered how to go about my search my eyes noticed something large outside the vehicle. It was a large concrete structure with a few entrances and exits.

"Is that the Central Interchange?" I asked the driver.

"Yes sir. Unfortunately only buses are allowed in, I will have to drop you here just outside," he replied. I nodded and when we stopped paid closer to four times what the fare should have been. I started out with a brisk walking pace, as I didn't want to draw too much attention to myself should I find Jackie. Additionally, I was concerned about rushing about too much and overlooking something important. I felt that she would most likely leave me a clue of some sort. I almost took out my phone and dialled her, then decided against it. If she was being tracked down, the ringing may expose her location. She needed as much time as possible for me to find her.

As I entered the Interchange I noticed that it consisted of a lot of bus stands with seats and shelters in front of each one. The road snaked between them, winding its way around the entire complex. It was a fair bit darker inside, once I was out of the sun. There was also a chill to the air that I did not expect. I began by picking a route that ensured I walked past each of the bus stands. As I passed each one, I took stock of the people milling around as well as anything that might direct me to Jackie. When I reached the stand where the one-three-two bus both terminated and began its return journey I paid extra attention. Since that was the bus she caught, there could have been some significance to the location. I loitered around, pretending to examine the timetable and small route map desperately trying to think of what clues could be around. Nobody waiting there seemed suspicious, and I didn't notice any graffiti or special markings on the signs in that area. Thinking that I had gotten the wrong idea, I resumed my plan and continued to investigate the rest of the stands.

The crowd seemed normal as I looked around. At first it was reassuring, but then it became worrisome. If there really were men after Jackie, shouldn't I see at least a few of them either moving around, or standing somewhere nearby? I finished up an entire lap of the Interchange with no sign of Jackie or her pursuers. I also didn't notice any hidden areas or security restricted doors in the general area either. Frustrated, I cursed myself for being so dense. Jackie was depending on me, and I was letting her down. Since I had no better ideas I headed back to the bus stand that she would have arrived at, to give it another look.

My second search was no better than the first. The bus had also just left, so the area was now devoid of people. I sat down on the provided bench and felt a sense of hopelessness well up within me. I stared out into space, feeling lost. I wondered whether I was too late, or if I had missed a crucial detail. At that point I noticed an unusual feature in the distance, one that seemed out-of-place. I stood up and looked closer, noticing that it was a toilet block. I had not noticed it before when wandering through the Interchange. I instantly thought that the men's toilet would be a good spot for a woman to hide. I rushed over, full of confidence now that I had what felt like a solid lead. I just hoped that I was in time.

I walked into the men's toilet and noticed a row of stalls on the left, urinals up the back and basins and mirrors to my right. The only place to hide would be in a stall. I walked past the stalls, and noticed they were all open. A quick inspection of each one showed that they were indeed empty, and there didn't seem to be anything that was left for me. I walked out of the toilet, my previous optimism fading. However I then realised that the women's toilet was still an option, and it was also my last option. I had to be sure. I rushed in, forgetting about being discreet. The layout of the women's toilet block was very similar, only with more stalls.

"Jackie!" I called out. There was no response. I called out again. The women standing around in front of the mirrors stopped applying makeup and looked at me strangely. I had come this far, so I had to leave no doubt in my mind. I walked up to the first stall and banged on the door.

"Answer me or I'll bring the door down."

"Please leave me alone," a female voice squeaked. I moved on to the next one and knocked once more.

"I'm not Jackie I swear," a voice answered. I continued this with every stall, some voices calling out before I could bang on the door. I reached the end, with only a larger stall left. However there was no answer when I banged on the door. I got down on the floor and looked under the door. I could see feet. Without any further delay I kicked the door with all my strength and it swung open. The sight before me was horrific. Jackie was sitting on the toilet seat, slumped back against the wall. Her eyes were closed, her mouth bound with tape and her bloodstained hands were resting on her waist. Blood pooled around her lap and dripped down the toilet.

I rushed forward, ripping off the tape as gently as I could to check if she was breathing. She was alive, but only just. I stepped back, wondering how to help. I noticed her opening her eyes and trying to speak. I moved in close and heard her whisper softly.

"Don't lose hope."

"I'm so sorry, let me get help."

"No time. What you need is in my lockbox, in a false drawer. The key is in my hands."

"That doesn't matter, this should never have happened to you. It's all my fault."

"It should matter. This time it wasn't for a story, it was for you."

"But.." I tried to say, then stopped when I saw her eyes closing. I didn't even hear the sound of the key clanking to the ground when her lifeless hands dropped it. The only thing I could think was that Jackie had been alive a moment ago, and would never be again. Another casualty of my pursuit of the truth.

PRIZE WINNING REPORTER SLAIN IN BUS TERMINAL BATHROOM

By Anton Horrowitz

Three time award-winning reporter Jacqueline Somers was found dead yesterday in the women's bathroom of the Central Bus Interchange and Terminal. Witnesses reported a man storming into the bathroom, discovering the body and then fleeing the scene.

In a statement today the police announced that Jacqueline was the victim of repeated stab wounds. They are working with witnesses to create a composite of the man who was last seen leaving the scene and have asked any civilians who may have knowledge to come forward. It is not yet known if Jacqueline was following a lead at the time.

Jacqueline Somers was a veteran reporter for the Ganford Gazette, breaking stories for over 11 years. She was awarded five Darley awards in her career for excellence in journalism.

"Jackie was such a unique person", colleague Ana stated, "she was just this amazing blend of caring and funny with real strength and an unrelenting commitment to stories." Jim Parsons, editor in chief at the Ganford Gazette, had this to say: "Jackie was a phenomenal reporter who would not only break incredible stories, but would take on the leads and be on the scene when nobody else would. She was an institution at our paper, and she will be sorely missed." An anonymous sponsor has put forward the money to establish a new award for investigative journalism formed in her honour.

In the coming days we will be publishing a special feature in dedication to her memory.

CHAPTER SEVENTEEN

SOMETHING BORROWED

I'm not sure how I got to the Ganford Gazette. Yet there I was, standing outside the building holding the key that Jackie that dropped in my hands. The last thing I could remember was her eyes closing. At some point night had fallen and now the Gazette was empty and locked. To enter I would have to break in. As I walked up the main steps towards the entrance I had the impression that I was removed from myself, as if in a dream. I stepped up to the after-hours door, ready to pick it or otherwise gain access. However I noticed that the door was slightly ajar. I pushed it open and entered the lobby.

My feet pushed forward on their own, I was merely following. I was headed directly for Jackie's office. I should have been wary of security, or other intruders but oddly I was not. I felt nothing except that I had a task to do. The light was on in her office, although the door was pulled to. I thought nothing of it and walked closer.

Hushed dialogue escaped the room, but I paid no attention to it. As I arrived at the office, I forced the door open and walked in. There were two men tearing the room apart looking for something. They stopped momentarily as I entered, frozen with surprise. I recognised them instantly as the two thugs that were smoking behind the bus stop earlier in the day. I wanted to say something, but no words came to me.

The closest one came at me with a knife, his initial lunge aimed at just above the hip. I caught his arm, twisted it at the wrist roughly and heard a snap. The knife fell from his grasp and landed softly on the carpet. He lashed out with his other arm but I leaned back, avoiding it easily. I noticed his companion reaching for a gun so I pulled the knife attacker closer putting him off-balance. I used this shift in momentum to spin him around and use him as a protective shield. I was just in time, two shots thudded into the man's chest and I shoved him off me. A few strides brought me closer to the gun wielding assailant and I effortlessly knocked the pistol from his hand with my arm. He stepped back in surprise and pivoted, aiming a kick at my head. I ducked and moved forward in one movement tackling the man against the wall and bringing him to the ground. I had the advantage, and rained several blows upon his face until he stopped struggling.

I stood up and surveyed the scene. The room was a mess, having been roughly searched and then further disrupted by the recent struggle. I spotted the pistol on the ground, picked it up and placed it in my jacket pocket. I sat down in Jackie's chair and systematically checked each drawer. I noticed that the last one had a false bottom and removed it. A large black strong-box was stored in the hidden compartment. I retrieved it and sat it on the desk. With the key I unlocked it, and found a dossier inside stuffed with documents. I took the dossier, returned the strong box to how I had found it and walked from the office with the documents under my arm.

I hailed a taxi and headed for my rental apartment. I didn't even look over the documents I had obtained, all I did was stare out of the window in a daze. When I arrived, a strange and heavy tiredness settled over me. I left the documents on my desk and lay down on my bed for a minute to rest and recover. I closed my eyes briefly and knew to open them a few seconds later so as not to fall asleep. I did so, but noticed that the room had become rather bright. I got up, confused, and walked around the room. It was clearly daylight. Somehow I had slept through the night, although the passage of time had not been noticeable in the slightest. In a panic I ran over to my desk to check on the documents I had left there. I breathed a sigh of relief when I noticed them untouched.

I relaxed, and sank down in the chair at the desk. Deep, powerful feelings and thoughts were surfacing as my head cleared and I awakened further, however I pushed them aside. I had no time for such encumbrances. I had a singular purpose, to find what Jackie had uncovered. I had already lost one night to sleep, I could not rest again until I had followed the trail to the end. I owed that much to her, and more. Behind that thought, a thousand others swelled up but I ignored them and opened the folder to examine the documents.

They were all records of financial transactions. All seemed to be initiated by different people, and some looked to be real estate sales. Other were charitable donations, loans or trusts. It was hard to make sense of them since I didn't have any context for my analysis. Yet somewhere in those pages was a secret, a clue, a marker so important that Jackie was tracked down and killed to keep it safe. Not only that but her office had been ransacked to recover the documents that I was now viewing. I tried looking at the details of the transactions to see if anything appeared suspicious. The real estate transactions were just addresses, so would need to be checked physically. The charity donations were to the Marchilde Foundation, which was hardly a revelation. The names on the loans and trusts had potential, but I had no frame of reference to give them meaning.

I stopped for a moment and poured myself a glass of water. I sipped it slowly, trying to think of what Jackie would have seen in those documents. What details would have tipped her off, put her on the trail and triggered an investigation? It was hard to draw conclusions when I didn't recognise a single one of the people mentioned. Then it occurred to me, that there had to be a connection between all of the different people. Jackie had assembled a specific collection of documents, and locked them all away together. Each one of them had to be significant, and part of the explanation.

I quickly downed the rest of my water and went back to the documents. I hovered above them for a second, then fetched myself pen and paper. I looked through each document and wrote down the names of each party in each transaction and what the transaction was for. Halfway through the process I noticed something. The Marchilde Foundation had been mentioned in several places. All of them were loans and donations, except for one. It was a real estate sale to a private individual. I circled the transaction and continued my list. I discovered a corresponding entry further down the list, where that same private individual had made a substantial donation to the foundation. That seemed like the kind of connection Jackie would investigate. I looked at the dates and noticed that the real estate sale was quite recent, but the donation was from a few years ago. So someone made a large donation to the Foundation, and then a few years bought a piece of real estate from them. At the very least it suggested that the location was important for some reason. That also made it important to Markus. In a way the link seemed tenuous, but I just had this feeling in my gut that it was more important. That it was crucial. I knew that I would find out for sure by visiting the address.

I splashed some water on my face, shoved all the documents back in the dossier and left my apartment. I took a taxi to the nominated address and leafed through the other documents while I waited. If I was wrong, there had to be other details I could follow-up. Even if I was right, there had to be more information that I was missing. Jackie was thorough and meticulous, she would not have stored useless documents in a secure location. I looked outside and stared up at the sky. What had seemed like a bright morning was beginning to darken. Clouds were rolling in, mostly white and innocent looking. I could see some more in the distance, which were darker and more menacing. The ones furthest from view looked almost black. There had to be a storm coming. I never really paid much attention to the weather, but it seemed significant in this instance. Within minutes the driver told me that we had arrived. I paid him and stepped out of the vehicle, looking at where I had ended up. It was a library.

I entered the library, feeling like I had missed something. I was just puzzled. I wandered around the foyer, wondering why I was there. Just then my eyes spotted something of interest. It was a small display area on the wall showing the history of the library. It was first established a few hundred years ago. However a few years ago it was purchased by the Marchilde Foundation. Accompanying this information was a newspaper clipping from the Ganford Gazette about the purchase. Jackie must have discovered that the Foundation bought this library, mere weeks after receiving a large donation from a private individual. One that had recently bought the library from the Foundation.

It wasn't a large step to consider that Markus, or an agent representing him had fronted the money to the Foundation to buy the library and then bought it from them years later. What seemed strange though, was why someone would pay for the same thing twice. Something seemed wrong with my deduction. I saw an older woman standing behind a counter nearby, so I walked up closer to see what she knew.

'Excuse me," I said.

"Yes, how can I help you?" she replied pleasantly.

"I just had a few questions about the history of this library."

"Certainly, ask away."

"I'm interested in the owners of the library."

"The library was founded by a rich philanthropist over two hundred years ago. Some of those original books are still here."

"What about more recently?"

"Well a few years back the last descendent of the original owner passed away, and left the library to the State in his will. The Marchilde Foundation made a bid to purchase the library, to preserve it and use it as an education center."

"But recently sold it to a private individual?"

"No, the library contents have been classified as National Treasures. That sale you are referring to was the building the library is in."

"I see, thanks for correcting me."

"You seem quite well informed on the library."

"Oh I'm just fact checking for a story," I replied, thinking on my feet.

"Ah are you working with that young woman that was in yesterday? I think she worked for the Gazette," the librarian inquired. I shifted uncomfortably, feeling the wall keeping back my emotions wavering.

"Yes. Thank you for your time," I answered and turned to leave. I needed a place to sit down, go through the new information and discover the next step. I had found the trail left by Jackie, I just had to see where it led. I turned my attention to the main library doors and noticed them opening. In stepped Alexis. I just stared in shock. She also stopped dead in her tracks, the two of us just watching each other. I studied her, trying to judge her reaction. However I couldn't interpret the look on her face. I took a step closer, but she didn't move. I took another step closer. She started to walk away, then stopped.

"Let's go talk," she said, then left. I rushed after her, I was not about to let her vanish from my sight for long. She was waiting for me outside. We walked for a few minutes in silence. So many questions came to me but I suppressed them all. First I wanted to hear what she had to say. We stopped at a park bench and she sat down. I sat down next to her and waited.

"I'm sorry about your reporter friend," Alexis said.

"She was special. She was also the reason I was able to find you," I said.

"I know. Markus has known of her efforts for some time."

"Why didn't you tell me? I could have protected her better."

"No you couldn't. When Markus wants someone dead there's no stopping him. Any effort is merely delaying the inevitable."

"What about you then?"

"He doesn't want me dead."

"Why not?"

"What's the point of winning, if nobody knows that you have won?" Alexis said before reaching out and taking the dossier off my lap. She flicked through it carefully.

"Is this what she found?" Alexis asked.

"Yes, she directed me to it before she died."

"My suspicions were right then, he bought the library. Under his real name too," Alexis commented. I took another look at the name on the purchase of the library address. The name was Mathew Arkus. I felt stupid for not noticing it.

"He used to sign his name as M. Arkus and someone once mistakenly referred to him as Markus. He liked that name so much he kept it as his alias," Alexis explained as my brain finally put two and two together.

"What brought you here then?" I said.

"I'm chasing down an artifact," Alexis replied.

"Now that you have mine you must have quite a few."

"They were never yours so don't refer to them as such. I need them to lure Markus out of hiding."

"Won't he just take them from you?"

"Not until I have them all. And when he does, he will come in person. That's when I'll kill him."

"Doesn't sound like much of a plan."

"Doesn't make it any less effective though. Come with me and I'll explain in more detail," Alexis offered as she handed me back the dossier and rose from the seat. I had to follow her, to see what she had in mind. She was now my best link to Markus. I walked over to the street to hail a taxi, but she grabbed my arm and restrained me.

"Don't use taxis, Markus has all the main providers paid off. They've probably been reporting on all your movements," Alexis said.

"What? That's not possible," I said with disbelief.

"You better believe it. Your reporter friend even worked it out," Alexis stated nonchalantly.

"Her name was Jackie."

"I know."

More questions bubbled to the surface, but I answered them all in my head before asking her. The simple fact that Alexis was collecting artifacts to get to Markus accounted for all but one.

"Why did you leave me when I got shot?"

"You would have slowed me down in your condition. I left you in good care, but you got paranoid and escaped. That proved my other concern, that you're unpredictable. However that also made you a good distraction for Markus."

"What about now?"

"Now I have a use for you."

"What might that be?"

"You'll find out soon enough. For now we have another artifact to research. I think the library is the key," Alexis said. She continued walking and I followed. We cut through a park, travelled down some narrow alleys and came to a small section of shops. There was a bakery, a corner store and a butcher. Alexis opened a small door to the right of the butcher, and we went upstairs.

"This location is more secure," she commented as we ascended. Once we entered the small apartment it was the same disorganised mess I had become accustomed to in her old safe house. I wandered through the small place, taking a look around but for nothing in particular.

"Looking for my artifacts?" Alexis asked.

"No, but how many do you have?" I asked in counter.

"Nine."

"I have two."

"I had hoped you did, that's good news. That means we only have one more to get."

"The one you have a lead on?"

"Yes. Finding you at the library provided some confirmation, and the documents you have with you prove it without a doubt."

"What is the lead?"

"I have a list of numbers, in pairs. My father believed that they were a cypher, referring to specific words in a book. Markus buying a library twice means that the book we want must be there," Alexis explained. I couldn't find fault with her reasoning, the information she provided looked to fill in the gaps. However to test the theory, we would need to find the right book and discover what the message was. Finding the artifact would be another matter altogether. However if by finding it we were to complete the collection, what would happen? That line of thinking also brought up another question.

"How many artifacts does Markus have?" I said.

"None," Alexis replied with a smile.

"That doesn't make sense."

"He did have one, but I stole it."

"Surely he can't be standing idly by while we amass the whole collection of artifacts."

"Why not, if he thinks he can take them whenever he wants."

"Do you even know what happens when you get them all?"

"No, but my father thought it was worth everything," Alexis replied with a hint of bitterness. I decided not to follow-up with the topic any longer. At any rate it seemed almost irrelevant. As soon as we had all the artifacts, Markus would find us. Then I could end things once and for all. I wasn't sure if I would get the answers I wanted, but at least I could prevent further tragedies. I asked Alexis about our next move and she explained that we could follow up that lead tomorrow at the library. I wondered why we could not go immediately, as I didn't feel the library security would be particularly tight but I stuck with the plan. There had to be a reason she wanted to go during the day. Alexis was hardly the patient type at all.

The couch I lay down on that night was old, lumpy and short. I didn't think that I would get a wink of sleep on it. Surprisingly though, I slept very deeply and didn't wake until well into the morning. When I awoke I discovered Alexis standing over me, looking intently at me.

"You look like you didn't get any sleep," I commented.

"That's because I didn't," she replied. My curiosity was raised substantially.

"Couldn't sleep? Or did you have something to do alone?"

"I retrieved your two artifacts."

"How did you.."

"I've been keeping tabs on you. I can guarantee that Markus has been as well."

"Saves me the hassle of handing them over," I said with some annoyance. It was not out of character for her, but I thought that perhaps by now I had earned some trust. Maybe it was foolish for me to believe that my standing with her would ever improve. Ultimately though it was only a minor detail. I had committed myself to discovering the truth and following things to their conclusion. Gathering the artifacts was part of that, so logically I had no reason to be irritated. Still, it grated on me that in her eyes I still had not proven my intentions.

Alexis didn't react to my comment and mentioned that we were heading to the library as soon as I was ready. I wasted no time, eager to be on the trail of the last artifact. As we retraced our steps from the previous day, it finally dawned on me that the end was in sight, perhaps for the first time. It wasn't for certain, but even if the library lead was no good, the simple truth was that only one more artifact remained. Finding Markus wouldn't even be an issue, at that point he would have to find us. We just had to be prepared.

At that moment another idea struck me. Once we had all the artifacts, perhaps we could discover their significance before Markus cottoned on. We could sabotage them even, or perform any of a countless list of other tricks. The ball was in our court and we would have the advantage. Markus's arrogance in letting us collect the artifacts for him would be his undoing. Due to this train of thought I was full of hope and expectations when we arrived at the library.

"What the plan?" I said.

"We find the book the cypher is linked to by collecting old books. We test the cypher on each one and then follow the message," Alexis replied.

"How will we filter out all the wrong books?"

"Think of how old the book must be, there can't be many which are of suitable age."

Alexis had made a good point. Surely only a handful of books in the library were of any significant age. It would be easy to find them and then by process of elimination see which one of those books, if any, was the book we wanted. The trick though, would be spotting them amongst the thousands of others.

We walked back into the library, passing through the foyer and proceeding into the main area. The library proper was roughly square in shape and comprised of a few levels. We decided to split up, I would take the top two floors, and Alexis the bottom two. We planned to meet back in the foyer afterwards and compare notes. The idea was to systematically wander through the aisles of books and grab anything that seemed to be of considerable age. I had some doubts about the plan, but it was better than anything I could think up so I followed along. I took the stairs, working my way up to the fifth level, the top, without stopping to look at any of the others in between.

Upon reaching the top level, I walked out and scanned the room. It looked like I was in a non-fiction area. It was dead quiet and seemed deserted. Yet at the same time I could hear a voice nearby, but just out of hearing range. I walked closer to the sound, noticing that it was coming from a separate room. I saw a sign on the door to the room, and approached it to satisfy my curiosity. The sign read as follows: 'Author Reading – 10am-11am'. I instinctively opened the door and entered.

The room was full of chairs, each occupied by a person. The people within were an equal blend of all different types, ages and dress. None of them seemed to notice my intrusion. At the far end of the room, seated apart from the rest was a man in his early thirties. He had long dark brown hair partially covering his face, rectangular glasses and strongly featured face littered with day old stubble. He was dressed casually in sneakers, jeans and a jumper. His was the voice I had heard, he was reading from a paperback while everyone else listened.

He stopped reading and looked up at me. The sudden silence awakened the rest in the room, and they all turned to face me as well. But I did not feel their gazes upon me. I was transfixed by the man. I was convinced that he was looking through me, that in some way he was teasing out all my secrets purely with his eyes. The feeling was extremely unnerving and uncomfortable, yet I could not move or look away. A few moments later, he resumed his reading, and the tension that had built up within me faded. I left the room as quickly as possible, and began my search of the top level for old books.

I am unsure of if there were no books matching the criteria that we had agreed upon, or whether I was still distracted by the strange gaze of that man, but I found myself back on the ground floor with nothing in my possession. I hoped that Alexis had fared better. As I could not see her, I wandered aimlessly, surrounded by books. It was so peaceful and comforting. I noticed however, that the perfectly symmetrical pattern of shelves was disrupted by a large space in the middle. I walked there directly to see what could be so important.

I was standing before a glass display case, surrounded by some prominent signage and red barrier ropes supported by golden poles. A quick glance suggested that the information was about the contents, but I disregarded it. I was drawn to what was inside. There was only one item. It was an incredibly old and dusty tome. The cover was inlaid with gold lettering that read 'Idle Thoughts'. I knew beyond any doubts that it was the key. Markus must have examined it cover to cover countless times with his connection to the library. I also knew that there was no way we could verify its contents without removing it from the library. Impulse, opportunity and determination combined within me in a heady mix and I grabbed the nearest pole and smashed it through the display case. With a great crash the case was split open, an ear-piercing alarm sounded and I had access to the book. I snatched it hastily, shoved it in my pocket and fled.

CHAPTER EIGHTEEN

PILGRIMAGE

I sprinted through the streets with little thought in regards to where I was heading. I glanced back periodically and only saw Alexis in pursuit. Any security or other parties in chase had fallen back or were seeking alternate means of transport. It was my chance to fade away and disappear. I stopped briefly in a quiet side street so that Alexis could catch up.

"Here," I said as I handed her the book. She had an annoyed yet surprised look on her face.

"I hope this is it," she replied.

"It definitely is. I'll meet you back at your new place."

"Sure. Don't take too long." Alexis turned quickly and walked away purposefully. I resumed a jog and looked around assessing what kind of attention I had on me. I could see some people pointing and shouting in the distance, which meant that I was still on their radar. A few blocks ahead I spotted an underground train station, that seemed to be the perfect solution.

As I descended the stairs I observed that the station was quite old and tiled. The ground was a dirty black and looked decidedly unhealthy. The corridors leading to the track entry area were rather narrow, which meant that there was a thick procession of people streaming in both directions. I pushed my way through hurriedly, unsure of how close any pursuers were. As I neared the ticket gates before the platform, I realised I didn't have a ticket. The idea of buying a ticket while being pursued seemed awfully silly, yet for some reason I still glanced over to see if it was possible. The lines of people waiting suggested that it was not. I took a fifty dollar note out from my wallet and hovered near one of the gates. An older man approached, I deftly pushed in front of him, swapped his ticket for the cash and went through the ticket gate before he could even blink.

I didn't hear any commotion as I ran down to the station, so in my head I surmised that the old man had been happy with the trade. A blinking sign indicated that a train had arrived at one of the platforms. I didn't care about where I was going, so I headed straight for it. I could barely see the train behind the throngs of people on the platform, so I pushed through them as quickly as possible with little regard for politeness. Once I got closer I made it to a space between two big groups of people, but the doors of the nearest carriage were closing fast. Summoning up a burst of speed I pressed on and squeezed through the doors just before they closed. Turning back I saw a few people struggling within the crowd, disappointed that they had missed the train. I was not sure if they were just unlucky civilians or among those looking for me.

I had decided to just ride for a few stops then get a train going back in the opposite direction. However before I had a chance to execute that plan, the train started to slow and then stop in the middle of the tunnel. A small stop didn't seem that out of the ordinary, although I was a bit surprised that we had stopped in the middle of nowhere. Minutes passed and there were no updates. That was of course until the train powered down completely. With scarce lighting and no air flow it was becoming quite an uncomfortable delay. My fellow passengers were becoming unsettled and disturbed. The questions running through my head were echoed by them all. Only I had an additional concern: that in some way the train stoppage was related to me.

A muffled announcement over the train PA system mentioned something about a passenger injury and requested the patience of all aboard. What was more interesting, was the frantic and disorganised communication between train staff over the same PA system. There had to be something seriously wrong if they needed to communicate with each other over a public channel. I weighed up my options, wondering whether I should stay put with the rest or find a way out. In the end I decided to not draw unnecessary attention to myself and stay with the other passengers. I told myself that it was just coincidental that I was on a stopped train.

A few minutes later I perceived some movement in the train cars ahead of me. Peering through the windows I saw people moving slowly down the length of the train. I felt as though my decision to be patient was still the right one. Eventually people from the carriage I was in started to move. I fell in line, joining the slow and plodding parade. As we moved along the train and passed through carriages we had to hold open the doors we encountered, the lack of power was making them remain closed. As I walked I wondered at what was ahead. Soon I spotted the platform, the train must have stopped just at the start.

In the next carriage I spotted a cluster of people standing around looking out the main window on the left side. I glanced through and saw smears of red on the platform wall. I wanted to continue and ignore it, but could not. I walked closer and looked over. There were some uniformed men zipping up a black bag, containing a man's body. Surrounding them and all over the wall was copious amounts of blood. Of course I caught sight of the man's head before they covered him completely and I recognised the face. It was one of Markus's henchmen. I stared incredulously. Was it purely coincidence that the man had died at this particular platform as I was on train heading in that direction? If it was not, how could it be connected to me? The other question that had me puzzled was who had killed that man?

I cursed myself for staring and wasting time, and reminded myself that I had a solid lead on the last artifact awaiting me. All I had to do was get back to Alexis at her new safe house. I rejoined the slow procession of passengers and wound my way out of the train and up the stairs. Eventually I reached the surface and left the station. I had forgotten all about my concerns of getting stopped, followed or chased. I was completely focused on returning to Alexis. Taking stock of my location, I realised that since I was only one station away, it wouldn't take long to walk back. I still vaguely remembered the way back, I just needed to get close enough for my memory to kick in.

During the journey back I turned my thoughts to my impetuous action in the library. It was of course the most expedient way to obtain the book, but what worried me was the way in which it was done. Such rash activity without any plan, right off the cuff was more Alexis' territory. Was I changing or was there another part of me that was becoming exposed? Forcing the thoughts away I returned my attention to the next artifact. If the book was the right one, then Alexis would be able to decode the message and we would have either the location or directions to the last artifact. Then I could focus on the problem of what to do with the full collection of artifacts.

My memory served me well, and I arrived at the small array of shops surrounding my destination shortly thereafter. I walked up the stairs and noticed the door was open. I stepped inside cautiously, listening for any sounds of a struggle or ransacking.

"Close the door behind you," Alexis called out from the next room. I did so quietly and then followed her voice. She was seated at a table working away with a pen and paper with the book open before her.

"This Cypher works by referring to specific words on specific pages and using the first letter of the word. While you were gone I worked out the first part. It was purely a test to make sure we had the right book," Alexis explained without looking up.

"I was delayed by a murder at the train station," I said. That got her attention. She stopped working and looked at me.

"Tell me the details."

"I'm not sure who did it, but it was messy. One of Markus's henchmen was killed right on the platform."

"Take over from me, I'll go consult the baker."

"Is that some sort of code word?"

"No, he's actually a baker. The one downstairs. He's got an amazingly large information network."

"If you say so," I said. I sat down where Alexis had been, and looked over the papers. One was a list of numbers, some of which had been circled. Another page was what appeared to be the message, judging by what Alexis had said. I checked a few of the numbers against the message to double-check that I understood the cypher correctly. Once I had satisfied myself that I was doing it right, I continued on from where Alexis had left off.

I paid no attention to the words as they emerged, focusing purely on getting the next letter. It was almost as if I didn't want to spoil the secret until the last possible moment when it had all been revealed. Finally when I had run out of numbers, I looked back at what I had written. The message was as follows:

Under the cross at St Mathews Church.

Before I had time to really process the revelation I heard Alexis returning.

"I have information," Alexis called out.

"And I have a location," I called back in response. Alexis ran into the room, grabbed the piece of paper and studied it closely.

"I know this place, it's in the centre of the city," Alexis said.

"That should make it easy. What information did you get?" I asked.

"It looks like some of Markus's old friends are returning some favours. That henchman was not the first one to fall."

"That may be the break we need."

"Perhaps, it will definitely help if his attention is spread out. Let's get going." Alexis shoved the message into her pocket and left the room hurriedly. I rushed after her, allowing myself to feel the excitement of discovery.

We had a location to investigate, and I was one step away from having all the artifacts. One step away from some answers, and perhaps even a solution to the problem of Markus. I thrust the book into one of my jacket pockets and headed out.

When I arrived downstairs I saw Alexis getting into a black vehicle with the engine running.

"Where'd this come from?" I asked.

"I asked the baker to arrange some transportation for me. I figured you'd finish the cypher," she replied with a smile as I approached. I walked around to the passenger side and got in.

"Do you know what to do once we have them all?"

"I know that they reveal a message when assembled correctly. I'm not really sure of the right way to do that though. But I'm confident that we can work it out."

"As long as we can work it out before Markus finds us," I said. Alexis didn't have a reply to that. I looked over at her as we drove, wondering what was going through her head. As well as I thought I knew her, I didn't know her that well. I thought about what might happen if we succeeded, and could not think of what she would do afterwards. All I had grasped of her ambitions and desires was inextricably linked to Markus and the artifacts.

"What will you do after all this is over?" Alexis asked me. I stared at her in stunned disbelief. How was it that we were thinking the exact same thing?

"I don't know, I've been too busy to even think about that."

"I've been thinking about it for a while now. I'm going to be a teacher."

"I'm not sure you have the patience for that."

"I think you'd be surprised at what I'm capable of, once I'm free of all this," Alexis said. She was right, I had no idea of what she would be like, if given a different life. I found it interesting that I had been so fixated on the struggles right before me, and my past, that I hadn't really looked to the future. Yet Alexis, the impulsive impetuous one had given it a lot of thought. I guess she never really picked a career before. Then again, I wasn't so sure I had either.

The drive over to the church took longer than I had expected. It was due to a combination of heavy traffic, narrow streets and the distance. By the time we arrived it was the afternoon and the sun was beginning its transition away from sight. As I stepped out from the vehicle I noticed my shadow was now elongated. Looking up, the church was quite small but appeared to be very old. I thought it looked like a classic design, with a cross up on the roof. I hoped that it was not the cross being referred to in the message. The main doors were open, so we ascended the short stairway out front and entered the church. Inside was rather dim, despite the stain glass windows evenly placed around the exterior walls. A few massive columns held up the ceiling, and the rest of the floor space was taken up with wooden pews.

Alexis knelt briefly, made a sign with her hands and then stood once more. We walked up the middle between the two sides of pews. I could see a large cross at the back of the room, with a golden box underneath it.

"Surely it's in there," I commented, pointing at the box.

"Not necessarily," Alexis replied. "Although we should start our search there." I nodded in assent and we continued on. Looking around, I couldn't see anyone else in the church. I noted when we were closer that the rear section of the room was raised off the floor. Alexis had some hesitation but I walked up with no reservations. Ignoring the furnishings I went straight for the golden box. It was secured with a thick sturdy lock.

"Can you take care of that?" Alexis asked.

"Sure, one minute," I said. I removed a lock pick from my pocket and set to work. The lock was particularly difficult, and it took me a few minutes of my best effort to get it open. My was mind racing the whole time, wondering if the artifact we sought was within. I slowly opened the door once I had finished to see what was inside. Alexis stood back and watched. I saw two objects in there, so pulled them both out. Both were metallic, however instead of silver I was hoping for they were gold. One was a cup and the other was a plate.

"No dice, put them back," Alexis said. I complied and returned the two objects, ensuring that the box was locked again.

"What are you doing?" a voice called out with an accusatory tone. I turned to see who was addressing us, and noticed that a short and elderly priest had entered from a side door. He hurriedly walked up to where we were standing.

"I'm sorry we were just taking a look around," I said. The priest regarded me with suspicion, then pushed past me and fished out some keys from his pocket. He opened the golden box, inspected inside, then locked it once more. Seemingly satisfied, he calmed down and addressed again.

"I'm sorry, but you shouldn't be up here," he said.

"Sorry for causing any trouble, we are just interested in the history of this church. It looks so old," Alexis replied innocently. The eyes of the priest lit up. It appeared as though Alexis had touched upon a topic he was passionate about. All the better for us, since we no ideas for where to search next.

"How about I give you a tour? That way you can both learn about the history of this place and stay out of trouble," the priest suggested. Alexis and I both readily agreed, it suited our needs perfectly. Since we had caught the attention of the priest, sneaking around was no longer an option.

The priest began by taking us around the main hall, explaining the detail in the stain glass windows and telling us a bit about the beginnings of the church. Apparently the church was designed by a local architect and commissioned by a local benefactor. He told us interesting facts about the wood used in the pews, the construction of the large columns and other details that were of interest, but ultimately not useful. My mind wandered, and I started to tune out. I felt that we were on a pointless tangent, one that would not produce results. When the priest offered to show us some of the small rooms not usually open to the public, I politely declined and let Alexis go.

I walked up to the front row of pews and sat down on the hard wood. I looked up at the fading light coming in through the stain glass windows. I thought about my future. I considered what I would do, once Markus and the artifacts were dealt with. I wondered whether I would ever solve the puzzle of my past. I pondered about my own purpose. The funny thing is what I decided upon. I decided that I didn't want to make any decisions. I felt that deciding upon something would limit me in some way, that I should be open to everything. Why pick a path when I could just wander until I chanced upon one that was suitable?

Thinking about paths and walking had me subconsciously staring at my feet. That led to me examining the tiled floor, following the intricate patterns of shapes and colours. I both admired the arrangement of tiles, but also felt drawn to follow the pattern with my eyes. The way the pattern morphed, merged and linked up with other pieces was fascinating. I forgot all about the important life defining issues that I was pondering mere moments before. Then I detected something that irritated me. It was a break in the pattern, a circular wooden shape. Something was set into the flooring. Inspecting the intruding object with more scrutiny I saw that there was a cross etched into it. The word from the message flowed through me and I recognised with perfect clarity that I was beholding the hiding place of the last artifact.

My excitement was so intense, I could feel my whole body tingling. I practically leapt up and ran over to the wooden circle. I dropped down to the ground, feeling around the shape for any way to open it or remove it from the floor. The surface was smooth and polished, and I could not discover any grooves or switches to press. I discovered a very small gap around the edge between the wood and the tiles. I figured that with the right implement, I might be able to lever the wood out revealing something underneath. I fumbled through my pockets, trying to find a suitable item. My lock pick seemed too flimsy, the pistol too noisy and potentially too destructive. I lay my hands on a swiss army knife next, and that seemed like the best option. I opened out the flat blade and inserted it into the gap. It was tight, but it fit. I tried to force the wooden shape out, but it was being held by something. I ran the blade around the edge of the circle hoping to find out what was blocking the movement. I was stopped by something, which felt like a rope or cord.

With a quick sawing motion I applied force to the obstruction and it fell away. I continued searching, finding two more cords and cut them both the same way. Once I had completed a full revolution I tried levering the shape one more time. I had more success, and the wooden object began to shift. When I had exposed enough of it I reached in with my hand and removed it completely. I saw something beneath where the wooden circle had been. I retrieved it from the hole, discovering that it was a cloth covering something else. With a degree of reverence I unwrapped the cloth to discover what was within. It was a small silver dish. I picked it up and had a closer look, slowly rotating it and examining it from all angles. The look and feel of it was distinctive, I was certain that it was an artifact. In this case the last one.

After basking in the discovery for a moment, I turned to more practical matters. Hiding the dish within my jacket, I set about replacing the cloth and wooden disc. I wanted to ensure that nothing seemed amiss, leaving no trace of what I had done. No sooner had I completed the task, I heard Alexis and the priest coming closer. She was thanking him for his hospitality and he was beaming, obviously happy to be have such a charming and attentive woman hanging on his words.

"I didn't really find anything worth investigating back there. How did you go?" Alexis asked quietly as she approached me.

"Oh alright I guess. I uncovered the last artifact and hid the evidence that anything was taken," I said nonchalantly. Surprise and delight crossed her face at the news.

"Where was it?"

"You're standing on the spot." Alexis stepped back and looked down intently. She nodded to herself then turned back to me.

"Good job, let's get out of here. The countdown begins now."

"I couldn't agree more, lead the way," I said. Now that we had the last artifact it was only a matter of time before Markus either found out or became suspicious of our actions. We had to do whatever we could to gain an advantage before that confrontation occurred. I followed behind Alexis thinking about all the possibilities. I wondered if anyone else had assembled them all together before. If they had, what had happened? What could I expect if we were successful and would I be able to recognise it?

Those thoughts and more like them occupied me and I only absent-mindedly followed Alexis. It was with great surprise that I walked right into her, as she had stopped dead just outside the church. Dusk was falling around us, the sky was darkening and no street lights were on yet. A single man stood in front of us, blocking the path to the street. He was tall, with unkept dark hair, intense green eyes and glasses. He was dressed in a long black cloak and the glint of a revolver could be seen in his right hand. Looking past him I saw a row of men in black suits lining the footpath. I could hear the church doors being locked behind us. We had nowhere to go.

"I was waiting for you to show up," Alexis said to the man, trying to mask her surprise. He didn't seem convinced by her display of bravado.

"Don't look so surprised, you should have known this was the only possible outcome," the man replied. He turned his attention to me.

"Please, show me the artifact. Don't try anything or I kill the girl," he said. I looked over at Alexis, at the man himself, and over to his entourage. It was too risky to make a run for it, and there wasn't really anywhere to go either. I concluded that my only option was to play along for the time being. I reached into my jacket, and slowly removed the silver dish.

"Bring it to me," he requested calmly and with a gesture. I looked him in the eyes, and walked over deliberately. I stopped before him and handed it over. As he touched it a look of ecstasy crossed his features.

"Come Alexis, let's go to where you have stashed the rest and finish this," the man said while beckoning at her.

"It's not over yet Markus," Alexis replied, her voice steeled with her resolve.

HOMECOMING

We were ushered into a black limousine, and I was re-minded of the book in my jacket pocket as I stepped inside. Markus and a few suits followed close behind before joining us. I was sitting right next to Alexis, and could feel her leg trembling. My first thoughts were of how to buy us more time. We were not ready for this confrontation.

"Where to?" Markus asked Alexis directly. She seemed to flinch at the question. I was unsure whether it was due to the nature of what he had asked, or if she was afraid of him. He did not seem that imposing to me.

"Home," Alexis replied.

"How clever," Markus replied thoughtfully before whispering to one of his men who conveyed a message to the driver. The vehicle came to life, and our journey began.

"I suspect you are wondering how I tracked you down at precisely the right moment," Markus said. Alexis looked over at him with a blank expression, I think she was still in some sort of shock. I expected a loud, rebellious response from her.

"Well," Markus continued, "the baker gave me all the details, he even put a tracking device in the car you used. His only loyalty is to cash, making him a very useful man." Alexis stared daggers at him after that remark.

"It's the beginning of the end for you, people won't suffer you any more," Alexis said.

"No, I'm afraid that's preposterous my dear. If you are referring to the fact that several of my men were found dead today, well that was at my request. I wanted you to feel bolder, and fed the baker that information as bait," Markus explained with an arrogant laugh. He really was detestable. He addressed me next.

"Whatever happened to you? I knew your methods were unusual, but I'm a little confused. Are you working with me or against me? You haven't become attached to the girl have you?"

"I'm working for myself," I replied. Markus chuckled, amused by my response. He did not say anything further. I wanted to talk to Alexis, to find out what she had planned or at least get some information, however we had no privacy. Markus was unlikely to leave us alone either, even though he now had the artifact we just retrieved. I felt so helpless. I just had to trust that when the time came I would know what to do. That didn't stop me worrying though, and endeavouring to think up ways to turn things around.

We stopped abruptly and I looked outside. The skies had darkened considerably, and rain had started to fall. What captured my attention was the large manor house before us. Alexis and I were almost pushed out of the vehicle and stood in the rain while Markus was sheltered by an umbrella held by one of his goons. Alexis shivered and I put an arm around her instinctively. She shrugged me off, and stepped forward digging a set of keys out of her handbag. She walked over to the towering metal gates, and unlocked them. What followed was a strange procession down the long driveway. Alexis in front, me following behind and Markus and a few men behind us. The rain increased in intensity, but I soon forgot about it. My eyes were fixated on Alexis. It was as if every step towards this place sapped her strength a little more. Yet she plodded on, the gravel under her feet both crunching and splashing as she went.

Pools of water started to form on the ground, but our pace did not change. The sound of thunder rumbled nearby and a flash of light temporarily lit up the sky. The grounds surrounding the driveway appeared wild and unkept. Looking ahead I saw that the house seemed almost derelict, like it had been abandoned for a long time. I wondered about the history of the place, and pondered its significance. My curiosity was soon sated.

Alexis paused outside the great doors and waited for everyone else to catch up. I wasn't sure whether she was just being compliant, or stalling to think of something.

"It's a lovely old place, I wonder why your father never moved in?" Markus asked.

"It intimidated him when my mother's parents lived here, and when it passed into his possession it just reminded him of her," Alexis replied. Markus nodded and gestured at the doors with his hands. Alexis unlocked them and pushed them open. The doors groaned as they swung, revealing an ornate entry area with marble flooring. A staircase leading upstairs was directly in front, with entrances to adjoining rooms on either side of a hallway extending before us. A chill hung in the air, which caused Alexis to shiver again.

She started walking, guiding us through a series of rooms and down a staircase into what appeared to be an extensive personal library. Bookcases lined all the walls, and a few padded leather chairs and small tables were littered around the available floor space. Alexis threaded her way through them and arrived at a small desk in the corner of the room. We all watched attentively, no one uttered a word not even the two men accompanying Markus. That said, they were probably under strict instruction to be quiet. I didn't think that Markus would put up with hired help that talked unless spoken to.

"My grandfather used to read me stories down here, just as he did with my mother," Alexis said without emotion. "He would regularly disappear in here when he was working on something and didn't want to be bothered." Alexis reached out to the nearest bookcase, tilted one of the books forward and pushed against the it. I heard a clicking sound and watched the bookcase rotate to reveal a small sitting room. Alexis stepped inside and pulled a cord, turning on a light hanging from the ceiling. We followed her inside. A desk was in the centre of the room directly below the light, with all of the artifacts laid out on it. A few chairs were the only other furnishings. One of Markus's followers blocked the exit, while the other rearranged the chairs. He put two on the library side of the desk, and the other one was on the opposite side. Markus seated himself at the opposite chair and pointed at the others, directing us to sit down.

I watched Alexis carefully, and after she sat down I sat next to her. Here we were, the artifacts all assembled, but completely in Markus's power. He removed the silver dish from underneath his coat and added it to the table.

"What were you planning to do next?" Markus asked.

"Discover their secret and use them against you," Alexis said, some defiance returning to her voice. Markus just laughed.

"Be my guest," he said before leaning back in his chair and resting his hands on his chest. Alexis sat bolt upright, looked at me then stood quickly. She went straight for the gun artifact.

"For your information, I know it doesn't actually function as a firearm," Markus said. Alexis appeared unfazed and swapped the gun with another artifact. She beckoned for me to come closer.

"Each artifact has two sets of markings, one is a unique identifier and the other is the message. If we can ascertain the message before he does..." she whispered to me. I looked back at Markus, and he met my eyes with a confident smile. I could tell that something was up, but went along with Alexis anyway. Maybe it was as simple as using this opportunity while Markus basked in what he thought was his impending victory. I picked up a few of the artifacts and examined the markings. There was definitely a pattern as Alexis had suggested, and I deduced that the identifier was the upper of the two sets of markings. However each identifier was a strange shape that didn't seem to have any corresponding pattern. There was a pen and paper on the desk, and I wrote out all the identifier shapes, hoping to see something I had missed when examining them individually. When nothing came to me I wrote out the messages under each symbol. The messages themselves also made no sense, consisting of a series of boxes and lines.

I racked my brains, struggling to pull out something that would help. Surely in the mind there had to be something to get me out of my predicament. It was clear in the past I had worked with Markus in some capacity. Why in my moment of need, was there no inspiration? I had to have something, I couldn't let him win.

"That's enough, you have both been most amusing," Markus called out.

"You're just afraid that we'll discover the secret before you," Alexis said.

"Quite the contrary, I know that you can't possibly succeed. Take a seat," Markus replied. I sat back down, wondering why he was so confident. My previous uneasiness had returned. Alexis followed my lead and sat down.

"Here ends your involvement. Tie them up," Markus said to his nearest associate. The man bound our hands together behind the backs of the chairs we were seated in. Markus himself got up and checked our bindings, to ensure they were satisfactory. He then resumed his seated position.

"It's quite sad really, you never had a chance. Intercepting you today was a kindness on my part," Markus said.

"What do you mean?" Alexis asked. Markus reached into his coat and pulled out an object encased in a plastic sleeve. It looked like a piece of paper covered with markings.

"This is the codex. It has instructions on how to arrange and translate the message from the artifacts," Markus explained. Alexis laughed.

"You really think that we could not have worked it out eventually?" she said in reply, unimpressed.

"Yes, in this instance no amount of hard work could overcome that which you lack," Markus teased. He was obviously enjoying himself. He slowly reached around the back of his neck, and lifted something over his head.

"The thirteenth artifact," he announced while dangling it in front of us. It was a circular pendant with an engraving on the front. Alexis swore audibly.

"You always wore it openly, I had no idea," she said.

"It came with the codex, and is the key to everything." Markus said with excitement. His eyes positively shone. Pieces of the puzzle connected in my mind. Markus was content to let others gather and collect artifacts because he was confident that nobody else could correctly assemble them. I had no doubts as to his arrogance, but he had actually maintained a secret advantage this whole time. Not even Alexis knew of his trump card.

"No wonder it was so easy to steal your artifact," Alexis grumbled. She had clearly come to the same conclusion as me. My face felt flush, I knew we were in trouble. Despite my best intentions, my disruptions and my choices, Markus had won. Everything had come together according to his wishes. I had no need to dwell on the subject further, Markus covered it quite well.

"All these years of careful planning, hiding my ace in plain view. It has all lead to this moment. I stand before you, the first man to complete the collection. In moments I will know their secret, something no man has known for centuries. I hope you feel grateful that I share this moment with you."

"What do you hope to achieve with this? Alexis asked.

"Many a night I have lain awake, contemplating what secret the artifacts hold. I believe they hold the power to fulfill my desires."

"So you have no idea either," I remarked.

"Rather than explain myself I'll quote the codex instead: 'Once combined the artifacts reveal the secret behind life itself'. Think of the possibilities, I will hold in my hand the power of life and death."

"So that's how you put my father on this search, you promised to bring her back!" Alexis accused Markus angrily.

"Such a simple man, just the mere suggestion of it set him on his path. I didn't even have to promise him anything," Markus laughed. I could see Alexis squirming in her chair, eagerly trying to escape from her bonds. The look she shot Markus was pure hatred, so harsh it even scared me. Markus appeared to be unconcerned though.

"Let us not delay any further," Markus said casually. He moved his chair forward and set to work, using the codex as a guide he translated the symbols and markings I had transcribed into a sequence of numbers and dashes. The numbers seemed familiar to me in some way. Not the numbers themselves, but the way in which they were arranged. It reminded me of the numbers we used to decode the message explaining where the last artifact was. That was too similar to be a coincidence. I glanced over at Alexis and she was staring at me, with what must have been the same realisation. If I was right we still had an advantage, the book. If only I had not taken it with me. Markus finished his transcription and looked up.

"Only one thing remains," he said before standing up and walking over to me. He inspected my jacket, and reached in to extract the book.

"You have good instincts, which I thank you for. This whole experience could have been drawn out much longer," Markus remarked. I had no doubt he was thankful, but he had worded it in a way to irritate me as much as possible.

"I know you had a similar task to deduce the location of the last artifact. In fact I had ascertained the location years ago, I was just waiting for the right time," he said with a chuckle.

"The difference here is in the interpretation and rules. It's not referring to pages and letters, but chapters and words. Please be patient, this won't take long." Markus sat back down, and opened the book. Using it as a reference he started to write out words. However his script was very small and at the bottom of the page so we could not read it. I watched him closely as he worked, and a range of emotions crossed his face. He started out elated, then delighted. This changed to interested, then concerned and then outright disbelief. Suddenly he banged the desk angrily with his right hand and stood up knocking his chair over.

"No, you've tricked me. What have you done?" he shouted out, pointing at Alexis. I looked over at her, and there was no satisfaction on her face just surprise. Whatever had happened was news to her as well.

"What are you talking about?" she asked. I think she was too shocked to try to take advantage of the situation. Markus lashed out smacking her across the face. He then appeared to withdraw somewhat, as if dealing with some internal conflict.

"No this can't be," he muttered. He ripped off the section of the page that he had written on and took a lighter out of his pocket, burning it. Next he took out his revolver and pointed it squarely at my forehead.

"Cut him loose and bring him here," he ordered. The nearest henchman stood behind me and I felt my restraints being removed. He shoved a gun barrel into my back and walked me over to where Markus was.

"Pick up that chair and sit," Markus commanded. I did as requested and found myself sitting in front of the list of numbers that he had decoded.

"I want you to decipher the message and whisper it to me. If I think you are trying to deceive me in any way I'll pull the trigger without hesitating," he said. Whatever Markus had gleaned from the message, it was clearly disturbing. He must have wanted me to be a source of verification. I weighed up my available options, and cooperating seemed like the best option. I could stall for time by being thorough in my work, and perhaps even use the secret of the artifacts for my own benefit.

I set to work, methodically checking and rechecking each word that I wrote down. As I progressed I recalled the changes I saw in Markus as he worked and began to understand. I could feel his gaze on me as I continued, it was as if I could feel the heat from his burning desire to know what my answer would be. Whether I would confirm the message that he had received. I was up to the last word, and I was both confused and puzzled by what was spelled out before me. However I reserved my judgement until I finished my task. I looked up the last word, taking my time. I knew it would be significant. I found it without realising that I had, I even double checked to see if I was correct. There was no mistake. Although I knew the meaning of the words before me, I read through them again as if I had to reassure myself. There was no mistake.

My reaction, however was different from Markus's. It was amazing. I had before me the answer to all my questions. My past, who I was and why everything had happened. The more I tried to question it, the more I knew that it was right. I looked up at Markus, and we exchanged a look. I cannot convey the meaning of that look in words, it was like an unspoken acknowledgement. I stood up slowly and walked over to him. I leaned in close and whispered the message into his left ear. It was merely a formality, he knew that I had come to the same answer as he had. The words had an effect on him though. Hearing them from me must have given them a new power, an edge they had not contained previously. It was if his mind was finally made up.

He turned to Alexis and aimed his weapon. I caught his arm as he pulled the trigger and swung it away. The errant shot hit the henchman behind me. Alexis dropped to the ground in her chair, obscured by the desk. I shoved Markus back and drew the pistol I still had on me. I fired at the other henchman blocking the exit. He took the bullet somewhere in his chest and fell down. As I turned to see if Alexis was alright I felt a searing hot pain shoot through my back and then my chest. I fell to the ground in agony. I managed to drag myself over to the nearest wall and prop myself up. By the time I had done so I saw Markus and Alexis in a stand-off. They were both facing each other, weapons drawn and ready to fire.

"Drop the weapon," Alexis said.

"So you can just shoot me? I know you'll shoot an unarmed man," Markus replied.

"Only if you cause me trouble, I have other plans for you," Alexis said. Markus had a strange look in his eyes. He then complied with her request, throwing his weapon over to her. Alexis turned away from him and came over to inspect my wound. I saw Markus take something from his jacket. It was a vial of some kind. He opened it and started pouring it on the documents on the desk. He looked at me as he did it, and I knew that he was destroying the means to discover the secret of the artifacts. I made no move to alert Alexis and let him complete his task.

"You should live," Alexis said to me and then turned to face Markus once more. She raised her weapon in anger as she saw what he had done. Markus had a twisted smile on his face.

"You know in the end, now that I think about it, all I can do is laugh," Markus said. He raised his arm and brought a small pistol up to under his chin and fired without a moment's hesitation. The sound of the shot rang around the small room and Markus crumpled in a heap. Watching him fall was the last thing I remember.

I now lie in a hospital bed. Alexis is seated near me, writing down my words on paper for me. It is kind of her to assist me in this way, but I also feel that she is doing so for a secondary reason. She believes that I will reveal the message of the artifacts. I'm sorry to say that I will not do so, but for two reasons. The first is that I don't want Alexis to know. I can see her expression change as I utter these words, but I will not change my mind. The second reason is that you already know the words I would be writing. You know the message that was revealed to me, and have known it since the beginning. It is something you take for granted. You know it without thinking. What's interesting is how I know that you already know. Telling you now would be redundant and cheapen my tale.

I see that old book 'Idle Thoughts' over on a table next to my bed. The cover looks so worn and scored with markings. They say not to judge a book by its cover which sounds like conventional wisdom. But we all do it anyway. If my writing was compiled, what would be on the cover? What would it say about my writing? What would it say about me?

To me idle thoughts are the most interesting. The ones that come to you in the dead of night, or over the sound of the shower. They invade your mind unbidden on wings of fancy. They are pure, untouched by purpose or bound by reasoning. They hold the power of creation. What truths are hidden in their fantastical nature? Maybe that's all we are, a collection of idle thoughts that stuck together.

As to what happens next, I'm not entirely sure. The doctors have assured me that my wound is not fatal, but I see the look in their eyes and know that nothing is certain. Regardless, I have completed all my objectives. I have seen this tale through to its conclusion and now it ends here. I can only hope that you enjoyed taking this journey with me. I have offered you all that I can, may it be enough. The future has not yet been written, and I feel a quiet excitement when I think of what could be. Now I feel sleep overtaking me, and with it a certain peace. I no longer worry about where I will be when I wake.

EPILOGUE

Adam put down his pen and closed the book with a deep sigh. He rubbed his forehead with his left hand and stared absently into the distance. The silence of the night was comforting, yet still a reminder of what he had not done. The sound of footsteps on the carpet awoke him from his trance-like state.

"How did you go?" his wife asked sleepily. Her eyes were still partially closed.

"It's a disaster. I just can't seem to get it right. The characters they..." Adam replied despondently before trailing off. He looked down at the book again, pondering whether he should resume writing.

"Come to bed honey," she said taking his hand in hers and kissing him on the cheek. Adam got up reluctantly and followed her into the bedroom. He got into bed, put his arms around his wife and felt her warmth against him. Yawning he realised that he really was tired. His last thought as he drifted off to sleep was: maybe things will be better tomorrow.

ABOUT THE AUTHOR

Vaughan W. Smith is a fiction writer from Sydney,
Australia, who explores big life questions through story.
His favourite genres are Thrillers, Mystery, Science
Fiction and Fantasy.

To connect with Vaughan check out his website:
http://www.vaughanwsmith.com